BROKEN BLADE

J.C. Daniels

This book is a work of fiction. The names, characters, places, and incidents are products of the writer's imagination or have been used fictitiously and are not to be construed as real. Any resemblance to persons, living or dead, actual events, locale or organizations is entirely coincidental.

ISBN-13: 978-0-9894605-1-4

DEDICATION

To my readers…thanks for sticking with me.

And to my husband and kids, who have always stood by me.

Also by J.C. Daniels

Blade Song

Night Blade

Part One

Broken

CHAPTER ONE

I am *aneira.* My heart was strong. Now it's broken.

I am broken.

Completely broken…sitting wide awake at ten in the morning, hiding in a closet, hiding from the memories of the time when a massive werewolf by the name of Goliath carried me out of hell.

I'd spent almost two weeks as a vampire's prisoner. He'd wanted to break me. He succeeded.

How much more broken can you get? Cowering in a closet, clutching a knife, praying the monsters wouldn't find me.

In the closet, where I could I hide.

In a closet where eyes wouldn't roam over my naked body—it didn't matter that I was dressed. In my dreams, yet again, I'd been helpless, naked, and trapped.

Hiding in a closet.

It infuriated me. But I couldn't stop it, either.

It had been four months since my rescue and although I no longer cringed in my room every second of every day, I still felt like a shadow of myself.

I could handle the nightmares. Those are nothing new. I've lived with nightmares off and on most of my life. But up until Jude Whittier kidnapped me, I'd gone years without waking to the sound of my screams.

I'd spent two weeks as his prisoner and he reduced me to a…thing. To a creature who hides in the closet.

I'd been a thing before…there for the abuse and the mockery and the pain others could mete out. He'd reduced me to this again. I hated him so much. I feared him so much. I wanted him dead with every bit of strength I had in me.

But even thinking his name reduced me to a pitiful pile of nothing and the nightmares sent me…here. Hiding in my closet and clutching a knife. How could I find a way to kill him when I was too weak to even face my nightmares?

I shifted and the stinging pain on my arms told me I'd done it again. Cut into myself. In my dreams, I lashed out at my attacker but there was nobody to fight. So I fought myself. Bloodied myself. I could feel the blood that had dried on my arms.

This was what he'd made me into. This was what I had become.

I hate this…

Coming off the heels of a bad nightmare was enough torture for one day, but the fun wasn't over.

I wasn't alone. Somebody was out there, prowling around in my room and even though my gut told me who it was, the fear inside me wouldn't let me breathe. I eased myself upright and did a mental check of all body systems.

Nothing on me hurt, except the muscles in my back from sleeping on the floor and the sting from those minor cuts, already healing. Nothing bad. I could fight. I could flee. All things in working order.

Or close enough.

My back complained as I moved into a crouch, preparing myself to face the man who awaited me. I'd locked my doors, but if it was who I thought it was, those locks wouldn't stop him.

He knocked.

The sound of it made me flinch and I rose to my feet, braced. Ready.

"Come on, Kit," Justin said quietly. "You can't keep living like this."

Justin. A friend. Or sort of. Once he'd been a lover. Then a partner. Then...just a part of my past. Now he was trying to drag me back into life, the way he'd done years ago, and I didn't want it. Closing my eyes, I pressed my head to door and swallowed. "Go away, Justin."

"For the love of all things holy, Kitty-kitty, you're sleeping in a closet."

"Go away."

The door opened with a suddenness that sent me sprawling forward. I caught myself before I could touch him and danced backward before he could touch me.

Dark brown dreadlocks hung down past his shoulders and his eyes, vivid, bright green stared at my face. "Hi, Kitty."

"Go away, Justin." I turned my back on him and now that I was out in the light, I studied my arms, my legs. The synthetic cotton yoga pants were trashed, slashes showing in the thighs, revealing my bloodied wounds. A few of them were already mostly healed so apparently I'd been tearing into myself throughout the night.

The shirt I'd worn was short-sleeved and black. It had blood on it, but since the dark color wouldn't show the stains as well, I could salvage it.

"The nightmares aren't getting any better," Justin said.

I managed, barely, not to flinch at the sound of his voice. Instead, I cleaned the blade and checked the sheath. It had managed to avoid getting bloodied, which was good. The leather wasn't cheap.

Once I'd put the knife away, I grabbed my med-kit and headed to my bathroom. It wasn't much bigger than the closet and when Justin came to stand in the doorway, it felt like the walls closed in around me even more.

I barely managed to keep my hands from shaking as I turned on the water to scrub the blood away. "What do you want, Justin?"

"How much longer are you going to hide in a closet and tear into yourself while the dreams eat you alive?"

I clenched my jaw and focused on the rust-colored water. "If that's all you needed to talk about, don't let the door hit you in the ass on the way out."

He swore and turned away, starting to pace. Oddly, having him a little farther away didn't make me feel any better.

I shut the door, finished scrubbing the blood and

slathered some ointment on the deep ones—the magic-infused gel started to tingle. The cuts would have started to heal by the time I left my room. Good enough.

I put the kit away and grabbed some clean clothes from the basket I'd yet to empty. Once I'd changed, I forced myself to open the door. I couldn't hide in there forever. I knew it for a fact…I kept trying to hide and people like Justin or TJ just kept showing up to drag me out of here, kicking and screaming.

Justin was still pacing out in my room. The dim light that filtered in through the narrow slits in my curtains danced over the silver worked into the sleeves of his jacket. I never had figured out what it was for, but lately, I didn't much care.

As I moved out of the bathroom, he paused by the foot of my bed and reached out, touching his fingers to the blade there. The sword rested against the bedframe. Just seeing her hurt. I made myself look away.

That sword…so much a part of me. Once.

Now it was just another bitter memory.

Tearing my gaze away, I looked at Justin. "I have to work in a little while. Was there something you needed?"

"Work. Shit." He spat it out and made a face. "Pulling drinks and serving half the lowlifes here who look at you like they want to eat you for lunch?"

"Lowlifes?" Wolf Haven was a breeding ground for all sorts of troublemakers, lowlifes and thugs. But the bar where I worked, TJ's, was my safe haven.

I'd run away from home when I'd been fifteen. The first two years, I'd continued to run, with nothing but the clothes on my back and that sword, so certain the monsters from my childhood would hunt me down and take me back. When I finally stopped running it had been here. TJ's had been my first real home. TJ had been my first real friend.

I shouldered past Justin. "Try to remember one of those lowlifes was there when you saved me."

"I haven't forgotten." He glared at me. "I was the one who got word to Goliath, remember? I know him, and I trust him. Him and TJ. But that doesn't mean I don't know the kind of people who come in there. And that's not the damn point. This isn't you, Kit. You're a fighter. A fucking warrior...not a bartender."

I shook my head. "I'm not a fighter anymore, Justin." I shot the blade another look. She no longer answered to me. I no longer heard her music. I wasn't a warrior. If the blade that made me strong enough to handle these people no longer answered me, what good was I? "I'm not anything."

Jude had made sure of that. The vampire had wanted to break me, and that's exactly what he'd done.

◊◊◊◊◊

Justin might not think this was my place, but I fit in here well enough.

You didn't need to be a warrior to serve drinks in a bar. Knowing how to fight didn't hurt. I wasn't the warrior I'd been, but I could still handle a weapon and I had a Desert Eagle strapped to my thigh as I headed down into the bar. It was one big-ass gun, especially in my hands, and that was one of the reasons I liked it. It looked big, it looked mean and it caught a man's attention damn quick.

Tucked inside my vest, I had several blades. Nestled just under the counter on a pair of hooks there was a silver-plated Louisville Slugger. It would knock sense into just about any shifter. And just in case, there was a solid length of sharpened wood—a little long and large to be called a stake, but it would go through a vampire's chest just fine.

I had enough weapons to buy the time needed for Goliath to get his giant ass in there. Relying on somebody else's strength…it churned and twisted my gut, but I couldn't trust myself anymore. I didn't even know myself anymore.

Although, in all honesty, I hadn't needed my weapons, or Goliath, even once. I'd been here for months and not a thing had happened.

It had taken TJ nearly two weeks to coax me out of my room. The first few days, though, I'd been flat on my back, healing up from blood loss and the other various traumas.

But the second week, that was just me cowering in the corner like a mouse.

Once she'd talked me into leaving the room, I'd spent the next couple of days cowering down here in the bar…like a mouse. Those first days had been the worst. Then she'd convinced me to help pull drinks one busy night. It had been hell. Every loud noise had freaked me out and I'd slept in awful stops and starts once I was done.

It was better, though. I could handle it. The job, I mean.

I still wasn't sleeping worth anything. I don't know if I'll ever sleep well again. Every time I closed my eyes, I fear I'll find myself back up in that cell, held prisoner by a vampire and I half-expect to be forced in wakefulness by the brutal dousing that had come from an industrial-strength water hose.

As I pushed through the doors, I felt the crawl of energy spread across my skin. Only one thing caused that.

Shifters. The bar was lousy with them. We got more than a few in here, yeah—it wasn't called Wolf Haven for nothing.

The place was crawling with cats, though, just like it had been for several weeks. If I could have given myself a minute to smash my head against a wall, I would have.

I didn't want to see cats.

Cats made me think of another thing I'd lost and I wasn't up to even crossing that line yet. I handled it the same way I handled everything else lately— shoving it down deep inside so I didn't have to think about it. Sooner or later, I was going to run out of room and maybe I'd bust open at the seams.

As I ducked under the bar, I found TJ back there with Gio. He was a new wolf she'd taken in, so skinny, his bones pressed against his skin and his eyes never seemed to rest in one place for longer than a second. He looked like he was going to attack at any given moment, but not because he wanted to hurt.

He just didn't trust people not to hurt him, so he'd rather take them out first. That was the impression I got from him.

I didn't give Gio my back. I didn't dislike the guy, but I didn't trust him any further than I could throw him.

Something about him bugged me, a lot. It wasn't just the way he kept eying everybody like he was trying to decide if he should kill them on sight or run.

"Heya, Kit," TJ said, her voice a rough, gravelly drawl. She didn't glance at me as she continued to go over things with Gio. She'd been doing the same thing every day for a week. The same material. Almost the same words. I think she was trying to get him used to her, the way she'd get a stray dog used to her voice before she tried to pet him.

If she tried to pet Gio, he'd try to take her hand off.

"Sexy-Sexy left in a bad mood," TJ said once she finished with Gio. He disappeared into the back, like he couldn't wait to be away from us people. People, bad. Smart kid.

I curled my lip at TJ. *Sexy-Sexy*. Yeah. Justin was that. And I didn't care. He could be as sexy as Adonis and it wouldn't matter. I didn't care if he was in a bad mood, either.

"So what was up his very fine ass?" TJ stared at me as I moved to settle in behind the bar.

A werewolf took the seat just off to my right and grumbled something. I heard the words beer in there and served him up, added a floater of Red to it, the specially-made grain alcohol that would hit even the metabolism of shifter hard. Of course, if a human tried it, they'd likely keel over dead of alcohol poisoning after more than a few sips.

Shifters still burned through it pretty fast and it took a lot to get them drunk. We didn't let them get drunk in here. Drunk and powerful didn't mix well. Especially when you were a werecreature. But there was something just...relaxing about sitting in a bar, talking crap, shooting pool.

It wasn't the best stress reliever in the world, but it worked as well as anything else, I guessed.

Giving him his drink, I turned to look at TJ. She was still waiting for me to answer her about Justin. I glared at her. "How am I supposed to know what his problem is?"

The werewolf dumped a fistful of bills on the counter—a hell of a lot more than the price of a beer. I scowled at him and fished out what I needed, leaving the rest.

Behind me, I heard a familiar whine—somebody else

trying the wards. Anybody who came into TJ's place had to fight them. Most people could get inside, but it wasn't just as easy as opening a door and walking through. The wards would have their way with you and it wasn't a fun way, either.

The wards resisted for a moment and then yielded, spitting somebody out onto the floor.

For a second, my heart stuttered. *Dark haired…cat…*

No. We don't think about him. Not ever.

But it wasn't him. This werecat was tall enough, but too leanly built. Too elegant.

Dressed too nice for Wolf Haven and that had my instincts humming. As he started for the bar, I turned my attention back to TJ, still keeping half of my attention tuned on the newcomer. He didn't belong in Wolf Haven. Didn't belong here at all.

That right there had me wary. People didn't come to Wolf Haven just for the ambience. Either they came because they wanted to hide, because they had no place left to go…or because they were looking for something. Somebody.

And automatically, even though it did me no good, I flexed my wrist.

"So what did Sexy-Sexy want?" TJ asked.

"You realize he has a name, right?" I asked, although I didn't know why I bothered. If TJ had decided she was going to call him Sexy-Sexy, then Justin might as well add that to his Banner ID. "Look, he's just aggravating me. I pissed him off. He pissed me off. End of story."

"What's he want?" TJ asked.

"Shit. What is this, twenty questions?" I glared at her and then looked at the werecat sitting at the bar, regarding us with unreadable eyes. "What do you want?"

"Redcat whiskey. Neat."

I sighed and got it for him. High-end stuff like that never used to be served here, but over the past month, more and more weres were showing up, asking for it.

TJ believed in supply and demand.

I dumped it in front of him as TJ said, "He ain't wrong, you know."

"TJ. Drop it."

"This isn't your place anymore."

"TJ..." I picked up the bottle of Redcat and turned to face her. "If you don't drop it, I'm dropping *this.*"

Her eyes narrowed on my face. "That shit costs a thousand a case. If you drop it, I'll beat it out of your ass."

Somewhere out in the bar, somebody growled. Swinging my head around, I glared out over the bar and tried to figure out where it had come from. The wolf still sitting at the bar? The cat? What the hell—?

Both of them seemed fixated on their drinks and it had seemed too faint to have come from so close.

Brushing it aside, I switched my attention back to TJ. "You are so full of shit, it's amazing you don't reek of it. You won't touch me and you know it. Now are you dropping the discussion or am I dropping more than a hundred bucks worth of booze?" I waggled the bottle in the air and held her gaze. She might be bluffing, but I wasn't. Maybe it made me childish, but I'd decided a little bit of regression felt good. I hadn't felt good in a long while.

"You can't hide forever, Kitty." She blew out a sigh and then shrugged. "You know that."

"I don't plan to." I put the Redcat back on the shelf and washed my hands. "I'll die sooner or later. That's good enough for me."

CHAPTER TWO

Two vampires walk into a bar...and naturally, it had to be mine. Of course, it wasn't the opening for a funny joke, either.

Gio had been on his way out, two cases full of booze in his skinny, strong arms, but from the corner of my eye, I saw him. Absently, I noted the way he stopped in the doorway, just out of sight of the vampires, watched the way he eyed them, saw his Adam's apple bob as he swallowed. And then, as quiet as he could be—and being a were, that was pretty damn quiet—he backed away.

I might have thought more of it, except I was dealing with my own level of panic and it was climbing higher and higher all the time as the vampires decided to settle at the bar just a few feet away.

Vampires.

My hands were sweating.

Why were they here? Vamps didn't come to TJ's much. She didn't like them and the feeling was pretty mutual. She didn't offer safe passage to people she didn't like and the blooddrinkers were outnumbered five to one in Wolf Haven. Wolf Haven was pretty much lawless territory and everybody knew it.

The few vamps who managed to survive here usually did so because they struck bargains with the right people.

But no vamps struck a deal with TJ. TJ just didn't strike deals. She did business and if she disliked you, it was entirely possible she would sooner set your ass on fire than do business. Part of me hoped desperately that TJ would take a rampant dislike to them.

I shouldn't have lingered around to help cover tonight.

The wererat who usually handled the bar after dark wasn't coming in and Gio had just hightailed it out of here. Just thinking about the vampires was enough to leave me half sick. My gut clenched into a tight knot and bile battled its way up my throat.

I swallowed it down and made sure I had everything under control before I approached them. Lingering over the empties, I shoved them into the dishwasher, then checked to make sure my hands were steady.

They weren't. The fine tremor would have been unnoticeable to humans, but a vampire would notice it in a heartbeat. Instinctively, my mind started to fall back on the one thing that had always steadied me.

I am aneira…

Immediately, I stopped myself.

That wasn't true anymore. I wasn't the warrior I'd once been so I had to rely on something else to get me through.

I shot them another look from the corner of my eye.

Evaluate your target, Kitasa—

The voice of one my aunts crept up from the well of my memories. Unwelcome at most times, but just then, it served to focus me. Target. Enemy. Same thing, right?

Okay. Evaluate.

They were young—younger than Jude. And they were on my turf now. I had a mean-ass gun strapped to my thigh. TJ had no issues with me carrying the weapon in the bar now, although before she would have raised hell. The ammo in that gun would take down an elephant. Or a vamp.

The sight of them still had my mind spinning away to dark and ugly places where time had no meaning and everything was pain and blood and hopelessness.

Now you're mine, and nobody will come for you...

Jude's voice, a sly whisper in the back of my mind, even now.

It didn't matter that he'd been wrong.

It didn't matter that people had come for me.

It didn't matter that I'd even managed to get out of that hell-hole on my own.

Yeah, I'd had a different idea of escape planned—the permanent kind.

It didn't even matter that he was locked inside a silver-lined box for the next five decades, his punishment for kidnapping a fellow member in good standing with the Assembly. That was how they'd phrased it. He'd kidnapped me and his punishment was confinement within a box.

I still had nightmares.

And I didn't know what was going to happen once he got out.

The fear was still enough to choke me.

A hand jabbed into my ribs and I looked up, found myself staring into TJ's dark brown eyes. She didn't say a word, but her nostrils flared wide and she breathed in slowly. I caught the drift.

I was throwing off fear so badly, she could scent it on the air. So could everybody else in there. I had to pull it in.

I couldn't rely on my sword, but I could rely on other things. Like the gun strapped to my thigh. I knew how to use it and I was fast. I could draw it in a second. I knew, because I'd timed myself. Turn, sight, fire. All in a blink. And a vampire's blood would run dark, ugly red across the floor.

Slowly, the fear eased back, because I knew I could do it.

I was terribly aware of how quiet the bar had become. I twisted the top of a bottle of Corona and delivered it to the were in front of me. She was a jaguar and although the Corona had no effect on her whatsoever, it was the only thing she'd drink.

She smiled at me but the look on her face was distracted and even before I turned around, I knew who she was looking at. The eerie glow rolling across her eyes was worrisome. TJ was going to get pissed if all of them lost it in here.

"Oh, somebody had fun with you..."

I looked up and found myself staring into red, red eyes.

That fear tried to scream at me again.

This time, I screamed back.

Somewhere in the back of the room, a were snarled.

I blocked the sound out. The weight of the Desert Eagle strapped to my thigh was the only thing that mattered right then. Like most modern weapons, the Eagle hadn't ever sang in the back of my head and sometimes I thought that made it easier. I didn't miss his music and it wasn't so painful now as I stared into those fiery eyes.

I missed my sword...I could see myself spinning, striking—

As those red eyes glowed, I forced myself to think past that. He was staring at my neck and that popped the bubble of terror as it tried to swell out of my control.

Fury punched through me, obliterating everything else.

"Not used to having vamps in here," I said levelly. "We've only got some cheap blood whiskey on hand."

Blood whiskey was the vampire's poison of choice when it came to bars. The older one smiled, a closed-lip kind that didn't show a hint of fang. "That will be fine."

I nodded and went to pull it up. TJ kept the blood whiskey on hand just in case—she did like making her money. It wasn't used often, a synthetic blood blend, mixed with alcohol. It was cut-rate whiskey, I could tell from the smell as I poured it, but TJ wasn't going to waste her good stuff on blood suckers. I poured their drinks into the heated glasses and carried them back to the bar, set them down, but before I could I could move away, the older leech reached out, brushing my hair aside. "He was careless."

I backed away, popping my wrist out of habit. I could imagine the weight of my blade…so easily. "No. He took great care, trust me. He did exactly as he wanted to do. Please don't touch me again."

The vampire inclined his head, nodded slowly.

His companion snickered. "He had a lot of fun, I think.

You were all but ripe with fear just moments ago."

My gut clenched and although the magic that connected me to my sword was gone, my hand started to itch and heat pooled there. It hadn't done that in…months. The need to draw the gun was strong. The need to hurt something was stronger.

I could control it, as long as he didn't make a move, but—

"I can show you it's not always bad," he whispered, flashing fangs at me.

I drew the Eagle and leveled it at his head before the last word had even left his lips.

The red in his eyes burned hotter, brighter.

"You can't kill me with that." Cold crashed through the room.

"Want to bet?" I cocked my head and studied him. "You're no more than thirty, thirty-five at the most. That's just a baby. If I bury enough silver in your brain, you're dead, and I mean for-real dead."

He swayed, the moves oddly snake-like. "You'd never be fast enough."

I kept my focus on him. "Yeah? You sure about that?"

His partner laid a hand on his arm. "Edison. You've upset her. Perhaps we should—"

The younger one leaped.

Vaguely, I was aware that the older one misted away. Edison, though...he came at me in a rush. I aimed, squeezed.

His head disappeared in an explosion of blood, brain and bone.

As his lifeless body dropped to the floor, I lowered my gun.

Nobody ever thought I was fast enough.

"I meant no harm in coming here."

The other vampire appeared behind TJ.

She tensed but said nothing, stroking a hand down her crossbow.

I stared at him.

Out in the bar, there was chaos. Shifters were snarling and

growling and in general, acting the way predators did when something died. I wasn't going back out there. Goliath was working the bar, something he only did in times of crisis.

"She doesn't like it when something comes at her back," I said to the leech. I still held my gun. Part of me knew I should put the damn thing back in its holster, but not yet. I'd known the vampire hadn't left and until he was gone, nope, not putting it up.

The vampire edged around, moving into her line of sight. He had his hands linked together in front of him and he was trying very hard to look nice and polite and not like a bloodsucker. He looked at TJ and then at me. "I meant no harm in coming here. I hadn't heard you…" He paused and then shook his head. "I am…working. I'm trying to track somebody down, but we didn't come here with the intent to cause any harm, or trouble. If I'd known—"

I narrowed my eyes and he went silent.

"Known what?" I asked. I had to force the words out. I was afraid I already knew.

His gaze dropped once more to my neck, and I knew.

My heart slammed against my ribs. Wonderful. I'm a legend. Jude's whore.

"Get out," I said quietly.

He bowed his head. "Of course. But..." He paused and then carefully, as though he was selecting each word, he continued, "I would like to offer you a kind suggestion."

"Leeches have no kindness."

"I do not blame you for feeling that way," he said, his mild brown eyes holding mine. I couldn't read anything in that gaze. "Every time one of my kind sees the marks on you, they will think, and wonder. Some will feel as I do and be displeased, and make no mistake. I am displeased. I realize you have no cause to believe me and I understand. But…"

His words trailed off and his gaze shifted past me. He knew what he wanted to say, I could see it. But I had a feeling he was trying to figure out if the words he had to say were going to result in TJ lifting her crossbow or me putting the Desert Eagle to use again.

"Just say what you need to say and get out." I wanted him gone.

Once more, he inclined his head. "Others will see it and look at you as a toy."

"All the more reason to stay the hell away from your kind, then."

"Who the fuck were they, TJ?"

She hunched over the computer. Her crossbow was on the massive mahogany length of her desk, just a whisper away.

The vampires had pissed her off.

She shot me a dark look from under the fringe of her bangs and then went back to glaring at the computer like that would pull the information up sooner.

"New players," she muttered. "I know that much."

Hell. I knew that much. If they weren't fairly new, I would have at least been able to place their faces and they probably would have recognized mine from the get-go—it wouldn't have taken the scars.

Ours wasn't so small a world that I knew every damned soul with a drop of non-human blood, but once upon a time, it had served my purposes to know the big guns. The one I'd killed wasn't a major anything, unless you counted the sleazeball circuit.

But the other one…he was smart. He was a cool, slick piece of work and he'd been on a mission. Plus, he wasn't a baby vamp—only had a century or two on him. Not old as far as vampires go, but comfortable in his skin. He wasn't full of his own sense of arrogance and when he'd looked at me, he hadn't written me off as a threat.

That, in and of itself, was a bit of a worry.

Right now, I wrote myself off as a threat.

I'd seen the measuring look in his eyes, though, and I knew what it meant.

I recognized my own kind well enough.

Maybe he wasn't a hired killer but he hadn't been in there

just for bad whiskey cut with fake blood, either. He'd been…looking. For something. Someone. Since he'd been unprepared to see me, it had nothing to do with me and it wouldn't have been any of TJ's people.

Nobody would go into TJ's place looking for one of hers. They wouldn't make it out alive if she found them out.

Judging by the grim look on her face, I suspected she was already regretting letting the other one leave.

A few minutes later, she grunted. "Fucker. Affiliated with Allerton House."

Allerton. A face flashed through my mind and I closed my eyes. Samuel Allerton. One of the men my…ex had killed a few months ago. It was a long and winding road that had placed me here and Allerton had been one of the pit stops.

The vampire had been an obstacle, somebody who might have been a danger. He'd been dealt with before I even knew about him.

And now somebody affiliated with his house was creeping around?

"Why would he be here?"

TJ shook her head, absently stroking a hand down her crossbow. "I don't know, Kit," she muttered. "This guy's name is Abraham. Died in 1894. Doesn't seem to be a total waste, as far as vampires go."

Snorting, I turned away from her and went over to stare at the bank of monitors. They faced out over the bar, the alley in the back, the halls upstairs, the gym, giving us a birds-eye view of TJ's domain. The only rooms not wired were the bedrooms. The bar was still crowded, roiling with an energy I could feel from here.

"Who is he looking for, TJ?"

"I really don't know."

I turned my head and looked back at her. "He didn't find whoever it was. So he'll probably be back."

She grunted and shrugged. "I'll call in a few more wolves to help for a while." Then she eased her chair back from the desk and swiveled it around, watching me with a brooding stare. "I guess that means you don't want to help cover nights anymore. Can't risk seeing another leech, huh?"

I managed not to flinch. But I suspected she knew what I was thinking.

She put her crossbow in her lap, stroking it absently. "Sooner or later, you'll see another vampire. What are you going to do, kill every last one who says something?"

I turned around and walked out.

TJ had never been one for letting something alone, though. She was like a dog with a bone. Or a werewolf. A pain in the ass.

When I ignored her knock, she just used her code to bypass mine and came in. I pretended to ignore her as I stayed where I was, staring at the fire I had crackling away merrily in the little fireplace. TJ's bar had been built in an old building and I had one of the few rooms with an actual fireplace.

TJ had always given me this room. There was enough of a chill in the air now, the weather about as cool as it ever got here in Florida. The warmth of the fire felt good on my skin, but it did nothing to thaw the ice inside me.

Nothing ever seemed to warm me.

Stop it. I closed my eyes and tightened my hand around the Eagle's grip, tried to pretend it was my blade.

It was a pitiful comparison. The gun, solid as it was, useful as it was, just wasn't the same.

"You can't hide away forever," TJ said quietly.

"I'm not hiding. I'm taking a break. It was a long day."

She sighed and wheeled her chair closer to me. I averted my face and focused back on the flames dancing in the fire. Much easier to look at them instead. Much easier.

"Kit, you're stronger than this."

"TJ, enough."

"Is it?"

Her hand stroked my arm and I closed my eyes against the

tears that threatened to cloud my vision. TJ never touched anybody. Suddenly I felt like a coward and I couldn't even look at her as she said, "Kit...you're stronger than I am. Please don't turn into me. Don't let him win like this."

Shame slid through me. "There are much worse things than being like you, TJ."

"Worse things?" She laughed sourly. "Yeah, sure. I could be like your bitch of a grandmother. I could have been born human and made a leech instead of born a weak werewolf and then tortured by the sadistic wolf who stole my legs. But he's not the one who stole my life, Kit. I gave it up. I stay in here…and I hide. I let him ruin me. I'm letting him win…and I know it."

"TJ, that's not—"

"Don't," she warned, and the thread of steel under her voice was enough to silence me.

"I stay in there," she murmured. "I hide. Even though that son of a bitch would never leave his mountain to find me, I stay here. And I hide. You face down everything that scares you, until now. Don't let him win, Kitty. You didn't let anything else take you down. Don't let this ruin you."

You didn't let anything else take you down…

Hard words.

Harsh words.

And as I made myself walk into the bathroom the next morning, I realized TJ wasn't really wrong.

My grandmother's voice, never far from my mind, rose up to haunt me. *Useless waste. I'll make a warrior out of you if it kills me…*

Sometimes, I think she'd meant if it killed me.

And damn if she didn't try. Try hard. But I'd run away from her, managed to build a life.

You face down everything that scares you.

But right now, everything scared me. Life. Leaving the safety of TJ's bar. And facing the woman in the mirror. It was a damned hard thing to do and for the past four months, I'd avoided it as much as I possibly could. As often as I could, because looking at myself was just too hard.

But today, I made myself look anyway.

It was almost a shock, the woman I saw staring back at me.

Leaner. Harder. Sadder.

The scars had paled. My neck was a mess of them. The ones on the left side of my neck were neat, a small circle of them, placed there back when I'd still mattered to somebody. When I'd still mattered, period.

No, we don't think about that… Immediately my brain started to skitter away even as memories danced closer.

Did you really think I wasn't coming for you? Damon's voice, raw and broken.

Tears burned inside me, but I swallowed them back. I couldn't handle that and this. Not now. So instead of looking at the mark he'd given me, I looked at the uglier scars. The ones that marked my ruin. My destruction.

The mess on the right side of my neck was what bothered me, the ones that told the awful, sickening story of what had been done to me.

The vampire's voice was a nasty mockery in the back of my mind. Every time one of my kind sees the marks on you, they will think, and wonder.

They'd see me as a toy.

It pissed me off because that was what I'd been.

I touched them, made myself do it even though I flinched. I memorized the feel of them.

Jude could have healed them after he'd fed, but he'd chosen not to. He'd wanted to mark me and he hadn't been neat about it. I'd fought, long and hard. Sometimes he'd almost let me get away, so there weren't just puncture wounds. Some of them were long slices down my neck from where his fangs had torn me. They started just below my ear and disappeared under the collar of my shirt. There was no hiding them, not unless I just started walking around in hooded cloaks.

I needed to make them part of me, somehow.

A voice, the one that now made me want to cry when I thought of it, murmured from the back of my mind.

It's the story of me...what put me on the road that made me what I am...

Damon had marked himself. Tattoos with charmed ink, etched onto his skin, back when he'd just been a kid, before he'd hit the spike—the period of change when a person with shifter blood went through that change prior to their first shift. The charmed ink, having it done before the first shift—those were the only ways a shapeshifter could probably keep a tattoo, otherwise the body would just absorb the marks as they were laid on him.

I didn't heal as fast as a shifter did, but I did heal fast.

Still, if charmed ink had been used on him then, why not on me now?

The story of me…

I stared at the scars a moment longer and then left the bathroom. On the way to my bed, I grabbed a notebook and pencil. If I was going to draw a story of me, I had to know what I was now.

The sheathed sword lay on my bed, a sad mockery of what I'd once been and I knew the answer.

I was a broken blade. A broken warrior.

That was the first thing I drew. A sword, with the blade shattered into pieces. A leopard, stalking along the ground. A vampire's fang. A giant python, his body curved into a coil. And a spear...my grandmother had always loved the spear.

I started to sketch a rat, but in the end, I didn't bother. The rat pack hadn't ever freaked me out that badly, and dreams about them didn't haunt my sleep.

Everything here, though...

Touching the tip of my finger to the leopard, I bit back a sigh. Maybe the dreams about him weren't exactly nightmares, but this was still something that had broken me.

It was time to start trying to put the pieces of myself back together.

I let TJ handle the initial phone calls.

No point doing this if it wouldn't work. I'd hoped for a few days to prepare myself after I'd asked her, but I didn't have even have half an hour.

Twenty-six minutes after I'd explained to her what I needed, she pushed an address in my hand.

"This..." I licked my lips and said, "This is here in Wolf Haven."

"Yes. Next street over," TJ replied, stroking a hand down her ever-present crossbow. She clung to that thing the way I'd once clung to my blade. Absently, I flexed my hand and made myself look away.

"So. Are you going to go see her?"

I looked down at the notebook I'd brought down with me. If I did this, it was a start. The first step, at least.

"This doesn't mean I'm quitting here," I said softly. "I'm not. I'm not what I used to be and..." I closed my eyes. What in the hell did I even say to her? I'm not strong enough to walk away from here? I'm not who I used to be and I'm not able to do what I need to do?

"You just take your time, Kit." The wheels of her chair squeaked as she moved over to me and I felt her pat my arm. "Why don't you come in and work half the day? Later in the afternoon? You can head over now. She's usually not that busy this time of day."

Then I was left alone with my thoughts.

CHAPTER THREE

It was almost painful leaving the bar.

Four months have passed since Goliath guided me through those doors. Once I came inside, I hadn't left, not even for a minute. I'd stayed inside, either working in the bar, or hiding away in my room.

Hiding…

I wanted to slam my fist against the dull concrete wall. Did I really want to spend the rest of my life doing that?

Logically, I knew it hadn't really been that long, but if I didn't force myself outside now, then when would I? In fifty years, when they let Jude out of that box?

The thought of it was enough to make me want to run back inside but instead I squared my shoulders and forced myself to move away from the bar. The bright light of the sun burned my eyes and I squinted against it as I took another slow, reluctant step.

A cool wind whipped down the street and I absently thought about going back inside to find something with long sleeves. I didn't have a jacket. But if I let myself go back in for anything, I wouldn't come back out.

It was edging up on the last few days of January and a cold front had blown through, leaving the temperature hovering in the low thirties. The chilly wind that came dancing down the street teased my flesh and made me think of things I'd rather forget, of that cold fortress in the mountains, snow stinging my flesh.

Swallowing the knot in my throat, I glanced down at the notebook and then looked up at the road. I could do this.

"You want me to come with, Kitty?" Goliath asked.

"No," I said and then I had to clear my throat and try again. I could fucking walk around the corner on my own. "I got this."

As I started down the corner, I saw something just ahead of me. I misstepped and almost tripped over my own feet but when I looked again, the puma was gone. All I saw was the black tip of its tail before it disappeared.

But it hadn't gone far. I could feel the heated presence of shifters, crowding all around me.

"Goliath?" I said quietly.

"'S'okay, Kit. Just some new cats been hanging around lately," he said, and his voice sounded tired. "But they won't bother you. You got my word."

If it had come from anybody else, I wouldn't have trusted it. But Goliath, I trusted him. Still, nerves chased me as I took the first step, then another and another, too painfully aware of the heated presence of were against my skin. Watching me. Why were they watching me?

Something in the back of my mind whispered the answer but I shoved it aside. That was something I didn't think about. Definitely not something I could think about now.

It was everything I could do just to walk. One step after the other until I made it to the tattoo parlor around the corner.

It was all of fifty yards from TJ's place, I realized. Fifty yards. It didn't have a name. There was no sign in the window and when I pushed inside, not a damn customer was waiting.

It was just me. Only me. And I needed to decide now if I was going to do this.

The tattoo artist was more than just an artist.

She was a witch, too, and as planned, she'd use charmed inks.

Her name was Paulie and she warned me, even before she started, that it would hurt. I could handle that.

I had a harder time with everything else.

As she pushed her magic into my body, it combined with everything else…all the memories. Awful, awful memories. I tried to fight them as she went to work and I could hear her voice.

"If you can just accept them and deal with them, it will make it easier," Paulie murmured as she bent over me. "They've become a poison inside you and we must deal with it."

Deal with it?

I clenched my teeth and swallowed the scream rising in me. It was like she was etching acid on my skin.

Baby girl…

Her magic danced inside me and the memories I tried so hard to forget edged closer and closer, while the pain grew.

"The pain works with the memories," she murmured some time later. I'd bitten my cheek bloody. "The harder you fight it…"

But I couldn't ignore it anymore.

Something about her magic changed and those memories screamed louder. Longer. And I heard his voice.

And I was caught, caught back in a web of those memories.

"I don't believe this," he muttered, turning away. He braced his hands on my desk, the muscles in his back bunching and moving under his shirt. "Fuck—everything I've...shit. No."

The disjointed ramble of words bothered me as much as the pain I saw in his eyes as he turned back around to glare at me. "A job, right? Fine," he bit off. "Day's done. Come home. With me now."

I opened my mouth to answer. Yes. Please. Just yes...

And my fucking phone rang.

Justin...I could hear the muffled ringtone of the Imperial March coming from the garbage can and I wanted to scream. "I have to talk to him right now," I whispered stiltedly. "I have the information I need to close this case and then I'm done. I just need—"

"I need you," he roared. "Now. Come with me now."

The phone rang again and anxiety rose to a wail in my mind as my office phone started to echo it as well. Calling both lines—not good.

And clear as crystal, I could see him speeding away from Assemblyman Marlowe's house.

Shit. I opened my mouth... I have to tell them you were doing it for me—

That was all I had to say. That was all.

But the binding spell kept the words locked inside me.

"Damon. It's two hours," I whispered.

"No." He shook his head. "It's more than that. Good-bye, Kit."

My heart cracked down the middle. "What?"

He backed away from me. "You don't trust me. Right now, you're half sick with fear and I can't get you to come with me when I need you like I need air. It's done."

"It's done, Kit."

I didn't even know how much time had passed when I surfaced from that well of pain. The memories that had consumed me were just...gone. Instead of being caught in them, consumed by them, they were tucked back inside my head and I felt like the ground had been jerked out from under me.

Shoving upright off the chair, I stumbled away from Paulie on shaky legs.

"Wuh..." I swallowed and my throat was so tight, even that hurt. Trying again, I glared at her. "What the hell was that?"

The witch had a troubled look on her face and sighed, looking away. "You have poison in you," she said quietly. "Just as I said. All of it is trying to come out through the memories. I warned you it would hurt."

Hurt? I glared at her.

Physical pain was one thing, but that…okay, yeah. She'd mentioned emotional pain, but I hadn't been expecting *that*. Passing the back of my hand over my mouth, I turned away and waited until I knew my voice would be level before I asked the next question. "Did you see anything? Feel anything while you were doing that? Are you…"

"I'm no healer. I have no empathic magic in me," she said.

I shot her a dark look.

She shrugged and rose from her chair to pace the small room. "I have an affinity for earth magics and small spells. But I see nothing when I do these things. And I'm grateful for that."

Silence lapsed and I ignored her for a moment as I tried to process what had happened. Memories, right? They were just memories. And I had them anyway. When I was asleep, they came out and taunted me and made merry with my sanity. During the day, I tried to ignore them, but no matter what, the memories were there and they were mine.

"You can't purge poison by ignoring it," Paulie said quietly.

Her words were a simple, brutal truth.

Slowly, I lifted my head and turned around to stare at her. Then I crossed over to stand in front the mirror.

Clad in just a bandeau bra, I stared at the leopard. He was frozen on my skin, muscles coiled, head down low and his body hid the worst of my scars. I'd never had time for whimsy in my life but maybe, if I hadn't been so broken inside, I might have thought there was something…protective about the way she'd drawn the leopard, stretching across the upper part of my chest, from my shoulder, down across my breastbone, spreading across the tops of my breasts.

Paulie had taken my sketch and made it into a tattoo that looked incredibly lifelike. She'd worked the design so that the scars were hidden in the curves and lines of the leopard's muscled body, in the dark shadows of the spots that darkened his pelt.

The color of his fur was a dusky stain against the pale ivory of my skin and I had to admit, it was beautiful work.

Beautiful. He looked like he was going to leap from my flesh, snarling into life in front of me. Swallowing, I turned away and found her standing there.

Waiting.

"If you were completely human, that would have taken a few trips to get all the color done."

I touched my hand to my skin and grimaced at the feel of how hot it was.

"It's going to take a while for the pain to fade," Paulie said, understanding flashing in her eyes. "We heal quicker than mortals do, but I explained how I made the inks last on your skin."

Copper.

She used copper inks on me. It was the only thing that would make sure the tattoo actually took. It would poison mortals, the way she used it on me, but with my makeup, it served to bind the tattoo to me.

Her assistant approached, lifting her hands. I eyed the compress and then angled my head, letting her place it on my flesh. I hissed—cooling, tingling magic exploded over my skin at the very first contact.

"It will help speed the healing." Her eyes caught and held mine. "Paulie says you wanted this done quickly."

I didn't say anything. She seemed to get the point. Talking wasn't anything I had in me just then.

It's done…

"Can I be alone?" I asked woodenly.

Once they left, I stumbled over to the chair and sank down on it.

Pain tore at me as I let the barest edge of those memories come out to taunt me. Poison… she wasn't wrong there. Yes, I had poison in me and she'd just cut me open.

Now I had to deal with all of the memories that were going to come creeping out.

I was nearly at the bar when I felt something—the warning prickle on my back made me tense.

What the hell…?

Hadn't I been through enough today?

If I'd had my sword, I would have drawn it. Instead, I sped up my pace, staring at the man standing guard at the door just a few yards ahead of me. Goliath. Once I got past him, I was in the clear.

His pale, watery gaze was focused on something…*somebody*…behind me.

I didn't dare turn to look.

My breath hitched in my lungs and I moved faster, all but running now. I knew that feeling, recognized the charge in the air and even if I didn't, I would have recognized the way my body reacted. Heart racing, breathing sped up and my skin felt flushed.

Stupid, stupid body, reacting that way.

Stupid, stupid heart.

I sped around Goliath as the heat of the presence at my back started to spread along my skin. From the corner of my eye, I saw his shadow and *damn* it, part of me wanted to stop.

It's done…

Instead, I ducked under the arm Goliath had spread across the door.

A low, furious snarl echoed around me and I heard my name.

"Kit."

That voice… I knew that voice.

But I wasn't ready to think about him anymore today. I *couldn't*. What in the hell was he doing here *now*, anyway?

The wards drifted across my skin, warm, soothing and gentle, the protections closing around me even as something else tried to shove inside. I heard Goliath's voice, a deep, bass rumble as he growled at somebody.

I ignored everything else from there on out.

Inside the bar, I found Gio cleaning down the tables and TJ working the bar with one of the other girls. Gio shot me a quick look; his eyes, all but colorless, bounced from my face to the tables, back to me, back to the tables, over and over, damned near making me motion sick.

Shoving him from my mind, I focused on TJ. Her gaze dropped to my neck, although she wouldn't be able to see anything more than the top edge of the leopard's body. I hunched my shoulders and made for the back door.

Hide—have to hide—

Then I stopped and squared my shoulders. No. No more hiding. Maybe I'd just run the hell away from somebody, but this was different. I wasn't ready to face him—I didn't think I'd ever be ready for that.

But I knew one thing—I had to stop hiding.

Once I'd done that, I could maybe figure who I was now. *What* I was.

"I have an idea for working everything together. Making a cohesive design."

Three days later, I sat back in Paulie's place. I'd used the back door and slipped in through the side entrance. I didn't know if anybody had seen me enter, but I'd left earlier than normal, planned to be done sooner.

As she held out the sheet of paper in front of me, I made myself look. I didn't care if it was cohesive or not. I just wanted...

But then I saw it. Struck, I reached out and touched my hand to it. The drawings were mine, but she'd made them beautiful. The broken blade that was me. The python, coiled and ready to strike. A vampire's fang. The spear burst up through all of it, everything twining around it. Each unique piece had been set into a vining, twisting garden of green.

There were flowers there as well. Vivid bursts and blooms of colors. I knew many of them. "Foxglove. Oleander. Belladonna. Angel's trumpet. Wolfsbane." I touched each as I named them. Then I looked up at her.

"These are all poisonous."

"Poisonous...deadly if used the right way. And lovely. Just like you." She caught my hand. "The leopard was one of the largest and we couldn't do anything else but him that first day, but if you have the time, and are up to it, we can get a third of this design done today."

Absently, I touched the leopard that stretched over my collarbone, up to the lower edge of my neck. "Yeah. We can do that."

Hours later, I reached up and touched the tattoo that covered more of my neck. She'd worked in the foxglove, angel's trumpet and leaves twining around the leopard, as well as the snake.

This had been almost a walk in the park compared to the last one. I could remember the fear of the snake—I *should*, the damn thing had tried to eat me—but it was nothing compared to what had happened with the first session.

The colors were surreal and vivid against my skin. Now I stood there, staring at the progress and shuddering at the pressure of that much magic crawling just under my skin. Behind me, Paulie went about cleaning up her supplies, an eclectic mix of mundane and arcane tools.

"I know it's a lot of pain, a lot of magic to deal with," she said, catching sight of me as another bout of chills wracked me. "Humans tend to do this sort of thing slowly…the outline first, then coloring it in. As it is, the only way to do it on our kind is to do as much of it as fast as we can."

I wondered if I was supposed to respond to that. I didn't really care anyway—yeah, I felt lousy, but I hadn't felt *good* in so long, I doubt I'd even recognize it. Instead of responding, I just studied the new marks laid on my skin.

"Come back in two or three more days, and we can get back to work on the next phase. If we keep to that pace, we can be done within two weeks, possibly less. It's all up to you and how you feel as we advance."

There was an odd hesitation and then she asked quietly,

"Are you coming back?"

I closed my eyes as I let myself touched the mess of scars along my neck, the ones that hadn't yet been covered. "Yes."

Jude had just about broken me. No chance of rescue…but one chance to escape. That was where the memories took me now.

I could even feel the ice of the cold air on my flesh as in my mind, I relived every brutal moment of that day.

They were chasing me now, but it didn't matter. I just had to get there—

Memories chased me as well.

TJ and Goliath, sitting at the bar as they showed me how to pull drinks. *You can hold a fucking blade but you can't pour a beer? That's shit, kid, TJ had groused. And Goliath had laughed.* She don't want to, TJ. But she'll do.

Then TJ's hand on my shoulder, years later. It's time you try to do something else, Kitty. You ain't made for hiding in a bar.

Justin, all fire and flash on the surface...and he'd made me realize I could come out of the shadows. Come on, Kitty-kitty. If you find that runner before I do, I'll let you try to beat me up. You won't win, though...*I had. It was the night he kissed me the first time.*

Colleen. Sitting at her daughter's bedside as Mandy breathed her last. The girl hadn't died easily...but Colleen had looked at me with a thankful smile and held my hand, cried on my shoulder and whispered, Thank you...

There was even a flicker of a memory from Rana, *one of my aunts.* We could make a warrior of you yet—*she'd stared at the bow in my hands and shook her head with something like admiration in her eyes.*

Memories, slamming into my mind...and then one nearly sent me to my knees.

Baby girl…

I stumbled to a halt as I reached the lip of the chasm. It was so far down, I couldn't see the bottom for the blowing snow.

The wind howled, raging and furious.

"Don't!"

I turned and looked at Jude's men, creeping closer.

I barely felt anything as I lifted the HK. Their blood painted the ground red and I went back to staring at the drop. Slinging the weapon's strap over my shoulder, I lifted the handgun and pressed it to my chin.

Shhh, it's okay, baby girl. It's okay...*Damon. After the first time Jude had fucked me over. Damon had been there. Had saved me. Hot tears burned my face but I managed to smile a little as another memory flickered through my mind.*

Reluctant humor in his eyes as he dragged me out of a drugstore after we'd narrowly avoided a run-in with those humans who'd helped hunt kids like Doyle. Come on. I'd rather not continue to lurk in the feminine hygiene area.

The look in his eyes the first time he'd marked me.

Good memories, I thought.

Not all of them were hurtful.

I needed to focus on those. They were more than I'd really ever expected when I'd broken free from my grandmother's iron grasp.

I squeezed the trigger, felt it giving way.

I nearly choked as I tried to swallow back the sob.

"Shhh…" Paulie covered me with a blanket after she'd covered my neck with the poultice. "Why don't you rest?"

Rest. Normally, the first thing I wanted to do when she finished was stumble off the damn chair and move, but all I could do now was curl up in a ball and shudder. Shake.

Eyes closed, I cringed and waited for the memories to fade.

But they weren't fading this time. They slammed into me, one right after the other.

If you think I'll kill you and let you escape me like that, you're sorely mistaken… I've had you a week. Even if your fucking cat could find you, he wouldn't want you after what I've done to you.

Oh, Kit…broken, already?

Shoving the blanket back, I sat up in the chair and lifted

my hands to my face, all but ready to scream. The memories swarmed. Swamped me. I couldn't breathe, damn it. I couldn't—

I could hear his laugh. Feel his hands pinning me down, the strength of him as he fed and the pain as he tore into me.

And the pain…the pain that ripped through me when he carried my blade away.

Broken…

Useless…

I jerked upright off the padded chair and stumbled out of the room.

Paulie was rising to meet me and I shook my head. "I'll be back in a few days," I said before she could start clucking and soothing at me. I didn't want to be comforted or patted or stroked.

Not when I had all those nightmares of Jude in my head.

I wanted to cut something. Hunt something. *Fight* something—

But I was broken.

I took off down the street at a run, ignoring the cats who loitered outside the tattoo parlor every time I went in. The damn puma again. And a lynx. They needed to leave me the hell alone and if I had the breath, I might have screamed at them.

Instead, I just hurled myself toward TJ's.

Goliath was staring at the cats as well, but looked up at me as I stumbled to a halt just in front of him. Couldn't go in there like this. If I did, I'd hate myself. TJ would see it and I couldn't hide from her. Couldn't hide from Goliath, either, but at least he'd let me keep my secrets. He looked at me and then lowered his head, staring at the tattoo that spiraled almost up to my jawline now. "That's some serious ink on you now. I like the snake. Looks mean."

My voice shook a little as I reached for some level of calm. "It tried to eat me once."

"Did it now?" Goliath resumed his watchful stare, looking out over the streets like the asphalt itself might attack. Nothing slid by his notice. Not even my skinny, scared ass.

"Yeah. I chopped off its head. Figured it was fair." Up until a few months ago, I'd still had nightmares about the snake. Whoever would have thought I'd miss those?

He nodded . "Sounds fair enough to me. I would have barbecued it and had it for lunch." He was quiet for a moment and then said, "I heard screaming come from Pauline's today. Bad screaming if I can hear it outside her spells. You sure you have to keep doing this?"

"Yes." I went to go inside, but he caught my arm.

"She has to use poison to make them stay," he said sadly. "You okay with letting her use poison on your skin?"

"It's just enough to make the ink settle and it fades," I said tiredly. It *was* poison…to the *aneira.* A fact I might have learned if I hung around home long enough to finish my training, but then again, if I'd stayed much longer, my grandmother's *training* might have killed me.

Goliath continued to study me and then he reached up and touched my chin, angling my face away so he could study the newest addition. "A fang, Kit? Why do that?"

"It's a reminder...these are all the things that have broken me." I'd rather cover the ugly ones Jude had left me with something of my own choosing. "Sooner or later, I've got to find a way to remake myself and it starts with this."

Somewhere close by, I heard a cat roar.

Deep and loud, it echoed. I flinched and instinctively moved closer to Goliath. One massive arm wrapped around me and he hugged me. Softly, he whispered, "Kit...nothing broke you. You got knocked down, but you ain't broken."

Everybody seemed to think that.

They were all wrong.

The cat roared again and it was closer. Goliath sighed. "If you aren't ready to face it yet, Kit, you better get on inside."

I got on inside, like the coward I was.

When the guy came inside this time, I knew who it was. The puma who'd been prowling the streets the past few days. I should have placed him before now, but my mind had been…occupied.

He also had been coming into the bar regularly for the past three weeks and he left tips that were almost painfully ridiculous.

That was fine. I had Goliath donate the money to one of the shelters set up in Wolf Haven. They had nearly half a dozen and they could always use money.

I dumped his Redcat in front of him. "If you want me to do a job, I don't do them anymore. Find somebody else."

He stared at me for a minute and then looked away.

"You're wasting your time."

He sipped his Redcat and then said quietly, "No, ma'am. I am not."

I sighed and turned away. Fine. Let him waste a hundred bucks a week here drinking TJ's whiskey. What did I care?

I pressed a hand to the tattoo burning on my neck and got to work. I only had to keep busy for another hour and then I could collapse. Sleep. Get up. Work. Repeat.

Yeah, the memories were a bitch, but once she finished the tats I *needed* done, maybe she could just think up her own designs. I might even ask her to keep going once she finished. And then do more. If I could sleep without nightmares, it would be worth it to walk around covered in ink from head to toe.

Maybe—

Something attacked the wards. Sometime over the past few months, TJ had been recharging them—or rather her witch friends were adding new ones, *powerful* ones—and these wards wanted to keep somebody specific *out.* I knew enough about magic to realize that.

I dropped the glass I held as I heard a cat's snarl.

"TJ?" I looked up and saw her sitting in the doorway that led to the back.

She had her crossbow in her lap and was staring at the

door.

"Nothing—and nobody—you need to worry about, Kitty. Not just yet." She nodded at the glass. "Clean it up, would you?

There was another attack.

And another.

I heard something growl in the back of the bar.

TJ lifted her cross bow and pointed it off in the shadows. "Sit down and shut up or leave. This doesn't concern you."

One of the werecats stood up at the table and bared his teeth at her.

TJ narrowed her eyes as she took aim.

I drew the Eagle strapped to my thigh, aiming at the middle of his head. He was strong; he was big. But if I put two or three rounds in his head, then two or three rounds in his heart, he'd be dead.

The man at the bar stood and turned, a rumbling sort of snarl trickling from his throat. Nobody else made a sound.

"Come on, Kit," TJ snapped. "Clean up the glass or I'll shove a boot up your ass."

I glared at her. "You don't fucking *wear* boots."

A bit of a smile tugged at her lips. "Nah. But Goliath does and his are huge."

"You get the last one today."

I stood in the bar, all but gagging as I made myself eat a piece of toast. Toast—about all I can handle these days. Today was the broken sword.

I nodded shortly and tried not to look at TJ.

"You going to be late?" she asked softly.

"I don't know. I—"

Something hit the wards with enough force that the very building shook. I should be used to it, because it had been happening every damned day since it had first occurred a few days earlier—the day I'd had the fang carved into my skin.

But this felt different.

Stronger.

Heavier.

And I could feel the wards giving under the blows.

Blue lightning whipped around the room. It hit again and the lightning turned into a frenzy. Again. Again. Again—

"What the fuck?" I whispered. I flexed my hand and longed for the weight of my blade. She wasn't there, though, and I had to make do with the gun. Mesmerized, I stared at it, barely even aware I'd drawn it. Why was I holding the damn gun?

"Kit."

I jerked my head to look at TJ.

She was watching me sadly. "He's hurting, too, Kit. Don't hate me too much. I'm just trying to help you, kid."

"What—"

It hit me then and I lunged for the back door.

Another frenzy of lightning hit and then the ward shattered with a groan. Bits and pieces of magic fell to the earth, sparkling in the air. I could see them from the corner of my eyes and the death of the ward sucked the air out of me. If I'd moved a few seconds sooner, I would have gotten away.

But I was sensitive to magic and the power of the ward death's left me reeling. As I stumbled against the bar, I was painfully aware of the roar echoing through the bar.

The doors opened and spat Damon's bloodied form at my feet.

I backed up, determined to get something between us.

Something. TJ. Goliath. Anything or anybody.

But TJ had disappeared.

And I was alone with Damon.

CHAPTER FOUR

He spat a mouthful of blood on the floor and then looked up at me.

"If you're going to take off running, now is your best chance. I'm going to need a few minutes to get back on my feet," he said hoarsely.

I darted a look at the back door. I could do that. Completely.

You can't keep hiding.

Wanna bet? Hiding was my specialty. I excelled at it. I was good at it. And lately, I was more comfortable with it than I was anything else, even my weapons.

He groaned and rolled over onto his back, staring up at the ceiling for a minute and then sat up. His arm was hanging wrong. His fingers were getting discolored and swollen and just looking at him made me hurt. As he climbed to his feet, I backed another step away.

I didn't want to see him.

He took a deep breath and slammed his shoulder against the wall. I winced and looked away.

When I looked back, he was flexing his hand and rotating his shoulder. The color of his hand was returning and I had to wonder—just what kind of wards had TJ put up and why hadn't anybody else been hit like that?

"She had set them up against me," Damon said quietly.

"I've been trying to talk to you for almost a month and that living mountain out there has been telling me to give you time."

He slid me a look. "Give you time…but you never leave. Then when you do, you take off running from me. So then I tried to come in here and it turns out TJ had new wards put up specifically to keep me out. They've been kicking my ass every time I tried."

My heart tripped a little as I focused on my feet. That sounded like TJ. Shooting him a look, I saw the blood still running wet down his face even though the wounds were already knitting back together. Setting my jaw, I grabbed one of the clean towels from the stack we kept on hand and threw it at him. If he bled all over her floor, TJ was mean enough to ask me to clean it up.

He caught the towel and swiped the blood away. "Kit—"

"I don't want to talk," I said quietly. Even hearing his voice hurt. Looking at him hurt. Thinking about him hurt. I couldn't handle talking to him. I jerked open the cooler where we kept the beer and grabbed a Corona. Popping the top, I guzzled half of it before I'd let myself try to say anything else.

Why wouldn't he just leave?

"I know you feel like you have things you want to say to me," I said quietly. "But I can't handle hearing anything yet." I drained the other half of the bottle and pitched it. "Next time, before you get yourself bloodied for nothing, maybe you should call before you waste your time trying to come after me."

I started for the back door.

His words froze me. "Coming after you is never a waste, Kit. And I'm not giving up."

"That's too bad for you. I have." I kept walking. I needed to get to Paulie's. Needed to get this next one—the last one—done.

I'd told myself when I had the scars covered I'd see about starting my life again. I'd see about trying to remake myself. But even looking at one thing from my past left me shattered.

How could I possibly rebuild anything?

"I..." Paulie's voice paused in the middle of the tattooing.

I floated in a haze of pain, heat and horror. I'd thought the fang would be the worst, but this was so much more horrible than I'd ever imagined.

"Close your eyes, Kit," Paulie said, her voice full of magic and power. Even as I struggled past the veil of her magic, I couldn't.

Voices raged around me.

I don't have to break you to fuck you up…Xavier. The witch who'd cut the bond with my blade.

You're mine now... Jude.

Useless waste... Fanis. My grandmother. The woman I'd fled from when I'd been fifteen.

Good-bye. Damon.

It wasn't just one piece of my past, it seemed. It was everything. I hadn't had any idea what I'd face when she put the broken blade on me, but I hadn't been prepared for this.

Behind my eyes, I saw the swirling silver of my blade, spinning brighter, brighter, but I couldn't reach her.

Something touched me and I screamed.

"Shhh," Paulie murmured. "It's me, Kit. We need to finish it. It's worse with this one. We weren't prepared, were we?"

I sobbed.

"Do I need to stop?"

"No!"

Hands pressed on my shoulders as I struggled. Strong, too strong—

"Then be still," Paulie said. "Let's be done with this."

I felt the hot burn of blood on my neck, the brush of a cloth as it was wiped away. The ache and misery as memories beat at me.

Nobody will come.

I don't have to break you.

Useless.

"Shhh," Paulie said again.

It was an awful, horrible spiral that lasted forever and in desperation, I retreated.

I wasn't even aware when she finished.

Cold and shivering, I floated in a numb haze, keenly aware of the burn in my neck. Somebody wrapped something warm around me. I shivered and huddled deeper into it.

And I felt the warm prickle of energy slamming against my skin.

Recognition slammed into me and I rolled off the chair to crouch next to it, ignoring the screaming pain in my neck as I stared at Damon. I was only vaguely aware that I was wearing his jacket.

He sat in the chair on the opposite side. The chair where Paulie's assistant had been each and every time I'd come out of this weird, magical haze. He held a bloodstained cloth in his hands, one he twisted around his hands, over and over.

"What in the hell are you doing here?" I asked. My voice was a hoarse croak.

"I heard you scream," he whispered. He wouldn't look up from the cloth. Muscles bunched in his hands as he continued to twist it and then it shredded and he stopped. For a moment, he looked confused and then swore, surging up off the chair to pace. "I was trying to tell to myself I needed to leave. Needed to give you more time. And I heard you scream."

He turned his head and I didn't look away in time. The impact of his gaze, dark gray and haunted, hit me square in the chest. "What the fuck, Kit?"

Shaking my head, I forced myself upright. My legs shook as I took a few steps away. Out in the main room, I could see Paulie and her assistant. They looked terrified. "You didn't have to frighten them," I said quietly.

"I heard you. Screaming. You think I care if they are scared?" The energy around him shivered, hot and tight for a moment and then he stopped, blew out a breath. "Why are you torturing yourself like that?"

Torturing myself.

Turning away from him, I moved over to the mirror and stared at my neck.

It was done, I realized.

Finally. The tattoo was still inflamed, the redness even more stark considering how pale I was but there was no denying the sheer beauty of what she'd done.

I couldn't see the broken sword but maybe that was best. And it didn't matter. What did matter was the fact that I couldn't see those marks. I couldn't see where Jude had all but branded me as his plaything.

Even though I knew where they were, the artistry of her design, the cleverly placed lines and swirls hid the marks.

"Why?" I asked quietly, turning to look at him after a long moment of studying my reflection. "Because now when I look in the mirror, I don't see the scars he put on me that marked me as his toy. I don't see him every time I see my own reflection. Maybe I can look at the mirror and start to see me again."

Something flashed through his eyes and an eerie green rolled over his gaze, the skin tightening around his mouth. Turning away from him, I went back to gazing at the mirror.

I saw the images of everything that had cut into me, the things that had left bruises on me, battered my heart and my soul. The things that had broken me.

And I also saw me. Now it was time to start rebuilding myself.

"I see me."

CHAPTER FIVE

TJ slipped a phone number in front of me three weeks later.

"What?"

"It's a job."

I crumpled it up and threw it in her face. "No," I said calmly as I went back to pulling a beer.

It was finally quieter in her place. Most of the regulars were werewolves and some roughneck offshoots. Offshoots were the odd magical breeds like me. I thought the guy in the corner might be part mer-something. Water kept trickling over his flesh when he thought people weren't looking. And he smelled like seaweed.

Even with the weird smell in the air, I was happy the cats were no longer crowding into the bar.

Very happy.

I could almost breathe.

And I'd been coasting along just fine until TJ had thrown that number in my face.

"It won't pay a whole lot, but if you don't take the job, nobody else is going to, and the poor girl is out of luck." TJ talked like she hadn't heard my *no*. Even though I knew she had. "I just hope she doesn't try to go down there herself. She tried talking to Sam one time and—"

"Sam."

The bottle of Redcat I'd been putting up shattered in my hand. The fumes of the alcohol were strong enough that I felt a little dizzy and it didn't help that the potent stuff was also seeping into the cuts on my hand from the bottle I'd busted.

"Damn it, Kit, that bottle was half full!" TJ snapped, wheeling herself over to me. She went still when she saw the blood on my hand and glanced up.

I felt the skin on the back of my neck crawl but there wasn't any upward spike in the tension in the air. It was early and no more vamps had come back into the bar since that day a few weeks ago. Still, never hurt to be safe. Swiping one of the bar towels from the counter, I wrapped it around my hand to staunch the blood.

"You can't do that, kid," TJ muttered. "You'll heal with glass in there."

She grabbed my hand despite my attempts to pull away—wheelchair or not, she was still a werewolf and had the strength to match.

I held still as she grumbled and reached for the first aid kit under the bar. "What are you rambling on about?" I asked. "You said Sam."

Sam.

I could still hear the sound of her voice in the back of my head. *Sorry, honey. He doesn't want you anymore...*Those were some of the last words I'd heard before I disappeared into darkness. They'd haunted me during those weeks. Even now, even now when I tried to console myself to the empty mess of the life I'd always expected to live, they haunted me.

A prickle of heat danced in the palm of my hand. But it could have just come from the booze. Could have been from the pain as TJ dug out the slivers of glass.

But rage pulsed inside me.

Aside from that night with the vampire, it was the first fiery whisper of real rage that I'd felt.

I'd felt everything from despair to self-pity to disgust and I'd contemplated all the options that seemed to be fitting—staying here with TJ. Leaving and trying to start over elsewhere. Suicide had trickled in a few times during those first few days, but it hadn't lasted for too long. I'd survived Fanis. I'd handle this; I'd get through it.

Lately, all I'd felt was just listlessness, though.

The burn of anger was almost welcome.

Sam.

Gritting my teeth, I waited until TJ had finished digging the slivers out of my palm. Then I turned, looking out over the bar. A couple of the regulars were tucked in the back, bent over a worn out deck of cards. They were TJ's men. Not employed by her, but they were hers. Unless TJ said otherwise, they saw nothing. Heard nothing. Said nothing.

"What does Sam have to do with anything?" I asked quietly.

TJ didn't answer and when I turned my head to look at her, she was watching with a little bit of a smile on her face. "You're pissed off."

I sneered. Turning away from her, I headed back to the counter. I needed to get to work on inventory. Inventory—

Something twisted inside me and I felt like screaming.

"Kit."

TJ laid the paper down on the counter, smoothing out the creases. "She doesn't need much help...just somebody who'll run interference with the cats for her. She needs to talk to the boy who used to own the phone. It's a quick job, although I'm telling you, she can't pay much of anything. Sam would have been able to tell her, but she won't and now the girl is too afraid to call again. It's an easy job, almost as easy as checking inventory."

I swallowed. "Then why don't you do it?"

"Because I'm not losing myself here. Because I'm not the investigator." She nudged the paper. "You are. You're not meant for working in a damn bar, Kit."

I picked up a box-cutter. I had shit to do.

Half way across the floor, I turned and stormed back to the bar. I slammed the box-cutter down and grabbed the number. "How the hell do I get in contact with her?"

For the first time in months, I had to leave Wolf Haven.

When I walked outside and found my car sitting there, my heart lurched up into my throat until I thought I just might choke on it. Instead of letting myself do it, I walked around and jerked the door open.

"That's a girl."

I glanced at Goliath before I went to duck inside.

"TJ said you might freak out about the car."

Others might not realize what he meant, but I knew. Anything and everything associated with Jude was going to give me bad moments, and as stupid as it seemed, and as unfair as it seemed, the damned car was associated with Jude now, too.

I'd been in the middle of leaving town when I was kidnapped. Bags packed, door open, ready to climb in and head out…and then Xavier had appeared.

The last clear thought was stumbling back against my car, and the last clear emotion was terror.

Shooting Goliath a narrow look, I shrugged. "I'm pretty damn close. But don't tell her."

"It's okay. When you freak out, you kick the things that scare you in the balls." He tossed my keys at me.

Snagging them out of the air, I climbed in. "I haven't been doing much of that lately."

"That's because the person you're fighting right now is yourself." He grinned at me and said, "I wouldn't intentionally kick myself in the balls, Kitty. Takes a bit more work to fight that battle. But you'll get there."

I wish I was half as sure of myself as he was.

Without letting myself think it through any longer, I started the car.

East Orlando was a good forty-five minutes away and the longer I thought about this, the more likely it was I'd lose what little nerve I had left.

Think about the girl.

Don't think about anything else. Just her. And maybe Sam. Because you'd really *like to kick her in the teeth.*

It was an easy job. I just had to track down a phone number and it wasn't like I couldn't do that, right? I'd think about her, figure out the steps to solving the job.

Forty-five minutes to plot out, figure out, try to decide just what her problem might be. I could do this…right?

The girl in the coffee shop had just a little bit of magic on her. I felt it as I walked inside and automatically, I tensed, bracing myself.

She looked at me with so much terror, some part of me felt sorry for her. As her gaze dropped to the Desert Eagle strapped to my thigh then bounced to the blade riding on my hip, I wondered if I should have left the weapons locked up.

Gut response—*no.*

Somebody approached me, eyes wide with terror and I flipped out my ID card. *Fraud!* The voice was a scream in the back of my head but I wasn't about to have my weapons taken away. "I work for the Assembly," I said, tapping my finger against the badge. "I'm meeting somebody here on the job."

"You can't carry weapons in here like that."

"I can." I tucked the badge back away and slid my hands into my pockets as I held his gaze. I didn't want to pick a fight with him. I wanted to go back home. "Assembly and human law are both clear on this. I'm recognized as an investigator under Assembly law and I'm often chasing after things that aren't human. In order to do that job, I need my weapons. If you'd like to argue the fact, I can call Banner and the Assembly, you can call the human cops and we can argue it all out, right here in front of your customers, which isn't going to reassure them. Or you can let me do my job and I'll leave a lot sooner."

Something ugly flickered in his eyes. "I'm not required to serve you. I have the right to refuse service to anybody."

"I don't recall asking for service." I edged around him and started toward the girl. She looked even more scared now.

I felt him moving at my back before I heard him. Ducking and spinning to the side, I turned to face him. "You don't want to put your hands on me."

Nobody would do that again. I itched to pull a blade. I hadn't brought my sword, but that didn't mean I wasn't carrying other sharp, shiny objects. The knife at my hip would work just fine.

He thought the gun was scary?

His throat worked as he glared at me, then he shot the girl behind me a dirty look. "Make it quick." He bit off the words like they tasted bad, his face twisted in a tight, ugly scowl.

I kept him in my line of sight as I moved over to the table. She'd picked a four-top. Instead of taking the seat across from her, I took the one at her left hand, keeping the counter—and the man behind it— in my line of sight. My new friend was shooting daggers at me.

I waved at him before focusing back on the girl.

She feels kinda witchy. Now that I was closer to her, that was how she read to me. *Kinda witchy.*

There was an odd twinge of magic in her blood that just felt strange to me. And there was something else.

I could feel the buzz of her soul, batting against my mind.

But it was more than that. She was terrified of me, but I caught an odd sense of hunger. Need. It flickered in the back of her eyes and as I studied her face, she licked her lips and looked away. Her hands, small and delicate, were clenched into bloodless fists.

Her respirations were too fast.

So was her heart.

And that weird something—

"You're pregnant," I said as it clicked.

Her skin, a soft olive gold, flushed and she hunched her shoulders. "How did you know?"

"I'm just that good," I snapped. It sounded better than *I don't know.*

Groaning, I braced my elbows on the table and ground the heels of my hands against my eyes. "It's a werecat's kid, isn't it?" No wonder she was so desperate to find him.

"Yes." Her voice came in a broken little gasp and I lowered my hands, staring at her face as darkness roared in the back of my mind.

She was *terrified.*

"Did he hurt you?"

"*No*!" Her dark eyes jerked my way and she shook her head. "He didn't. We were..." She bit her lip and looked around before scooting in closer. "We were seeing each other but my dad didn't know. Then we…uh…he stopped calling me a few months ago. I...I didn't realize at first what was going on. But now I can't get a hold of him and I need to let him know and I—"

"Slow down," I said as the words came spilling out of her.

Pulling out the paper that held the number, I tapped it. "This is his number? Or was?"

She nodded. "But that number is dead. There's no forwarding address or anything. He...well, sometimes he used to hang out at the rec club on Bart Street."

Bart Street.

My brain filed that away even as I processed everything else. She was hiding something. I'd caught that little pause. A fight, maybe? Made sense. Everything else added up, even how she didn't know she was pregnant. Shifters carried longer and if she was carrying a baby with shifter blood, she'd carry longer, too. Typical shifter pregnancies, if I remembered right, were thirteen months and she might not have even noticed for the first four or five months. And it was a *damn* good thing she had non-human blood in her, otherwise we'd have an entirely different set of problems to deal with.

Swiping a hand down my face, I studied her and then braced my elbows on the table. "So when you couldn't get a hold of him, what did you do? Try to find him? Go to his house?"

"I tried to call. Well… um. Look, we had a fight."

Bingo. I thought so.

She glanced around nervously and then gave me a sad, almost broken look. "I thought my dad knew about us and I was…I was scared. So I broke up with him. But when I found out about the baby, I tried to call." She darted a look to the front of the coffee shop.

Fear spiked. Swelled.

Something lurked in the back of her eyes, a chained, caged beast looking out from behind her eyes. It wasn't *her*…not entirely. But the baby inside her wasn't human.

And it showed. In that odd, inhuman hunger, in the weird, not-quite-there look to her eyes.

The fear was the worst, though. It was gutting me. She looked like a girl who'd lived her whole life afraid. I knew what that was like.

Don't, I told myself. I was going to remain detached. This was just a quick and easy job because I was going out of my mind—I wasn't getting sucked back in.

It was already too late.

I found myself reaching out before I could stop myself. My hand on hers. "Why are you afraid?"

"I'm not!" It was a high-pitched, strident whisper. And a lie.

Her eyes wheeled around and I saw as her gaze landed on the man behind the counter. The blood slowly drained out of her face. "You have to leave," she said. "Please." She scrawled a name on the back of the piece of paper. "His name is Kent. Call me when you know something."

Lies... lies...lies...

The air was thick with them, but her fear was growing hotter and thicker, clinging to me. "Are you okay?"

She gave me a desperate look. "Just please, leave now."

I left.

CHAPTER SIX

The rec club on Bart Street had an official name, but nobody used it. It was just the rec club. If you needed clarification, it was the rec club on Bart Street. The official name was used in legal documentation or on Chang's credit cards, the bills, that kind of stuff.

Today was the first time I'd been here in almost five months.

I didn't let myself count the exact days, although I could.

I could count them to the hour. My heart slammed away inside my chest as I climbed out of my car and stood there, staring at the unassuming pile of cinderblocks. I didn't want to go inside, because if I did, they were likely to make me surrender my weapons and I didn't think I could do my job without them.

Not since my sword—

Stop it, I told myself.

I couldn't think about that without the fear raging out of control and if that happened, I'd start smelling like dinner. It didn't mean they'd want to attack. Shifters had serious control and they had to, but that didn't mean I wanted to walk around smelling like an all-you-can-eat buffet.

I locked the car and headed across the street. The men at the gates were watching me. Like all Assembly territories, the grounds were marked. Ideally, the signs should warn humans:

ANH turf, people. Enter at your own risk. But us non-humans had only been out of the closet for five decades and we were still struggling to be accepted as rational, thinking creatures capable of more than mayhem and murder.

It didn't matter that we'd all been sharing the same world for more centuries than any of us could count. Humans had only known about us for a few years and they were still struggling to accept it. It didn't always go well.

If a human got hurt inside those gates, even if he was trying to *kill* somebody else and the non-human—the NH—was acting in his or her own defense, it wouldn't matter.

The NHs would suffer the consequences. That was why the NH population worked to keep all but a few humans on the outside. Why they built up the reputation for being homicidal and bloodthirsty. If they kept the humans away through fear, they had fewer idiots to deal with. Safer, in the long run.

But I wasn't human.

"Ms. Colbana." That came from the one nearest my left. He had one meaty hand gripping his left wrist and his gaze was locked somewhere around the vicinity of my toes. "Chang has said you're welcome to go straight to his office."

"I'd rather speak to him out here," I said. Resting my hand on the butt of the Desert Eagle, I glanced past him to his cohort and saw that he was standing in about the same fashion. Hands in front, eyes on my feet.

What the hell was so intriguing about my boots?

"Of course, Ms. Colbana," the older one said. Dude in the back. He didn't look up as he gestured toward the guardhouse, just past the entry. "If you'd wait inside, I'll call Chang."

"I'll wait here. I'm not removing my weapons."

Older Dude shot me a look. "You needn't remove your arms, Ms. Colbana. If you'd wish to speak to Chang here or inside, it's all the same. You're welcome to carry the weapons." The eye contact lasted for ten seconds and then he went back to studying my toes.

What. The. Hell.

I couldn't stay outside here where they wouldn't look at me. It was hard enough being around people who looked at me out of the corner of their eyes and guessed about what had happened, but when they just wouldn't *look* at me?

Without saying anything else, I headed inside. Just before I pushed through the doors, I glanced back. They weren't watching me. They still had their gazes on their damn feet.

As did the men standing just inside the doors of the rec club.

This was the place where I'd once had a man grab my tits under the pretense of giving me a pat-down for weapons. As I started toward the security set up, one of them stepped forward, gaze downcast.

"Ms. Colbana."

He gestured to the door off to the side. I knew where it led. Chang's office.

I all but lunged for it, so relieved to get out of there. Away from people who couldn't look at me.

Shame and disgust and fear and humiliation crawled inside me. It was like it was written on my skin what had been done to me. Was *that* why they wouldn't look at me? Was that why they didn't want to see me? Because of what Jude had made me into?

His bloodwhore.

Bile churned in my throat and when a door caught my eye, I hurled myself inside.

It was a restroom, far more opulent than one would expect just from looking at the outside of the club, and even the general makeup of it. It was a teen's club, made for them to roughhouse, run wild and cause trouble, all without getting into *too* much trouble. It wasn't built with elegance in mind. But that was on the other side of the door.

This was Chang's territory and his stamp was everywhere, even in the damned women's room. Walls the color of burnt umber surrounded me as I leaned back against the door, sucking in one desperate breath after another. After about sixty seconds, I thought I could move without shattering, so I shoved away from the door and stumbled over to the sink. It was black marble, threaded with gold and cool under my hands.

Staring into the mirror at the pale circle of my face, I tried to understand what they'd seen that kept them from looking at me. Was it that obvious? Or did they just *know*?

They just know…

This time, when the bile crowded up my throat, I couldn't swallow it back down and I doubled over the sink, emptying my stomach. The sour, acrid stink of sickness wrapped around me as I convulsed, time and again.

Even when there was nothing left inside me, I retched. When the spasms finally passed, I rested my head against the marble and waited for the burning sting of shame to fade away.

It would take years, though.

The taste in my mouth, the stink of my own vomit pushed me to move. I straightened up and turned on the water, washing away the evidence of my weakness, while in the back of my mind I heard a familiar, mocking voice. *Useless waste. Pathetic weakling—*

"Shut up, you vile old bitch." Cupping my hands under the stream of water, I splashed it on my burning face. With the water dripping from my hands, cheeks and nose, I straightened up and looked at my reflection. The woman staring back at me was red-eyed, tired.

And she looked weak.

Not entirely broken, but she didn't look strong.

The tattoos spiraling up my neck were a stark splash of color against the pallor of my skin and I focused on them, on each mark etched on me. The broken blade that I could barely see. The spear. The snake. The fang. Hidden by my shirt was the leopard. Not easily seen by others, but still a mark I carried on me.

I looked at myself and saw something, *somebody* who was broken.

If I acted broken, I was going to be treated that way.

Chang had the door open before I reached his office and when I walked inside, he was standing in front of the desk.

When I saw his head lower, I wanted to take off running.

But the anger inside me took over and spilled out.

"I'm getting damn sick and tired of seeing the top of everybody's head. Am I that fucking hard to look at now? Do you look at me and see *Jude's Whore* tattooed on my forehead?"

Chang flinched, like I'd stabbed him with silver.

"No, Kit. Of course not."

And he still stared at his damned feet.

"Then why in the *hell* is everybody suddenly so interested in their shoes when I walk up?" I demanded.

A quiet sigh escaped him and he turned away. As he did, he lifted his head and it was just another lash across my heart. He could look up now. If he wasn't face-to-face with me, he'd look up. Son of a bitch.

I'd called him my friend—

"It's not you, Kit," he said quietly. "It's us. We failed you."

Staring at the back of his head, I flexed my hand absently. Even though I *knew* it was a waste of time, it was still a punch in the gut, knowing I couldn't call her.

Useless…broken…

Still, I didn't need a sword to relieve the fury inside me. Pounding my fists against the nearest hard surface might help; Chang's head would suffice.

"You're the woman Damon chose for himself."

I tensed at his voice.

Now *I* was the one to turn away. Averting my head, I shoved my hands into my pockets. "Chang, don't."

But it was like he didn't hear me. "You're his," he continued. "And by extension...ours. If you were a shifter, this would translate to different things for us. Had he chosen a shifter for his partner, she may or may not have been somebody who'd been his equal. We don't hold to any mindset that he has to pick his physical match."

I snorted. "He'd never find *that*."

"No. He wouldn't. But he found somebody who suited him, and somebody who was his match in other ways. It was you. And as you weren't as strong physically as a shifter, it was up to us, those who hold ourselves loyal to him, to protect you in the ways you couldn't. If you aren't as strong as some, we could make up for that. If you aren't as fast, we are. It was our duty to make sure you were cared for. And we failed. You proved yourself worthy of him, but we've proven ourselves not worthy of you."

I couldn't even describe what was going through me as those words fell between us. *You're his…*

No. No, I wasn't. But I guess they didn't know that. They were beating themselves up over nothing.

Spinning on my heel, I headed over to Chang's weapons wall. It had always soothed me. Maybe I couldn't call them anymore, but weapons were my security blanket and just looking at them made me feel better.

There was one katana that had always drawn my eye. He gleamed like silver magic under the lights. Absently, I touched my fingers to his hilt. His music was gone, too.

I'd lost them all. No connection to any of them now.

"You're all getting worked up over nothing then," I said, forcing the words out as I continued to stroke my hand down the blade's hilt. "It ended the night Jude kidnapped me. Damon had dumped me. I guess word didn't get around. You're all kicking yourself for no reason, so just stop it already. I'm getting sick and tired of staring at people's skulls and I don't care what the reason is."

"It isn't over for Damon, Kit. His connection to you is permanent."

Goodbye, Kit.

I closed my eyes against the ache inside me. "No. It wasn't. He walked away from me. I was in the middle of a job and I had to see it done. But it was something that was hurting him and he needed something I couldn't give him. In the end, what he needed and what I needed didn't meet up and he ended—"

"If I may interrupt," Chang said and his voice was no longer quite so malleable. No longer quite so gentle and polite. "I'm aware of what the job was."

I felt a flicker of heat—it was enough of a shock that I turned, hand instinctively going to the Eagle that rode my hip, but Chang was still staring outside. "I'm quite familiar with the Banner job at this point," he said. "And it doesn't matter. Damon was angry. But despite his anger, he wouldn't have stayed that way."

I absorbed those words and tried to let them settle inside. In the end, though, there was only one thing that I could think of. "What does it matter?" I asked quietly. The thick, lush carpet muffled my footsteps as I crossed over and settled in the seat across from his desk. It was the narrower one, the one he'd often pointed subordinates to when he was questioning them, dressing them down. It was a miserably hard affair, but I couldn't sit in the other one. It had my back to the door and I couldn't defend myself as easily from it.

I sat down and focused on his back. "Whether he would have stayed angry or not, whether he and I would have tried to get things to work, none of that matters because that life is no longer mine." I brushed my fingers along the tattoo on my neck. "The woman who left here five months ago no longer exists, Chang. She died up in the mountains in Canada. I'm not her."

"No?" He turned around and for the first time, he looked at me. There was sadness in his eyes and it bothered me. I didn't like seeing my friends sad. I guess I still considered him a friend. "She's not dead—I see her in front of me, Kit. *You* are still her."

"No." I held his gaze. Not that many knew just how much had changed. I wasn't going to educate them. But the very basic part that made me who I was—she was *gone*. "Jude broke her and then he killed her. I'm all that's left and I'm still trying to figure out what that is."

His gaze shifted to the tattoos on my neck, lingering there. Slowly, he nodded and then he looked away again. "If that is how you choose to view it, then very well. Why are you here, Kit?"

Pulling the phone number from my pocket, I held it up for him. "I'm looking for the cat who used to have this number. I was given the name Kent. I was also lied to. But I need to find him."

"Kent isn't the name of any shifter I know." He flicked a look in my direction, studied the number. "Cat, rat or wolf. It's not the first name or last, to my recollection."

"It could be a middle name. I don't know." Shrugging it off, I tossed the number on his desk. I trusted his recollections but I wasn't letting it go at that. "As I said, I was lied to. A girl is involved. She's scared. Said he used to hang around here. She tried to call the Lair and Sam gave her the run around, I'm told. The number is the one thing I have to go on and she wasn't lying about the number or the fact that he's a shifter. Can you find out who had that number?" He shifted his gaze to me, his black eyes troubled. Finally, though, he moved to his computer. "Computer, search database," he said, reciting the number.

"*Working...*"

He tapped something on the keyboard. I couldn't tell what from where I was sitting.

The skin around his eyes tightened a little and then he looked back up at me. "I believe the cat you need works at the Lair. Whether or not he's on shift now, I don't know. Doyle would be of more use to you."

Doyle.

I thought of the kid I'd rescued almost seven months ago. The boy who'd *then* rescued me.

"I'll just call him," I said woodenly. Shoving out of the seat, I headed for the door.

"Kit. Why did you come here instead of going to the Lair? If Sam knows the number, why not just ask her?"

"Because I didn't want to go to the fucking Lair," I snapped, shooting him a dark look.

He watched me soberly. "You have some issue asking Sam for the information you need?"

I stopped in my tracks and turned to face him. "The day

that idiot bitch stops me from doing anything is the day I take up knitting."

"Then I must assume it's because of Damon." He cocked his head. "Why is it a problem for you, though? If it's over...and the woman you used to be is dead?"

I glared at him for a long moment and then fantasized about drawing my gun and shooting nice, watermelon-sized holes in the walls of his oh-so-lovely office. Instead, I turned on my heel and left.

Still, I carried that image with me all the way down to my car.

I tried to hold on to it even as I drove to the Lair. Going there really shouldn't be a problem. Not if the woman I'd been was dead. The problem was I that I knew I'd lied.

It was just easier to think about things if the woman I had been was completely dead.

Dead sounded so much better than broken.

There had been a time when I couldn't show up here without Damon being on the walk, coming toward me the minute I parked in the spot that he'd set aside for me, almost always with that faint smile on his face, the one that made my heart skip.

Even now, I was having a hard time controlling my heart and damned if I could figure *that* out.

I drove past the empty spot that had once been mine and turned down one of the side streets, parking nearly a half-mile away. Parking wasn't exactly substantial around here, but that spot wasn't mine anymore.

A couple of the cats I saw glanced at me—weird little double-takes and then I got the same damn behavior from them that I'd gotten from Chang and it pissed me off, but what in the hell was I supposed to do about it?

A year ago—hell, six months ago—the Lair had been a quiet place. Heavy with tension, pain and ugliness, the silence broken by the raised voices of those who'd been in good standing with the former Alpha. She'd been a crazy, evil bitch and those who were crazy, evil pieces of work had done well under her hand.

Since her rather timely death, Damon had been doing his best to turn things around and after a few rough months, things had changed. Usually, it was noisier here. He was doing a lot of rebuilding, putting his stamp on the massive building that was known as the Lair. Sounds of construction filled the air, people laughing, shouting.

Some of the cats lived there. I think he had about two hundred people total living at the Lair and a handful were kids. Sometimes, you could hear them laughing. When I'd driven past, I'd heard the faintest strains of voices drifting over the resounding *whack* of a hammer, somebody blasting music.

But the closer I moved to the Lair, the quieter it became.

Nausea churned in my gut as I popped my wrist, wishing like hell that faint tingling I sensed in my palm was something, *anything* that would bring my blade to me, but it wasn't.

Because I needed to touch something, I rested my hand on my belt and rubbed my thumb over the silver wire worked into the leather.

I wasn't even afraid of them really.

I was just—

A tiger's roar ripped through the air and I tensed as I saw the flash of orange just before he came leaping over the fence—that damn thing was eight feet high. He took it like it was a bump on the road.

I came to a halt as Doyle crouched on the ground in front of me, a long, sleek tiger that was nearly double the size of a natural one. He waited there, staring at me with intelligence in his eyes.

Swallowing the knot in my throat, I forced myself to talk. "Hi, Doyle."

He stretched out on his belly and rested his head on his paws, eyes on my face, just watching me.

"Ah...is this your way of telling me I can't go in? Using

that giant, tiger-skin rug to block me?"

He sneezed and sat up, still watching me.

I took a step forward and he didn't do anything, so I moved a little more.

By the time I was even with him, I was almost breathing normal. As he leaned in, he lifted his head to butt it against my chest. It was almost enough to knock me off my feet. Sighing a little, I wrapped my arm around his neck.

"If I didn't know better, I'd think you missed me," I said quietly. It hadn't been *that* long ago that the overgrown house cat had acted like he couldn't stand me. And now this?

He rubbed his head against me. Sinking my hand into the thick, dense fur around his neck, I dipped my head and pressed it to his. "Thanks again for finding me, Doyle."

He'd been the one to track me down. I still didn't know how. If I could ever get to where—

Just before my mind could take that nasty sideways journey into fear, he made a harsh sound, deep in his chest and then eased away, still watching me with those alien, inhuman eyes.

"I need to talk to you," I said, darting a glance around. I could do this out here, I thought. If he'd just change—

He moved his big head in a nod and then turned, flicking his tail as he walked.

I stared at him.

He stopped and looked back at me.

"I guess that means I'm coming inside."

Another dip of his head and he started to walk. At the gated entry, the guards fell back aside, staring at their feet. Since they didn't make any comment about my weapons, I wasn't about to mention them. They would have seen them; I had no doubt about that.

Oxygen seemed a little too sparse in this part of East Orlando all of a sudden. I completely blamed the atmosphere, too, because it was easier to think it was some weird thing with the air than to think about being afraid.

Curling my hand around my belt, I followed Doyle's orange-and-black hide into the Lair, focusing on nothing but him, the scents of fresh-cut wood and paint. He wound through, taking corridors I hadn't previously used. Everywhere there were signs that the renovations had expanded well past Damon's quarters. I guessed that explained why we were winding in circles.

He paused in the middle of the hallway and I stood so close, I could feel the brush of his fur against my hip. Golden eyes stared through a pane of glass and I followed his gaze, wondering what it was that held him so enthralled.

Somebody came flying at the glass right as I looked up.

I managed not to flinch. Barely. It would have been reinforced, otherwise Doyle would have moved.

Blood splattered the glass as the dark-haired woman crumpled to the floor. A few seconds later, she was upright. Swaying, but upright. I took a second to look past her—recognition hit. This was the training hall. They were putting in a viewing section. It had used to be grim and gray, more like a dungeon than anything else.

It was still grim, but that had more to do with the blood all over the place than anything else. It wasn't the windowless pit it had once been and the walls were white—had to be charmed or specially made to repel stains or something, because cats didn't spar like human combatants. They fought to the blood. Then they healed up and did it again. When weres had to fight, it wasn't about fair play and rules.

It involved life and death. That was how they trained.

The woman was upright now, moving with a limp as she headed back into the circle, blood flowing down at her back. The man in the middle looked familiar, I thought. Dark hair, almost black. Golden skin. Very pretty. Out of place in the middle of that circle—then he looked at me and I knew.

It was the puma I'd seen back in Wolf Haven.

One of Damon's cats.

Clenching my jaw, I looked away from him to the woman, but as she turned around and I saw her face, rage sizzled inside me, a low-level burn.

Sam.

He doesn't want you now...

The mocking edge of her words screamed loudly in my mind as I watched her. Her gaze slanted my way and that rage, a sleeping beast in the pit of my belly, snarled to waking life within me.

A smile curled her lips. Mocking and cold.

I imagined pulling the gun at my hip. Those windows might be strong, but the ammo in my gun would cut through a tank—and her.

The man in front of her said something—I couldn't hear what. The walls, the glass, all of it was soundproof. I imagined not even Doyle heard what he said.

She just continued to stare at me. A split second later, she was on the floor.

I blinked and looked at Doyle. "Ah, isn't she one of the lieutenants?"

Doyle made an odd *hnk* sound in his throat. It almost sounded like a laugh. Then he rubbed his cheek against my arm and started to walk. Lingering just long enough to watch Sam shove up onto her hands and feet, I fell back into pace behind Doyle. As long as I focused on him, I didn't have to think about all the others around me.

So far, the majority of them either backed out of the hallway at the sight of me or they took up the rapt study of Kit's feet.

The kids were different, though.

Although they sensed the tension in the air and fell silent over that, they didn't look away from me. One came hurtling down the hall, a little scrap of a thing, moving quicker than anybody had a right to, especially when she was all of three feet tall.

Her hair was bright red and her eyes were as green as grass. She stopped dead in the center of the hall for a minute when she saw Doyle. Then she squealed and lunged for him. As soon as she caught him, he rolled, going to his back so that the girl was now sitting on top of him. "Are you ready to play with me?" she demanded, bending down and glaring at him, nose to nose.

Doyle growled.

She growled back and it was the cutest damn thing, because she wasn't even close to coming up on her shift. It sounded just like what it was—a human throat trying to make an animal sound, but Doyle pretended to be afraid.

I found myself smiling at them. Bumping his hindquarter with my toe, I asked him, "Am I interrupting a play-date, Doyle?"

He swung his head over to look at me just as the girl noticed me.

She blinked up at me, her eyes rounding.

"Who are you?"

Somebody came rushing around the corner before I had an answer. "Chelsea, what are—"

The words froze in her throat when she saw me and her eyes widened in the same way the girl's had. I had no doubt this was the mother and the horror on her face hit me right in the pit of my stomach. As she jerked her head down, I tore my gaze away from her and focused on the hallway.

"Chelsea, sweetheart, come with me now," the woman whispered, the sound all but silent.

The girl didn't seem too interested in listening.

She swung a leg off the living, breathing toy she'd discovered in Doyle and slid to the floor, leaning against him like he was a nice, cozy pillow. Her red hair spread around her like a fan as she smiled. "You look mean," she decided.

"Do I?" I asked.

The mom inched a step forward.

Screw you, I decided, hunkering down in front of the girl. She looked like a little fairy. Delicate and soft and pretty.

Fairies weren't exactly soft *or* delicate, but she still put me in the mind of one. And if she was a cat, she'd end up being deadly later on. Maybe it was a good comparison, after all.

So far, the little fairy was the only one besides Doyle who didn't treat me like I was either breakable or contagious. *Mean* sounded so much better.

Bracing my elbows on my knees, I peered into her face.

"Just how mean do I look?"

"Even meaner than Doyle when he acts like he's going to eat me," she said. A dimple appeared in her cheek.

"*Chelsea*."

Her mom sounded like she was going to have a panic attack. I should probably stop talking to the girl, stop distracting her, but it was nice to not be treated like a pariah. Resting my chin on one fist, I said, "If I look *that* mean, then why are you talking to me?"

"Cuz you're with Doyle. If you were really mean, he would have eaten you."

"Do you really think he'd try to eat me? I don't think tigers eat people."

She scrunched up her face. "If you were mean, he would."

"Chelsea..." the woman's voice was near tears now and I was so disgusted, I wanted to kick something. Hit something. *Somebody*.

I slid Doyle a look. "Think so?" I leaned in a little closer and said, "I think your mom thinks *I'm* the one who's going to start making snacks out of people. Either that, or she thinks standing near me is going to give you a deadly disease. Who knows, maybe you'll catch *human*."

Chelsea gulped. "You can't *catch* that." Then she darted her mother a quick look and her thin shoulders drooped.

I patted her on the head. "Go on, Miss Chelsea. I'm not hungry today anyway."

She laughed a little as she clambered back over Doyle. As her mom snatched her up, she whispered, "She's funny, Mama. You can't really *catch* human—"

"Chelsea, *hush*," the woman said, still staring at the ground. "You're being rude."

"Actually, she's the *only* person who isn't being rude," I snapped. Screw these nerves. I nudged Doyle again and watched as he stretched out before climbing to his feet. "Other than your kid and the lap-cat here, everybody else is acting like I'm a leper. Didn't the humans cure that finally?" Disgusted, I buried my hand in his pelt. "Wherever we're going, can we *go*?"

I was so pissed off, I thought I could have maybe handled seeing Damon without falling apart.

Maybe.

CHAPTER SEVEN

Then again…

I wanted to take off running down the long dim hall when Doyle reached the end of it and bumped his head against the wall. A wall that wasn't a wall. My gut went tight, turning into slippery knots as a section eased forward.

Even before it moved completely out of the way, I knew where Doyle had brought me. "You damned overgrown fur rug," I grumbled while the knots in my gut went taut, drawing tighter and tighter with panic. Damon's quarters. I knew it. Just from the change in the air—I knew the light, the feel, the scent of it.

And I reacted the way I always did when I thought I might see him. Belly tight, hot. Hands sweating. Heart racing. Mouth dry. My body went on red alert while my brain kept replaying moments that I tried too hard to forget.

Goodbye, Kit.

Damon's voice, rough and raw in my ears.

Did you really think I wasn't coming…

I realized I was standing there in the middle of the hall, a shaking, terrified mess, all because Doyle had pushed open a door. Six months ago, I would have been in that room and happy with it. *Had* been happy, as happy as I'd ever been.

Then the job from hell ended everything. Damon and I'd fought, because I'd been investigating *him*, trying to save his life and I'd been bound from telling him. He'd told me goodbye and those were some of the last words I'd had in my head, words that haunted me during the two weeks I had been Jude's prisoner.

Did you really think I wasn't coming for you?

"Shit." I drove the heel of my hand against my head, wishing I could silence all of those memories. Now wasn't the time for inner contemplation or self-reflection.

He did come—

"Job first," I muttered. Job first. Breakdown later.

My legs were only shaking a little as I pushed past Doyle and headed into the main room.

The scent of him wrapped around me and for a moment, just a moment, the world spun away and I was back in that time. When life made sense, and I felt secure in who I was…when I had *mattered.* When I had been something. Somebody. When I'd been somebody worthy…

Swallowing the knot in my throat, I cast a furtive look around and couldn't decide if I was relieved or disappointed to see he wasn't here. Although part of me had already known that. If he was in here, I would have realized it already.

Sucking in one slow breath, I turned in a circle, taking in the room. Nothing had changed.

Nothing except everything outside this room. Shaking it off, I turned and faced Doyle.

"Why am I in here, kid?"

Hot, prickling energy rolled across my skin and I wasn't surprised when I heard him speak a few seconds later.

Some people had to fight to shift from one form to another.

Doyle made it look easy.

"Sorry, Kit. I figured you'd rather talk about this privately. Most of your jobs are usually stuff you don't talk about on the street."

I glanced up and saw him standing behind the couch, tugging a shirt over his head. As he moved out from behind the couch, he dropped down on it and stared at me, his blue eyes calm.

Once his face had given me some bad, bad moments. He reminded me of somebody I hated, feared, despised, but I didn't see so much of that now. And it helped that he didn't seem to hate, fear or despise me, I'll admit.

"You don't seem to have any trouble looking me in the face," I said levelly.

He shrugged, something dark and unhappy moving through his eyes. "Don't be angry at them. I know you see it as an insult, but they're just…ashamed." He shoved off the couch and started to pace. Doyle had as much trouble being still as I did; always had, it seemed. "Seeing that you're out working and about ready to kick us all in the teeth will probably help a little."

"I'm not working," I muttered, hunching my shoulders. I had to fight the urge to hide. I could curl up in that chair and press my face against the fabric of the upholstery. It smelled like Damon and if I didn't think about what had happened…

You need *to think about it* , the rational voice in my mind whispered. *What really did happen? Jude was wrong. You got out. And your friends* did *come, all of them. Damon came.*

I couldn't do this here. I was too close to falling apart already and I knew I'd been lying to Chang. I knew it, because it hurt too much to think about the disaster I saw when I looked at myself. If the woman I had been was dead, it wouldn't hurt so much. I'd be a shell, starting over from new and the memories wouldn't cut so deeply; the pain wouldn't tear into me with hooked claws.

Yes, I'd lied.

I was angry with Damon. Not because he'd told me good-bye. Not because he'd been angry with me.

It was because he hadn't *been* there when Jude had me grabbed. That he hadn't stopped it. There was no way he could have known, but it didn't matter.

Nobody hurts you, Kit…

He'd made that promise to me. That foolish, unrealistic promise. And some part of me had wanted to believe it. That same part of me was *furious* that he hadn't kept that promise.

That wasn't fair.

Swallowing the knot in my throat, I forced myself to focus on Doyle, on why I was here. "I'm not working...exactly. I don't know if I'm going to."

Liar.

A half-hysterical laugh bubbled in my throat but I kept it trapped inside. "Look, let's not talk about work, okay?" I looked at my hands and realized I'd managed to keep hold of the phone number. "Right now, I just need to focus on one thing—finding whoever used to have this phone number. Chang says you'd be able to help me."

Doyle glanced at it. "Yeah. I know who used to have it. Why?"

"That's personal."

He grimaced and went to flop back on the couch, rubbing the back of his neck in a way that reminded me too much of Damon. "Well, that's a problem, because I can't tell you unless I know. Damon could, but then you'll probably have to explain to him why you need to know." With a look of wide-eyed innocence, he stared at me. "You want to ask Damon?"

The knot in my throat was about the size of the Epcot Center, lodged there. Choking me. Shooting to my feet, I crossed the room to the small bar area. There was a stock of packaged water and I needed something. "Sure. You can have him call me when he gets in—"

The prickle of heat that I'd felt from Doyle was nothing like the wave of it that rolled across of my skin in the next moment. Gripping my water in my hand, I stared at the bar. "Damon's in the Lair, isn't he?"

"Yeah." Doyle stayed on the couch. I could see him from the corner of my eye and he was watching me.

I could see the concealed entrance where we'd entered. I hadn't been aware of it until Doyle had brought me through just moments earlier. As the wave of heat grew stronger and hotter, I tried to decide. Did I run for it?

Doyle wouldn't stop me. I knew that.

Not his fault.

Closing my eyes, I twisted the top of my water and lifted it to my lips.

Damon.

My heart raced. It had been three weeks since I'd seen him. It seemed like longer. But it wasn't long enough. I couldn't—

The door opened. My hand convulsed on the water and the plastic crumpled. Lowering my gaze, I stared at the water and sighed. Dumping it in the recycler, I dried my hands off. I was surprised to see they weren't shaking. That was nice, I thought. At least I could face him without showing how much of a mess I was.

He'd know, of course.

Damon always knew.

My heart bumped against my ribs as I turned around and saw him standing in the door. His hair had grown out longer than I'd ever seen it, maybe even close to an inch all over. Eyes the color of thunderheads stared at me as I stood there. A muscle pulsed in his jaw.

The silence was weighted, a heavy burden settling on my shoulders as I fought the urge to back away. Run. Hide.

Nearly a month had passed since he'd barreled his way through the wards at TJ's. An eternity seemed to stretch out between us, words hung unspoken, the pain in my heart, in my soul, so vivid and all consuming, it all but doubled me over.

Doyle was the one to shatter it. "Kit needs some information on somebody in the Clan."

Damon shot me a look and then focused on Doyle. "What for?"

"Work."

Damon looked back at me, taking in the gun, the K-bar strapped to my thigh and although he didn't say anything, I suspected he was fully aware of the fact that I was pretty much loaded for bear. His gaze dropped to my belt—at least that was what I figured he was looking at, although some part of me, the part that wasn't instinctively cowering in fear, felt a warm, shivery little tingle spark, then spread. I rested my hand on my belt and stroked the silver wire of the garrote, needing something to ground myself.

"You looking to kill one of my cats, kitten?" he asked tiredly.

"No." I shouldn't have thrown the damn water out. I needed a drink. My throat was dry. Stroking the wire, I made myself think about the girl. Her scared eyes… the silent plea I'd seen there.

Looking down at the scrap of paper I held, I rubbed my thumb over it. *An easy job, TJ. Supposed to just be an easy job*, I thought. And here I was. Standing in front of a man I still dreamed about even though I tried to convince myself that part of me was dead.

"I just need to find a kid." Wow. I sounded nice and level. Almost like myself. Not bad. "There's a girl who needs to talk to him."

Feeling the weight of that gaze, I made myself look up. He hadn't moved. But Doyle had. He was on his feet and heading out the door. *Leaving*—

The muscles in Damon's arms bunched hard, rigid for a moment and then I watched as he relaxed, bit by bit. I had to make myself do the same thing. I wasn't going to be afraid to be someplace alone with Damon. I wasn't.

I wasn't *afraid* of him, either. There was no reason to be. *He* hadn't hurt me and I knew that. The pulse slamming away in my heart, fluttering in my wrists, the adrenaline crashing through my veins, my body would get the message in a minute, too, and I would calm down.

I wasn't afraid to be alone with him.

I wouldn't *let* myself be afraid.

Spinning away, I shoved my hands through my hair and locked my fingers behind my neck. "I just need to know who he is, Damon. I'm not looking to bring him any trouble and I'm not—"

The rest of the words caught in my throat as I spun around and saw him standing closer.

Not too close. Ten feet separated us, easily.

One hand curled into a fist at his side, beat against his

thigh. "Why you need to talk to one of my cats, Kit? If you aren't looking to kill him, then it shouldn't be that hard to give me a reason."

"And what if I am here to kill him?"

It popped out of me for no real reason. Other than the fact that I needed to distract my brain. Nothing did it quite the way my smart mouth and trouble could.

"You already *said* you weren't here to kill him," Damon pointed out.

"Well, that's not my plan." I shrugged and absently reached down and stroked my hand down the butt of the Desert Eagle. The weight of it wasn't as comforting as my sword, but it was there. "But you probably know by now that my plans have a habit of going to hell and I do better if I don't operate with one."

His eyes narrowed on my eyes and then he shoved a hand back over his hair. "Okay. Explain what the problem is so I can understand why you think you might or might not have to kill him so I can decide if I need to help you or not."

"I don't recall asking for *your* help," I said sourly. I'd come here to ask for Doyle's.

"You're in the Lair," he pointed out. "You want information on one of my cats? You're going to need my help."

Now *that* rubbed me the wrong way. "You know, I was doing shit like this on my own, without your help, for a long while and I often had to do it when I wasn't fucking the damn Alpha," I snapped.

"You're not fucking him now either." Something flashed in his eyes. Pain. Regret. Misery. A low, ugly curse left him and he turned away.

As he moved over to the couch, I rubbed my thumb along the surface of my belt. I think this would be easier if I just wrapped the garrote around my fist, pulled tighter until the wires dug into my skin and sliced me open. *Quick. Just get it over with quick.*

He sat on the couch, elbows braced on his knees, staring at nothing.

Easy job. I just need to find a kid…

Swearing, I stormed over to him and threw the phone number down on the stone-and-glass coffee table in front of him. "I need to know who use to have that number. He hooked up with a girl—she's mostly human. Not entirely. That's a good thing, otherwise you might be dealing with Banner instead of me. She's pregnant."

A hiss escaped him and he jerked his head up, staring at me. "Mostly human?"

"Yes." I held his gaze for a minute, to prove that I could more than anything else. "She won't catch it." If she'd been fully human, it could be a touch and go thing in the first few weeks after sexual activity. It could lay dormant in the body and not emerge until some major stress was placed on the body—pregnancy would do it. But the girl was months pregnant and more; she wasn't going to be able to catch the virus. The magic in her blood wouldn't let it take root. It was the same reason I couldn't catch any of the were-viruses. The blood we'd been born with wouldn't let an invasive virus take over.

He scrubbed his hands over his face. "How did it come to this?"

"She lost contact with him for a little while. They were dating—sounds like her dad is a prick and a half and she's scared of him. Whoever the cat is, she broke up with him. Didn't realize she was pregnant until recently, but when she tried to reach him, the number had changed." I shrugged and moved around, pacing the living room, keeping a wide distance between me and him. Getting close to him was more than I could handle right then. "I don't know if she's too nervous to try and come out here, if she'd rather talk to him on the phone or what. But she did try to call and get in touch with him and..."I paused, felt that tug of anger unfurl inside me. "Sam answered the call. Told the girl that if she wanted to talk to a cat, she needed to grow some balls and come down here."

I slanted a look at him. "I don't like that woman, Damon. I don't like her at all."

A muscle in his jaw pulsed. "She's a bitch, but the clan doesn't exactly give out phone numbers just because a human girl calls up looking for one."

"And what about when your girlfriend calls to talk to you after a fight?" I don't know if I'd meant to talk about that or not. But the words ripped out of me and…and they were just *there*. Thrown out like a sucker-punch and now they hung between us like an ugly, red stain.

Silence struck, heavy and weighted, crackling with more tension that I could stand.

Damon came off the couch in a smooth, controlled motion, his eyes locked on my face and everything inside him seemed…quiet.

Too quiet. All of that caged, restless energy was sucked down and he just stared at me, unblinking. It was damned unnerving.

Seconds ticked by and finally, he said softly, "What did you just say?"

"You heard me well enough," I muttered, spinning away from him. Crossing my arms over my chest, I focused on the cold, empty fireplace.

"Kit, what did you just say?" Damon asked, his voice still calm and gentle.

Lulling me…and it worked. I shot him a nasty look. "Oh, come off it. Are you going to give me the kid's name or not?"

"My question first, Kit," he said quietly.

My heart slammed once against my ribs as I glared at him. "Forget it, Damon. Okay? Are you going to help me with the kid or not?"

"In a minute." He started to pace around the room, not circling *me* exactly, because he kept too much distance. "We need to back up a bit…you're going to answer *my* damn question this time, or I'm going bring Sam in here and I'll get the answer out of her. I can tell you now, she won't answer the first time I ask." As he circled in front of me this time, he came in closer, stopping just a few feet away. His gaze locked on my face and the look in his eyes was enough to have my heart slam against my ribs, just from the sheer intensity of it. "I want answers and I'm going to get them, so if you don't give them to me, I'll drag them out of her. And she's stubborn, so I'll probably have to break a few bones, starting with her hands and then I'll work my way up. If that doesn't do it, I'll snap her neck."

He wasn't calm now. Rage danced across his face and it was an icy sting on my skin. Swallowing the spit that had pooled in my mouth, I said, "Well, that will do you a fat lot of good, breaking her neck."

"Baby girl...she's a cat." A slow smile curled his lips. "She'll live through it. If I'm careful, she could even heal. I'm not overly worried about her healing, though. Are you going to tell me or do I get to get some practice in on breaking bones?"

Son of a bitch. He'd do it, too.

I might have serious rage piled inside me towards Sam. I realized it wasn't fair—it was like being mad at Damon for him not *being* there when I was kidnapped. But emotions don't much care about being fair. Maybe I could eventually handle how I felt about what happened between us; I don't know.

And *shit*, I was fooling myself. I wasn't going to get over what had happened with Damon and me. I'd deal with it. I'd accept it. I'd move past it. But get over it? That wasn't going to happen.

Sam was a different issue altogether—I wasn't about to *accept* how pissed off I was with her, and I don't care that it didn't make sense. Still, I didn't necessarily want to see him batter her into the ground.

Maybe I'd feel better if *I* hurt her a little.

But there was a difference between what I would do and what he was planning.

Absently, I pulled one of the blades out from my vest and started to toy with it. I was slow—it had been too long since I'd let myself find comfort in any of my weapons. The silver wasn't a blur in the air over my hands. A couple of times, I almost dropped it before I found the rhythm again, but it was comforting just to try.

"I don't see what you're so fucking pissed about," I said, focusing on the blade instead of what I felt. Instead of the fear, the anger and the shame. "I told everybody up on the mountain that I'd called. Sam just passed on your message."

"My message," he said, his voice hovering just above a growl.

I moved my hand wrong and the blade caught my palm. I snagged it with my left hand, lowering it as I stood there.

"Kit," he whispered, my name a ragged snarl on the air.

I ignored him, staring at the blood welling from the gash across my palm. It was deep. Tucking the blade away with my good hand, I closed my fist and watched as blood seeped through my fingers.

A booted pair of feet drew near and I looked up, saw him reaching for my wrist. My heart slammed against my ribs and his mouth went flat. "I just want to see your hand," he said softly.

Translation: *I'm not going to hurt you.*

I didn't need the translation. I already knew he wouldn't hurt me. Doesn't mean my body was automatically ready to listen. It's amazing the damage that a few days, a few weeks can do.

Most of my *life*, I'd just been a *thing*—something that was just there for the battering and the abuse. I'd made myself stronger.

It pissed me off that Jude had taken that from me.

Take it back, a voice inside me whispered. *Maybe you're broken, but you can fix yourself. You did it before.*

Because I knew it was what had to be done, and because I couldn't do it if I kept flinching away from everybody who came near, I uncurled my fist and let Damon take my hand.

"I've never seen you slip up and grab the blade wrong." He gently inspected my bleeding palm.

"I didn't get enough caffeine this morning."

He snorted and tugged on my wrist, guiding me back to the bar. The first aid kit under it probably didn't get much use; it was entirely likely he'd put it there for me. Damon, like most shifters, healed with amazing speed and kits like this were wasted on him. He gripped my wrist with a steely grasp, slowing the flow of blood. It hurt but it wasn't too bad.

"Are you going to explain or do I need to get ready to break bones?" he asked again as he started cleaning up my hand.

"You're always ready to break bones," I muttered. "I think it's one of the things you miss from when you weren't Alpha."

Once he had the blood cleaned up, he swiped the wound with an antiseptic wipe and then applied a couple of butterfly strips to keep it closed.

"I also miss how much easier my life was. And you haven't answered. Ten seconds, Kit."

Through my lashes, I studied him. "I don't care to be bullied," I said softly. "Just be aware of that."

"If I wanted to bully you, I just would have called Sam in here and started breaking right away." He leaned in a little closer.

Close. So close—closer than he'd been in months and the smell of him flooded my head, made my heart race.

His thumb stroked over my wrist, just above the bounding pulse. "I didn't do that, because I'm trying here. But I'll get an answer."

Blood roared in my ears and I barely even realized what he was talking about for a few, blissful seconds. I only knew that he was close. The mantle of his energy, as warm as the summer sun, beat down on me and I didn't feel cold; I didn't ache, and I didn't feel empty and alone.

Seconds spun away and I swayed forward without realizing what I was doing. Damon's eyes widened and then he groaned just as my lips met his.

His free hand came up, pushing into my hair.

One hand on my wrist. His hand cupping the back of my head. His mouth on mine, again.

Bliss...for those few, short moments. Stroking my tongue across his lower lip, I whimpered as he opened, shuddered as the taste of him hit my senses and the hunger for him flared to burning, forceful life.

More...

That was all I could think.

I needed more—

I moved against him, blind and deaf to everything. Even the fear inside had faded away. Nothing mattered.

Damon growled against my lips but didn't move. Even when I shoved my free hand under his shirt, he didn't move. I raked my nails across the muscles that ridged his back, felt him shudder. Against my belly, I could feel the heated warmth of him and it sucked all of the oxygen out of me.

Tearing my mouth away, I gasped for air.

Damon muttered my name, the low, ragged growl a velvet caress. He moved his mouth across my cheek. My jaw…

You're mine.

Pain ripping through me…

As his mouth brushed over my neck, all desire disappeared, crushed under a brutal, unwanted reminder. Terror slammed into me and I struck out, driving my fist into a hard, warm body.

The hand fisted in my hair fell away and I was free, backpedaling and tripping in my haste. I ended up falling, landing with my weight on my injured hand. A scream rose in my throat but I bit it back.

The pain shot through me and although it was a nasty way to clear to the fog of terror, it worked.

I found myself sitting on the floor, staring up at Damon.

And he looked horrified.

For the longest time, neither of us spoke and then he spun away. "Fuck. Kit, I'm sorry—"

"No." I swallowed, closed my eyes. Now that the terror had faded, now that the adrenaline rush was leveling out, my brain settled back into its normal rhythm and I knew what had caused it.

"I'm sorry," he said again. I watched as he lifted his hands, drove the heels of his palms against his eyes while the muscles of his back strained and swelled against his shirt.

"Damon, stop." I stayed on the floor, folding my knees. Because it was easier to think if I didn't look at him, I stared at my palm. I'd made it start bleeding again. "I'm the one who kissed you, remember? And I was fine, but..."

I stopped and reached up, touching my neck.

Realizing he had turned back around, I looked up at him. "Every damn time he touched me, he bit me. When you touched my neck, it just put me in a bad place, okay?"

"I shouldn't have—"

I glared at him. "Shouldn't have what? I kissed you and it felt pretty damn good so would you stop..."

Thick black lashes fell over his eyes, shielding them from me.

"Stop what?"

I shoved to my feet and headed back over to the first aid kit. The strips were nasty with blood again. Peeling them off, I tried to figure out just what to say. What I could say. What I *should* say. Damn it. "You didn't do anything wrong," I said softly. "And if I could find a way to turn off everything in my head that made me freak out, I'd probably have been very happy to keep going just as we were. But if you keep..."

His hand brushed down my back.

I stilled, staring down at the bloody gash in my palm. Damon moved around me and stroked my arm and once more silence fell as he cleaned the blood from my hand and rebandaged it. I wiggled my fingers and flexed my hand instead of looking at him even though I could feel the weight of his stare boring through my skull.

"Three weeks ago, you said you'd given up. And now...now what?" he asked softly.

"Now I'm just trying to figure out who I am." I darted a look up at him and it was enough to make my heart ache. A huge part of me wanted to lean against him and just stay there. Right there, lost in the warmth of his body. I'd felt safe there. I missed it. Needed it.

But I had to remember that I could stand on my own.

Be on my own. I don't think I'd ever really done it all that well to begin with. It was time to fix that.

"Everything I thought I was, everything I am, it still feels broken, Damon. I have to find me again. Sometimes it feels like I'm coming back, but other times, I remember..." I stopped, looking down at my palm. The silence in the back of my mind was like a mockery. I kept waiting to hear her. Hear that voice...*Call me...I am here. I am here.*

But she wasn't.

The bond with my blade was gone and it wasn't coming back.

Swallowing, I shook my head. "I just need to find out who I am again."

"And you have to do it without me."

"I can't stand on my own if you're always there to pick me up." He didn't have to know that it hurt to say it. Hurt like I was cutting out my heart.

"And when you're ready to stand on your own?" he whispered.

He was so close. I could feel the heat of him through my clothes. Need, confusion and fear were a morass inside me. I wanted him so much. I *needed* him like I needed air. But in the back of my mind, I could still hear that mocking laughter and my body hadn't forgotten that pain, either.

I wanted to rip out my hair, scream, kick something, hit something, break something.

"I don't know if that's going to happen," I said flatly.

"You're one of the strongest people I've ever met, baby girl." He stroked a hand up my back, stopped with it resting high between my shoulders. "You'll make it happen. You don't know how to stay down. When you're ready, I'll be waiting."

I looked at him from the corner of my eye. "And what if it takes the rest of my life?"

"I don't care how long it takes. I'll wait. I…" He clenched his jaw and went silent. Then, each word coming slowly, he said, "You told me you weren't ready to hear what I had to say, and that's fine. I'll wait for that, too. I'll wait forever."

A knot swelled in my throat. Needing to move, I eased

away from him.

Silence stretched out and it was awful, awkward and I desperately needed to get out of there.

"Are you going to give me the cat's name?" I asked softly.

He blew out a breath and I heard the frustration. "We're back to square one, Kit. I can give you the name, but if you don't tell me what I want to know about Sam, the second you leave here, I'm going after her and I'll get it out of her on my own."

From the corner of my eye, I saw him lift his face to the ceiling, eyes closed while a strange little smile curled his lips. "I'll be honest, I'd probably have fun with that. Sam's been a problem for a few months. I've been thinking I'd have to curb the problem and there's no time better than the present."

Bastard. Fighting dirty was his favorite way. He had no problem using pain or anything else to get what he needed out of people.

It bothered me, though, and he knew it.

Flexing my sore hand, I dropped onto the couch. "I tell you, then you give me the cat's name. No discussion."

He slanted a look my way. "I'll bring him here. The girl can meet him here. I can't endanger one of my cats. You know that."

"No. The girl's scared of this place." Absently scratching at my arm with my uninjured hand, I muttered, "She's scared of her own shadow."

"I'm not having it happen off my land," he said flatly. "If she's young, then it's one of my kids and I'm not risking them getting hurt. Too many of them don't think for any longer than it takes to eat or get laid and being stupid isn't a good enough reason to get dead."

"You think I'd let that happen?"

"Not willingly, but until I know more about the girl, I'm not taking chances. We can find a neutral place…" He cocked his head to the side. "Your office."

My heart lurched in my chest. Hell, I hadn't even paid

the damn rent in months. "That might not be doable," I said woodenly. "I haven't kept up with the place."

"You can make it doable. We can compromise on this. That's my compromise. You need neutral ground if you won't bring her here." The storms in his eyes darkened. "You know it's not wise for one of the younger ones to leave clan territory without others from the clan with him, Kit. And he needs somebody else to act as witness. The girl can bring her mother or something and we'll all sit down like rational adults."

I curled my lip. "If you plan on coming, who is going to be the rational adult for the kid?"

A faint smile came and went on his face.

Because I didn't have much choice, I agreed. "But if my office isn't doable, we find someplace else." I didn't even know if I could get *in* to my office. Five months was a long time to stay away from a place of business. I had a fair landlord, but that fair? I just didn't know.

"Deal. Now...talk."

Swiping the back of my hand over my mouth, I surged off the couch and started to pace.

Memories from that night slammed into me. The fight between us. Justin telling me, *You can't let it go so easily—*

The jerk wasn't right often, but when he was right, he was *really* right.

"Look, this isn't any big secret," I said, swiping my uninjured hand down the side of my jeans and shooting him a look. "I said I called here, remember?"

His lashes swept low, shielding his eyes.

"Yes. I thought you weren't able to reach anybody." A muscle pulsed in his jaw. "I take it that wasn't the case."

"No." I shrugged jerkily. "I…look, we were over with anyway, right?" I swallowed, jerked a look at him, fast and then I dragged my eyes away. "I'm trying not to be mad about that. Not matter what, you couldn't always be there, right? And I'm trying not to be angry that."

A snarl ripped out of him. "You're trying not to be angry?"

I shot him a look. "Damon—"

His eyes glowed, savage and hot. "*I* am angry." He went to take a step forward and my breath caught. A look of pure hell crawled across his face and he turned away. "You go ahead. Try not to be angry. I'm pissed enough for both of us. I should have been there."

"But we were over." I shook my head. I didn't want to be angry about this. I was so tired of being angry. Of being afraid.

"Kit…just tell me what you need to tell me."

Okay, maybe I wasn't as tired of being angry as I thought. "Just tell you." It ripped out of me and I slammed my fist down as I fought not to yell, as the rage bubbled and brewed inside. "Fine. I'll fucking tell you. Sam gave me your message. One fight, Damon."

He stared at me and my skin burned under that gaze.

One fight, damn it. We had one *serious* fight and he walked? "I don't get it, Damon, okay? I know I'm still fucked up over everything and I'm going to be for a long, long time. I *wanted* to tell you what was going on, but I couldn't. I couldn't tell you, I couldn't write you a fucking note, I couldn't even *think* about it thanks to that fucking spell Justin put on me."

Oh, yeah. I wanted to be angry, all right. I'd lied. Or maybe I just hadn't realized.

The rage inside me pulsed in the air. I could feel it. Sucking in a breath, I tried to calm my breathing and I made the mistake of looking at him. His eyes glowed, that eerie glow, rolling from gray to green-gold and back. That was all, the only sign he felt anything, but it was enough.

"What the *fuck*, Damon!" I shouted. "We had one fight and all of a sudden you won't even *talk* to me? One *damn* fight and you don't want me anymore? You have that bitch Sam passing on your messages to me?"

The tension ratcheted up in the room, swelling hotter, tighter. Choking the oxygen out of the room until I couldn't even breathe. "Kit…" His voice was ragged.

I didn't care. Whirling around, I glared at him. "One

fucking fight. You said you loved me and that's how you showed it?"

There was even more rage inside me than I had realized and now it was ready to explode out.

He dodged and I didn't even realize why until a knife was vibrating in the wall behind him.

Missed—

I'd missed…

Useless waste, an ugly, hated voice whispered from the depths of my memory. "Shut *up*!" I screamed. I reached out for something else—the only thing that came to hand was the first aid kit, but I hurled it too. It smashed into his chest, the box a ruined mess, the contents spilling out all over the floor. Before I could grab something else, Damon caught my wrists.

"Kit," he whispered. "Stop…just stop."

I jerked back away from him, but he didn't let go. "Get the fuck off me."

But he didn't even seem to hear me. He let go of my wrists and shoved his hands into my hair, tugging my face back and forcing me to look at him. His eyes, glowing and burning, stared down at me. "Kit…" His voice came in hard, uneven pants, like he'd just run a hundred miles. "Kit, I never gave *anybody* any message."

I stared at him and for a moment, the words just didn't connect.

And then, abruptly…they did.

CHAPTER EIGHT

Sam entered Damon's chambers looking just as cocky as she had the first day I'd met her.

Just as cocky, but not quite so elegant with it. That first time, she'd been wearing all black. Black pants that clung to her like they'd been painted on her lush body. A leather corset.

Her long dark hair was pulled back in the same ponytail, leaving the flawless lines of her face unframed.

But instead of the Dominatrix-in-training garb, she was wearing the kind of clinging cotton pants I'd wear to work out in, and a close-fitting black shirt that looked like it was both sport bra and tank in one.

She'd healed from her sparring session earlier. That was nice. I wanted to bloody her again, all by myself.

I never gave anybody any message,

Bloody her? Screw that. I wanted to take her damned head off.

Damon was standing just a few feet away from me and the heated energy I'd felt from him all this time was gone, sucked inside him. I felt nothing—he was giving off about as much as Chang did. That in and of itself was scary.

Sam stood a few feet away, flicking a bored look at me before acknowledging Damon. The look that danced in her eyes was one I recognized. I'd seen it before. Damon was hot.

Women wanted him. Some of the men did. But most people tried to least cover it or be a little more discreet.

She didn't, although she did do the nice, submissive little cat thing, clasping her hands in front of her and lowering her head a bit. If I had my blade…

"Want to tell me why you decided it was okay for you to speak for me, Sam?" Damon asked, his voice all silky menace and deadly promise. I knew that tone. If she was smart, she'd get scared. Fast. Like as in yesterday.

"Sir?"

I knew how swift he was. I'd seen evidence of it. But it still caught me by surprise—especially when the threat wasn't aimed at me. I sensed the blur of movement, but that was the only warning I had.

And to be honest, I was more concerned about Sam. Ugly hate glittered in her eyes and I was ready to move, to act or react. . I didn't have my bow. But I had my gun—

No.

No, I didn't.

Stunned, I saw my Desert Eagle in Damon's hand. And it looked a hell of a lot more at home in his than mine.

How in the hell—?

Swallowing, I followed the line of his aim and saw that it was leveled at Sam's gut.

She was no longer staring at me with hate. She was watching him. And that cocky-ass attitude was gone. Caution showed in her eyes, finally. "Damon, I—"

"It's not Damon to you," he said. "It's sir, it's Alpha. It's anything but Damon. Now I asked a question and if you don't answer it, I pull the trigger. If I know anything about Kit, she's loaded this with silver, so when I empty it into your belly, it's going to hurt."

She went white. "Alpha, I was only trying to help. I heard you talking to Chang and I—"

He fired and she went down with an eerie, inhuman scream. The scent of her blood flooded the air.

"I'm asking again," Damon said, his voice flat. "And I'm now pissed off that you think you've got the right to listen in when I speak with my adviser."

"I just overhead you tell him you didn't want to talk about the silly bitch," Sam said, her voice a pathetic whine. She writhed on the floor and slammed her head against it as the poison ate its way through her system.

Damon hadn't been wrong. The Eagle had been loaded with silver-wrapped ammo. She was lucky I hadn't loaded it with magically charged bullets. I'd considered it but thought it might be overkill.

He studied her for a minute and then, quicker than a snake, shoved his free hand against her belly, pressed against the open wound. She screamed and reached down, clutching at his hand. Bile churned in my throat, but I said nothing.

"Please," she whimpered. "Please...call Ella, please, Da...Alpha, please call Ella."

"No. And if you call Kit one more name, I'm going to rip your throat out. You can bleed to death for all I care," he said. He added more weight—I could see the muscles bulging in his arm as he applied pressure.

She puked. The rancid, foul odor wrapped around us, adding to the miasma of blood, fear, pain. The stench triggered memories and I had to dig my nails into my palm to stay grounded. *Focus...just focus, Kit...*

Scent is a strong trigger and I'd spent a lot of time wrapped in the stink of my own blood, fear and pain. But I wasn't letting this shove me back there.

As her retching passed, Sam moaned. "I need Ella...get this silver out me, Alpha...please—" She shrieked and spasmed.

A wet, meaty sound filled the air. Closing my eyes, I said, "Damon, if you plan on torturing her, can you do it later?"

"Be quiet, Kit." His voice was impassive. "She violated my trust. She lied. Stepping out of line like that endangers the pack—Sam's a soldier, she knows that. She endangered the pack when she decided she'd speak for me."

Slowly, he lifted his head and stared at me. "And *fuck* all of that—she endangered *you*." He shifted his attention back to her and twisted his wrist. Sam screamed. "I want to know why."

I forced myself to watch. I wasn't going to be stupid enough to blame myself for this…I had enough shit in my head and I didn't need to add to it, but this was all about me. And Damon.

Crossing the floor, I stood beside them, keeping my boots out of the ever-spreading pool of blood. "I already know the damn answer, Damon." I held out my hand for the gun. He didn't need it to hurt her and I'd rather he not use it for whatever else he had planned. He slid me a look and then turned it over. I stayed out of her reach. Wounded or not, she was still a shifter and faster, stronger than me.

"In case you haven't noticed, Damon, she wants in your pants. How much that has to do with this, I don't know. But she also hates me." I stared at Sam, saw the way her energy flickered around her. "Somehow she heard we'd broken up and she wanted to make sure it stayed that way, so when I called, she took her shot."

"I want the answer from her," Damon said quietly.

"And she's going to lay there, whining like a little girl and begging for help," I pointed out. I eyed the nasty mess of her belly. "Are you going to call her a healer?"

"No." He rose to his feet, blood dripping from one hand. "If I'd talked to you—"

The muscles in his arms bulged and I could all but taste the violence coming off him. "No *if*s, Damon. It's already done."

Staring down at Sam's face, I wondered if she realized. And in the depths of her eyes, I saw the answer. She realized what a difference it might have made. And she didn't care. And worse, I saw the *hatred* there…this woman would see me dead if she could.

"You went through and cleaned house, Damon, but you missed some of the dirt," I said quietly. "This bitch is evil. I wouldn't trust her at my back."

"A fact I've figured out myself." A grim, ugly smile curled his lips as he stared down at her. "She's going to really regret that fact in a while. She'll be begging for a quick death."

I eyed him narrowly and then looked back down at Sam.

He tried to stop me, but by the time he realized what I was going to do, I'd already pulled the trigger. He's fast, but it doesn't take much time for me to aim and squeeze.

Sam's scream cut off abruptly and I looked up and met his gaze. I suppose I could have let him kill her. Could have let him torture her. But now, every time I thought about the fact that her lie might have contributed to my hell up in the mountains, I could look back at this.

It was some small piece of myself that I'd taken back. Maybe not a big piece, but a piece nonetheless.

As Damon's people came inside to deal with the body, I left the main room. It didn't occur to me to ask if it was okay as I pushed through the door that led to his private area. Maybe that should tell me something; I don't know. Nobody had access to his personal space.

Chang didn't even come through this door.

But I wasn't staying out there, smelling death.

In the bathroom, I turned on the faucet, deliberately keeping my attention away from the shower. Memories danced in the back of my mind, but they'd have to come out to play some other time.

I had to get the information I needed and get the hell out of here.

Soon.

A whisper of air brushed across my skin as I cupped my hands and splashed water over my face.

It was still dripping down my cheeks and neck when I lifted my head and saw him standing behind me. He'd already changed clothes and washed up. Violence and temper all but clung to him.

His eyes rested on the tattoo on my neck and my skin burned. "Is it done?"

Looking down at the colorful lines and images, I studied

it.

"It's done."

He gave a short nod and then moved away. I breathed a little easier when he wasn't so close. The heat of him didn't beat against me so strongly and I didn't have the struggle raging so hard inside me—where part of me wanted to just fling myself against him even as the rest of me wanted to get away. As far away as I could, as fast as I could.

I felt the heat of his gaze burning into me as I dried my hands and face off. Without looking at him, I said, "If you expect an apology from me over Sam, you're going to wait a long time."

"She was mine to handle."

I flicked him a glance. "Yours to handle…maybe. But I'm the one who laid in her own waste and blood in the mountains, and if she'd minded her own business…?" I shrugged. "I figured she owed me the blood more than you."

The storm clouds in his eyes turned nearly black. "If you wanted blood from her, you should have done more than just shoot her."

"I didn't need more." I'd lived through torture. I'd never be able to dish it out now. Even if Jude was put in front of me, completely helpless, I don't know if I'd be able to torture him—kill him, oh, yes. My hands trembled a little as I hung the towel back up, smoothing it down so that it hung precisely centered on the sculpted metal bar. Unable to avoid it any longer, I turned around and looked at Damon. "It's your turn now. I need that kid's name."

He stared at me, long seconds ticking away as he said nothing, just watching me.

The very air in the room seemed to weigh down on us as I waited for a response. Then finally, he dipped his head in a slow nod. "Chang says Doyle would know the number, right?"

The tension slowly melted away. I cleared my throat and hooked my thumbs in my pockets to keep from fidgeting. "That's what he told me."

Damon shoved away from the wall, prowling the

bathroom. Unable to look away, I stared at him and then my heart slammed against my ribs hard as he stopped by the shower, resting one hand against the glass wall.

Why did he have to stop *there*? By the damn shower.

Jerking my attention away, I busied myself with the toes of my boots. Everybody else found them so damned fascinating. Maybe I'd just see if I couldn't find what it was that was so interesting.

"I'll talk to the kid, then. Once I have the information, I'll call you, set up the time to meet at your office."

Nodding, I twisted the towel and then grimaced as it rubbed against my bandaged palm. I needed to brush up on my knife skills again. I had to be doing something with my hands—being still just wasn't something that came naturally. "There might be a problem with the office. If there is—"

"There's not going to be."

Eyes narrowed, I slid him a glance.

He had that implacable *I-know-what-in-the-hell-I'm-talking-about* tone to his voice. Damon was an arrogant son of a bitch, but he only had that tone when he was absolutely sure about things. He didn't do *wrong* very well. So he didn't use that *I'm-right* tone unless he was, in fact, right.

"And how are you so certain of that?" I asked him.

"I just am." He still wasn't looking at me and I knew he wasn't going to explain anything any further than that.

My belly churned.

"Damon, if you've been paying my rent, I'm going to bloody you."

He slid me a dark look. "Go ahead." Shoving away from the shower, he came closer. Violence, danger and anger radiated from him and fear pulsed inside me, despite the fact that I *knew*, deep inside, that he wouldn't hurt me. Damon was one of the few people who *was* safe.

Too bad my body didn't get that message.

He reached up and my breath froze in my lungs as he slid a hand inside my vest. The back of his hand brushed against my breast and the black band of terror grabbed me, held tight.

"You're so fucking afraid now, Kit," he whispered, dipping his head to murmur into my ear. "It's killing me."

Then he lifted his head and reached down. He caught my left hand and pushed one of my knives into it. "Bloody me."

I jerked my hand away—or I *tried*. He still held my wrist and he wasn't letting go.

"That's a silver blade, you son of a bitch."

"I know." He guided my blade to his chest, his grip relentless. "Bloody me. I'd feel better for it. And if it would do something to take that fear away..." A muscle pulsed in his jaw and he was standing close enough, I could hear the thunderous sound of his heart, racing far too fast. I didn't have ears as sensitive as his—if he'd been standing any farther away, I couldn't have heard it. As it was, though, the roar of blood in my ears, the racing of his heart, the adrenaline crashing inside me and the torment I saw on his face...the torment I felt in *me*...it was too much. "Sam's not the only one who owes you blood, baby girl."

Once more, I tried to twist out of his grip. "Damn it, let *go*."

Swearing, he dropped my wrist. I put the knife away and darted toward the door.

He slammed it shut before I managed to get it open an inch.

"Kit..."

"Don't, okay?" I leaned my brow against the wood and closed my eyes. "I need to get out of here. I need to breathe. I need to..."

His fingers brushed across my shoulder and he pressed his head to the back of mine. "I miss you."

Tears burned my eyes and although it didn't seem possible, the ache in my heart spread.

I really, really wish that what I'd told Chang was true. That the woman I'd been was dead and gone, that nothing of my old life mattered. If I could *believe* that, then it wouldn't hurt so much to stand there.

But I wasn't going to make myself better, or stronger, or fight my way out of this hell I currently lived in if I kept lying to myself. About anything. "I miss you, too."

He reached up, resting a hand on my hip.

"But that doesn't mean anything," I told him. "Not if I can't find *me* again. I'm still lost, Damon. I have to find who I am...I have to find my way again."

Easing around, I stared into his eyes. Close. He was so close.

And even though I *knew* he wouldn't hurt me, the fear was there. He went to pull back and I surprised us both by reaching up and fisting my hands in his shirt, holding him there.

His eyes widened and he stilled, stayed there, one arm braced on the wall by my head while his hand rested on my hip. I could handle this, I decided. The fear was there, but I couldn't expect that to go away so easily. And…hell. It was Damon. Just having him this close had my heart racing and not *all* of it had to do with fearful things.

Curious, I placed my hand to his chest and as his heart slammed against my palm, I felt the way my own sped up in answer.

I did miss this…even when it wasn't a spur of the moment kiss. I missed this. I missed us.

But I wasn't ready.

"That day, up in the mountains," I said quietly. "I told you that I was broken...so far from me that I didn't think I'd ever find my way back."

A harsh, ragged breath escaped him. "I know."

"You told me you'd find it for me." The heat of him scalded me, even as it warmed me. "I didn't want to hear it then...and I can't be sorry for that. I can't let somebody find my way *for* me. I just can't. I've got to do it for myself. But I'm trying. Okay?"

He stroked a hand down my hair. "I told you…I'll be waiting."

"It may never happen." Turning my face into his hand, I kissed his rough palm. It hurt more than a little as I pushed him away. "You have to understand that."

He was quiet as he stepped back.

Just before I slipped out the door, he asked softly, "Do you *want* it to happen?"

The question stopped me in my tracks and I looked back at him. "Do I want what?"

"Us. This." Those eyes watched me, so carefully. "I'll wait. Forever. It doesn't matter how long. But is that what you want from me? Are you coming back to me?"

"I…" I licked my lips and shook my head. It shouldn't be such a hard question. "I don't know."

He smiled sadly, looking away. "That's fine. Like I said. I'll be waiting."

"Even if I don't know?"

"Yeah. Even if."

CHAPTER NINE

Damon had been right—big surprise. I had come into my office with half a mind of calling my landlord and figuring out just *how* my office was still mine, but then I'd made the mistake of looking out the window.

Right there.

It had happened *right there.*

That was where I'd been standing when Xavier had appeared out of the shadows.

Seconds later, a dart had appeared in my chest.

I don't have to break you to fuck you up.

He'd been right—he'd fucked me up and then Jude had been the one to break me.

And here I was, huddling on the floor again, clutching a knife and wondering if there was a way to cut the memories out of me.

The phone rang. The noise of it was so loud, so unexpected, when I gasped, it caught in my throat, choking me.

Such a simple sound, really, but one I hadn't heard in months. It flooded me with apprehension and instead of taking the call, I let it roll over to voice mail.

I could take a few more minutes, enjoy my little breakdown.

I could ignore the calls, after all. I still hadn't decided I was going to go back to work, right?

I could even ignore the rippling presence of something…*other* that I could sense just outside my office. A were. He'd been trailing me off and on half the day and I didn't want to deal with him. Her. Whichever it was.

Whoever it was. I wasn't ready for this. Whoever it was, he or she was coming closer.

I'm not here, I mouthed. *Office closed. I've closed up shop.*

But even as I thought that, the presence retreated and I blew out a relieved breath. Good. Very good. I didn't need to think about working. Not at all. I was barely able to handle the cakewalk job that TJ had thrown at me. No way could I handle anything more complicated.

I'd just…sit here. Catch my breath.

Ten minutes later, I was still doing just that when the phone started to ring again.

"I can't keep doing this," I whispered. My voice sounded terribly loud, terribly raw.

The phone went silent and I closed my eyes. My world had already ended.

The monster had already grabbed me.

And despite what I tried to tell other people, despite what I'd tried to tell *myself*, I had lived to tell about it.

Gritting my teeth, I shoved myself upright and looked around. The walls were bare. All my lovely, lovely weapons were either stashed on my body—and there weren't many of those—or they were back in my room at TJ's. The place was naked without them.

I felt naked without them.

But I didn't need a damned sword to talk to a couple of cats about a pregnant girl.

The phone started to ring again.

Once.

As I continued to stare at the bare walls, the seconds ticked away. When the phone rang again a minute later, I groaned. There was only one person who'd call like that and I'd just gotten done talking to him about—

Frowning, I checked the time.

Damn. It had been more than two hours. Apparently, my little mental breakdown had cost me more time than I'd realized. Crossing to my desk, I caught the phone in the middle of the ring and lifted it to my ear.

"I'm already a nervous wreck," I said bluntly without waiting for Damon to say anything. "The last thing I need is for you to start that annoying ring thing. It's like an ice pick in my ear."

"You answered," he said levelly. "I have the kid. It's Marcus...remember him?"

Yes. I remembered him. One of Doyle's friends. Charming. Liked to play Mortal Kombat. Had an annoying habit of referring to me as food. If he did it again, I'd hurt him.

I didn't even realize I'd pulled a blade until just then, when I looked down and saw I'd buried the tip of it in my desk. Swallowing, I said, "Yes. I remember."

"He mentioned a girl. Hard to say if it's the right one since you won't give me much info on her, but he did have a human, or mostly, human girlfriend. He remembered that she smelled like magic…sorta. Reminded him of you. Think that could be her?"

I frowned. "Yeah, maybe." A lot of people took me for a witch at first. Marcus was young enough, inexperienced enough, that it was a fair assumption. Tugging the phone number from my pocket, I rubbed my finger over it and tried to figure this whole puzzle out.

Marcus was a mouthy brat of a kid, but he didn't have anything really mean inside him.

What made her so afraid?

"Is he willing to talk to her?"

Damon's voice went flat. "If he's the father, he'll live up to his responsibilities."

And that was pretty much that. If Damon said it, it would be done. "Fine. I'll get in touch with her and see when I can work out for her to come here. I'll call."

Hanging up, I leaned against the desk and closed my eyes. *Here we go.*

An hour after I placed the first phone call, my skin went tight.

I pulled my gun out and rested it on my thigh as I listened, ears pricked, ready. *Quiet. Male. Full of magic. Knows how to move—*

My brain put together all of those little clues and fed me a picture but I was still processing it when the knock thudded and Justin called out, "Open up."

I don't want to, I mouthed at the door.

"I don't give a shit if you want to or not."

I flinched as the wards sparked around me. Justin was a witch. The wards would fight him but if he really wanted to power through, he could. Not everybody could do it, but he most definitely could.

"Fine," I muttered, shoving back from the desk. I still held my gun in my right hand and it rubbed against the slowly-healing wound. I gripped it tighter and took a little bit of relief in the pain that jolted through me as the bandage dug into tender flesh.

Wards hissed and hummed in my head as I deactivated them, one at a time. As the last one went down with a sigh, I opened the door and glared at Justin.

He grinned back at me. The fading sunlight glowed off the silver worked into the sleeves of his black jacket, the only thing from his Banner uniform that he wore; under it, he had on a green tank top and a pair of battered jeans. "You're out of uniform," I said. "If you're not here officially, I don't have to talk to you and I don't want to."

Before I could slam the door in his face, he slapped a hand against it. "Actually, I'm on probation. I had a...slipup...with one of my superiors and I'm being disciplined."

"They're wasting their time. You and discipline don't even have a passing acquaintance." I put my shoulder into it as I shoved the door closed. One thing about not being entirely human–I was strong. And I was actually stronger *physically* than he was.

But then I felt the burn of magic rush into the door as he

decided to level the playing field. “That’s cheating,” I said. “If you can’t do it with your muscles, you shouldn’t be able to fall back on magic.”

He smiled at me. “Hey, I’m the one who taught you some of the dirty tricks to use when you *can’t* rely on muscles.” With a wink, he sauntered inside. “I mean, I wonder, where on earth did Damon Lee get the idea to use magically charged ammo against one of the witches he took out?”

I glared at his back. “Hey, it’s not like somebody couldn’t come to the logical conclusion on their own.”

“It’s not all that logical for weres.” He shrugged. “They aren’t human. They’re were. They think with claws and teeth first. Weapons are a nuisance and unless you make them the option, weapons aren’t going to be their default choice.”

I curled my lip at him, but he wasn’t paying attention to me. He was staring at the bare walls that had once held all my weapons. “Are you going to put them back up?”

“I’m not back,” I said, crossing my arms over my chest and staring at the dull tiles of my floor. Easier to do that than to stare at the naked walls. “I’m just helping out somebody TJ knows.”

“Hmm.”

The tone in his voice had me looking up.

I narrowed my eyes when I saw the expression on his face.

“What?”

He just held up his hands. “Nothing. Not a thing, Kitty. Not a thing.”

The look on his face wasn’t a *nothing* sort.

But fine. If he kept his *nothing* to himself, then I didn’t have to worry about it. Heading over to my desk, I settled down and laid the Desert Eagle on the surface, eying the phone. Maybe I should call again. Maybe—

Justin settled in the seat across from me.

I rubbed a finger down the small strip of recycled paper and eyed him narrowly. “If you’re not here to nag me into working and you’re not here for something official, why are you here?"

"I felt the wards." He shrugged and glanced around. "Colleen and I have been trading off on charging them. Figured it wouldn't hurt to keep them ready for you..." He smiled at me. "Just in case."

Great. Now I owed him, too.

Not that I didn't already. He'd been there—

My breath hitched.

That awful darkness started to creep back in but as it tried to suck me under, a hand closed around my wrist. A jolt of magic snaked through me. Wincing, I shook the shock of it away and glared at Justin. He was still holding my wrist. "Do you mind?"

"Nah. Always happy to help." He smiled and settled back in his chair. "You know there's somebody slinking around outside, right?"

I sighed and shoved a hand through my hair. "Yeah. Vaguely."

"Is it a problem?"

I stared at him. "I don't know. Whoever it is hasn't come inside yet."

Justin just lifted a brow. I knew what he was offering. If I needed him to, or if I asked him to, he'd move the visitor along. But I wasn't going to start cringing at the very presence of something more than human. Jude was a different story and if I could figure out the right way to kill him while he was still in the box, I'd do it.

Part of me thought that maybe I should just demolish the Assembly Hall. Burn it, and while it was burning, get to the area set aside for…problem prisoners and find Jude's box. I had a sword, one that could penetrate any barrier known to man—or beast—and if I drove that piece of metal through Jude's silver prison…

"Dark thoughts there, Kit," Justin murmured.

I shot him a look and then, just as quickly, turned away. It wouldn't do to let him know just how dark those thoughts were. Whether he was being disciplined or not, if I did decide to go all vigilante on Jude, I'd be the prime suspect and I didn't need my friends being pulled in and questioned.

"Just thoughts," I said, shrugging. "Don't worry about whoever is out there. If they become a problem, I'll deal with it then. Having a were slink around my office is no reason for you to go whipping your magic dick around."

I wanted this day done.

Justin laughed. "My magic dick? Kit…I don't need *that* to deal with whoever it is out there."

Despite myself, I realized I was grinning. I rolled my eyes and flipped him off before bending back over my desk and eying the mountainous pile of mail. It was neatly sorted and the only bills were recent ones. Somebody had been dealing with those for me. I had a feeling I knew who that someone was. From the corner of my eye, I saw Justin slump in his seat, that vaguely amused smile still on his face.

After he continued to stare, I sighed and shifted my gaze upward, meeting his eyes. "What?" I demanded.

He just shrugged and shifted his attention downward, eyeing my neck. "Damn, that's a piece of work."

Magic pricked the air. I might have gotten pissed off, but I knew Justin too well to expect any less. He'd sensed the magic in the tattoo the second he'd seen it. He wouldn't be who he was if he didn't ask about it. "Don't go pulling a mama hen act, Justin," I warned him. "I've already had a bitch of a day."

"No mama hen." He leaned forward, the silver on his sleeves catching the light. "Hell, since I flash magic dick around, if I pull anything, I'd think I'd pull a daddy rooster act anyway. Besides, if you're crazy enough to let some fetish witch carve copper ink into your skin, that's your concern."

His smile faded and those intense green eyes held mine. "You made yourself who you are, Kit. Nothing's changed that."

I looked away.

"Are you ready to let me help you with your sword yet?"

Blowing out a tired sigh, I climbed out of the chair and started to pace. "Justin, stop. There's nothing to *help*. It's just gone. I know what the bond feels like and it's just not *there*."

"So you're too afraid to try."

Stopping in my tracks, I turned to face him. Every muscle in me was tensed and I felt like I might shatter. "Don't. You son of a bitch. Don't."

"Don't *what*?" The rage coming out of him caught me by surprise. He closed the distance between us and fisted his hand in my shirt, jerking me onto my toes. "Don't ruin your life? I did that. Don't put your life in danger? I did that, too. What am I *not* supposed to do? Everything bad that I could to do to you, I already did."

I swung out and punched him in the throat, putting every bit of strength I had behind it. It pissed me off that there wasn't as much as there should be, but he still staggered, gasping for air as he dropped me. Stepping backward, I glared at him.

"What in the hell do you want?" I demanded.

Anger raged inside him as he glared at me. But I knew it wasn't directed at me. He opened his mouth and tried to speak. No words came out at first but finally, he managed to choke out, "A chance to make it better."

I blinked back the tears. "You *can't*."

"I can't make it *right*." He shook his head and said, "I *know* that. I can't make it right and no matter what in the hell I do, I have no chance at that. But if I can undo some of the damage? Maybe…"

His voice trailed off.

I turned away and stared at the bare, stark walls of my office. "If you tell me you're feeling *guilty*, Justin, I think I'm going to kill you."

He laughed. It was a raw, ugly sound. "Guilty, Kit?"

That laugh echoed around me and it went on, and on. It was like a living, breathing wound and just *hearing* it hurt me. Finally, I turned around and glared at him because the very *sound* made me want to weep.

"Guilty?" he whispered. "Do you honestly think the word *guilt* touches what I feel?"

He leaned his back against the wall and slid down to the floor, his gaze locked on nothing. "Guilt," he muttered again.

"I helped track you across a continent and the entire time, I was linked into that tiger…feeling what he felt, hearing what he heard. He was keyed into you the whole time. And you think I feel *guilty*."

He shifted his eyes to me. "I had to make a choice, Kit. I knew what that motherfucking cat meant to you, even though I hated it. I knew. I could let him die. Or I could use you to save him." His lids drooped down and he said quietly, "Not a day goes by when I don't wish I hadn't just let the motherfucker die."

It hit me in the heart. "You're not helping."

In a blur of motion, he surged to his feet, his hair flying around him and his eyes burning with the heat of his rage. "I'm not *helping*?" he growled. "No. I'm *not* helping. I've not done a damn *fucking* thing to make this better since I ruined your life. But I'll tell you one thing… if I had to choose between letting that bastard cat die and sparing *you*?" He sneered at me. "You'd be grieving at his graveside even now and I don't care if that makes you hate me."

A fist banged on the door and seconds later, it flew open.

I didn't even have to look. I knew who it was. The warmth rolling over my skin told me everything I needed to know.

Damon came prowling inside and I sighed, flinging myself onto the couch and closing my eyes as the two men faced off with each other.

CHAPTER TEN

Damon's gaze rolled between storm-cloud gray and green-gold.

The cat inside warred with the man and I didn't know which one was going to take control at the moment.

Magic rolled around Justin as he glared at the shifter standing in the door and for the first time, I noticed that the silver on his sleeves was sparking. Not *sparkling*, but *sparking*, like it was shooting off energy. It wasn't just a trick of the light, either.

A growl trickled out of Damon's throat as he stared at Justin.

Justin curled his lip at him. "You want to go a round or two, pussy cat?"

I reached for the gun at my thigh and drew it. It wouldn't kill Damon. I knew that. It would probably do a hell of a lot of damage to Justin, but unless I had it loaded with pure iron bullets—and I didn't—it would only slow the witch down. Still, I didn't want to hurt them. Well, I didn't *think* I wanted to.

So I aimed at the floor between them and pulled the trigger. It was concrete under the carpet and while it tore the carpet up to hell and back, the floor itself wasn't torn up too bad. Maybe they had injuries from the shrapnel. That thought made me feel better.

And now I had their attention.

"I'm not doing this," I said quietly as I lowered the Desert Eagle. A pang of regret rolled through me. The gun just wasn't as…poetic as my blade. But nobody could *hear* a blade the way they heard a mean-ass bitch like a Desert Eagle.

Justin shot a look at the floor and then at my gun. Damon just stared at him, face impassive. I crossed over to my desk and settled down, keeping the Eagle in my right hand. "If the two of you wanted to have a go, you could have done it without me in the picture. It's been months and I'm sure you two can figure out how to track each other down. Right now, I've got a job to do and I don't give a *flying fuck* what your problems are with each other."

The magic surrounding Justin sparked a hard, cold silver.

Damon's rage was hot and fiery.

"Tone it down," I told them. "Or get out of my office. Personally, I don't care which because I don't want to deal with this…" I hated that my voice cracked. "And I *can't* deal with it."

I paused and swallowed, shifting my gaze away from them to stare at the painfully bare walls of my office. I missed my weapons, I realized. Not just the music of them, but the sight of them. The feel of them. Even the comfort of them. "If the two of you are going to go at it, get the hell out of my office," I said again once I knew my voice would be level.

"I'm here because you wanted to see one of my cats," Damon said and although his eyes were still flickering with an eerie glow, his voice was calm, like he was just discussing the weather. "If you want to kick Harry Potter outside? I don't give a damn."

Justin's lip curled. "Harry Potter, huh? If I was Harry Potter, I would have *Avada Kedavraed* your ass straight into hell." Then he prowled over to my desk and leaned a hip against it.

The air went tight again with Damon's anger, but at the moment there wasn't a damn thing I was going to do about it. Truth be told, I felt a little easier with Justin sitting there. He was a barrier and I needed the breathing room.

The testosterone in there was going to kill me. Damon, I had to deal with for a little while. Justin…if he was there for any reason other than guilt or to jerk Damon around, I don't know if I needed the trouble, even if I *did* need the barrier.

Sliding him a look, I asked, "I assume you're here for a reason, right? Other than just to hassle me?"

"You assume right, Kitty-kitty." The jackass smiled and winked at me as he reached out and tugged on a lock of my hair.

Damon growled.

I stroked the butt of my gun and debated on whether or not I was going to put a bullet in one of them next time.

"Behave," I warned Justin.

"Don't I always?"

"Yes." Disgustedly, I batted his hand away when he went to touch me again. "You behave badly. Damon, where the hell is this cat?" I glanced over at the clock before I let myself meet the shifter's burning gray eyes. "She's going to be here in fifteen minutes."

Almost a minute passed before he answered me. A minute of that unyielding, unblinking stare and then finally, he glanced back over his shoulder. He said nothing; he did nothing else, just looked back out the door he hadn't closed.

Vaguely I felt the prickle of another's presence rolling over my skin and then Damon moved farther into the room.

Marcus stood in the doorway, still a lean kid with lots of attitude, lots of nerve. His father was with him and while Marcus shot me a quick look and a weak smile, the dad was another one of those idiots who was fascinated with the floor.

"Damon," I said, hearing the rage as it pulsed in my voice. "If that ass can't seem to meet my eyes, then he needs to get out of my office."

Damon stared at me. And then he flicked a look at the other shifter. "Conley."

The man's shoulders tightened but his gaze stayed locked on the floor. "Alpha, I need to be with my kid," he said quietly.

"For fuck's sake," Damon snarled. "Just look at her."

Slowly, like somebody had to force him physically, Conley lifted his head, bit by bit. But *finally*, somebody met my eyes and actually looked at me. Conley looked like he'd rather be looking at anything, anybody else, but he held my gaze.

I gave him a sharp-edged smile. "Wow. Look at that. I still exist. Jude didn't turn me into nothing, after all."

They all flinched.

Clara, I thought, nearly an hour later.

It suited her.

Simple and sweet.

She was sweet, although I couldn't exactly call her simple, considering she had a shifter's baby in her belly and the blood of something not quite human pumping through her veins. Plus, despite the fear inside her, she'd done something a lot of people wouldn't have done. She'd taken a risk.

The bruise on her face told me a story. She hadn't wanted to voice it and if it wasn't for the fact that Marcus had been getting all growly and snarly, she probably wouldn't have said a damn thing.

But as Marcus's anger got worse, I managed to get her attention. Catching her hands, I crouched in front of her. Giving anybody my back these days was harder than it had ever been, but I did it and waited until Clara's frightened eyes left the men to focus on me. "You know he's not going to hurt you, right?"

"I…yeah. I think so," she whispered, nodding jerkily.

"Good." I squeezed her hands just this shy of too hard, keeping her attention focused on me. "Listen, these cats, they're like most shifters and they aren't always operating on the same cylinders that humans do. They've got too much of a beast in them. He's not working with a full deck, so to speak. You got me?"

A faint smile curled her lips. "Yeah."

"He won't hurt you." Part of me wondered if I was talking to somebody other than her. *I* knew what I was saying. I believed it even. But maybe I had to voice it, so somebody would understand that I knew. Even if I needed time to get around to it. "It might not be easy to accept it all right away, but he's not going to hurt you."

She nodded it and shot Marcus another quick look. He wasn't pacing and growling so much, and that helped. I flicked him a glance myself. "Now if he'd actually use that *human* brain of his, and not whatever Tarzan complex is in control, maybe things could settle down a bit." Then I looked back at Clara and added, "I think it would be easier for him if you could explain what happened."

That's when the fear came back. I was ready for it.

Marcus wasn't. And it didn't even matter much right then that she wasn't afraid of him. Damn it, the poor girl. Poor Marcus. Poor both of them. What in the hell was going on? Her fear spiked harder and harder and it was worse, because she wasn't just afraid…she was hurting. I could feel it clawing at me, swarming in the air all around us and it hurt. Just sitting there hurt.

If it was that hard on me, I knew it had to be hell on Marcus.

But it was even harder on her, and his anger wasn't helping.

As she stuttered the words out, I could feel him getting angrier and it was almost too much for me to take, sitting there with my back to him as she explained. "My father," she whispered. "He knows now. I was trying to leave…I just…" Her voice tripped, hesitated and I watched as tears flooded her eyes, saw as the pain danced across her face. "I told him I needed to leave for a while and I think he knew something was going on. He yelled at me and didn't want me to leave. I was going to go to my room and just hide, but something about his eyes, the way he was watching me, it scared me. And I knew if I went in my room, I'd never get out."

Trapped…nobody is coming for you…

Shoving those memories away, I squeezed her hands

again, tighter and tighter until she looked at me. "You aren't there. Remember, no matter what, you aren't there, okay?"

A growl, low and wild, drifted through the room, and I tugged on her hands, forcing her focus back to me.

She nodded. It made it that much easier for me to remember *I* wasn't there, either. I'd gotten out. So had she.

"He hit me when I said no. He hit me so hard, I hit the wall and our neighbors…they were worried. He's never been that angry before and I think they thought somebody was breaking in."

"Let's hear it for concerned neighbors," I said, forcing myself to smile at her when she paused. "Keep going."

Behind me, Marcus growled again and I felt the punch of tension as his anger crawled and whipped across my skin. Shooting a look over my shoulder, I looked for him, but the closer person was Damon. He was no more than a few feet away. Standing guard, some part of me realized absently. Standing there…watching over me. *Nobody hurts you, Kit…*

Too bad it hadn't worked out that way. I made myself meet his eyes. "Calm him down, Damon."

Something not quite human stared back at me but he only nodded and then he turned away. Clara, the poor girl, was going to break my heart. She was rocking a little now, staring off at something none of us could see. I don't think she was even aware of Marcus. "He wanted to hit me again, but they were at the door," she whispered . "One of them is on the school board and Dad had this idea about me teaching once I got out of college." She gave me a ghost of a smile, the kind a teenager might give another close to them in age. "Teaching, you know? I'm no teacher. He tells me that I had to go with him and tell them everything was okay. I had to help him *diffuse* the situation I'd created. And I told him no. I told him I wouldn't help, and I told him that things had to stop. He just stared at me and then he said, *If you leave me, I don't have a daughter.* Just like that. Just like that I'm an orphan."

Just like that…

Something about the tone of her voice made it clear that

the man wouldn't be one who'd change his mind. But I didn't want to point out to her that maybe she was better off without him if he was the kind of man who'd raise his hand to his daughter. It hadn't been the first time. I could see that in her eyes.

No. Now wasn't the time. Not the time at all. She was getting ready to step into an entirely different world and her road here had already been bumpy.

"Just like that," I agreed softly, stroking my hand down her arm. "But you got away from a man who beat you because you did something as human as fall for a nice-looking kid. You got knocked up—it's going to be rough, but it's not the end of the world, right?"

Blood leaped to her cheeks and she looked down.

I touched her chin and forced her to look back at me. "These people here won't harm you. They won't harm your child. They'd sooner cut off their arms than hurt a kid. I've seen how they are with the little ones. You, your child, you'll be safe there. You can go from a place where you were mistreated to a place where you'll be cared for…" Then I slid Marcus a look. "Maybe even have a chance at something more. You can make your own choices and nobody will demonize you for this. It's not the life you'd set out to live…but it's not a bad one, either."

Marcus, Clara and Conley were the first to leave.

As they all piled into the car, I had to swallow the nerves crowding my throat.

Damon slumped on the couch, his chin resting on his chest and for all the world, he looked like a man who had no desire to leave.

As the sound of the engine faded, I crossed my arms over my chest and forced myself to face him. "Job's done," I said tightly.

His lashes lifted. "She never paid you."

"It wasn't about the money." Hell, the fifty bucks she'd offered didn't even cover the gas from Wolf Haven and that wasn't the point.

A little stunned, I turned away but before I could stare out, I caught Justin looking at me. His green eyes glinted in the dying light and I saw the knowledge there.

He knew.

Maybe Damon hadn't quite made the connection there and that was understandable. He hadn't been there when I'd first dragged my sorry ass out into the world of the living all those years ago, so he might not understand how hard this was.

Swallowing the knot that threatened to choke me, I whispered softly, "I saw it through."

"You did."

The tension mounted in my office until we could have sliced through it with a knife. I didn't hear the sound behind me so much as I just knew he was moving. Slowly, I turned around just in time to see Damon uncoiling and rising to his feet. His gaze all but bored into me. Like a blade, it sliced me open and laid me bare and I was helpless to stop it.

But then, as I saw him slipping a hand into his pocket, whatever had held me frozen evaporated. "If you pull any money out of your pocket, I'm going to tell Justin to burn your ass," I snapped.

Something flashed in his eyes. "Can't handle me on your own anymore, kitten?" he asked, his voice low and soft. All too intimate. It brought back memories that were better off tucked in the back of my mind.

I couldn't be dwelling on those parts of me right now.

Holding his gaze levelly, I summoned up a cocky smile. It felt fake on my face, stretching my lips unnaturally. But I did it, damn it. I stared at him with a smile and I kept that awful, hideous smile on my face as I replied, "Oh, it's got nothing to do with handling you, honey. It has to do with the fact it's always fun to watch a cat dancing around trying to avoid getting his feet singed."

As far as quips went, it was a damned miserable one and I knew it.

Damon knew it, too, but he didn't say anything.

Instead, he just looked at me for another minute and

then a faint smile curled his lips. He crossed the floor and stopped, just inches away. I held my breath as he dipped his head.

Against my ear, he murmured, "I'll be waiting."

He didn't say or do anything else, just headed for the door.

I didn't breathe as it shut behind him.

Didn't let myself breathe until I thought my lungs might explode.

One minute ticked by.

Then another.

I hiccupped a little.

Justin touched my shoulder. I swung at his hand and stumbled away. But when I fell against my desk, blinded by the tears, he wasn't so easily deterred.

As the storm hit me, I ended up pressed against his chest and all but starving for oxygen.

Justin had been the one to help me put the pieces of me together all those years ago.

Maybe it was fitting that he was there when I fell apart again.

Part Two

ReMade

CHAPTER ELEVEN

Now what?

I stood in the driveway of my home, staring at the door.

Why was every damn thing a battle?

Justin had offered to come home with me. I'd told him no. I knew better. If I let myself lean on him too much, take comfort in him too much, I'd end up using him.

And then I'd keep on using him.

It was even an appealing thought, I had to be honest. Just standing there, I found myself thinking about calling him.

I couldn't deny that I was absolutely terrified of being alone. Justin knew how to get past all the barriers I had inside me, including the terror that now gripped me in a cold, sweaty fist.

I could call him; he'd come. I wouldn't have to be alone. He'd stay the night. On the couch if I asked him to. In my bed, if I wanted.

Comfort sex might even make me feel a little better, once I got past the sweaty panic. Comfort sex had gotten me through some rough things before— *comfort* sex had been the only thing that had made me appreciate sex, really. Justin had been my lover and healer, all in one, for the first few months. It wasn't until later that we moved past that into just *lover* territory.

But I wasn't going to do it.

I'll wait…

Damn him to hell, but I still loved Damon. Even though thinking about him was an ache in my heart, I still loved him and that's all there was to it. Another reason why comfort sex with anybody was a big, fat *out.*

Morosely, I stared at the front door. Why in the hell was it so hard to think about walking into my *home*?

Because I was alone.

Because night was coming.

Because the first step of any journey was always the hardest, blah-blah-blah and I wasn't just taking *one* fricking journey, I was taking a hundred of them, and this was the next one.

I had to do it. I had to walk into that place by myself. I had to disengage the wards and reset them the second I was inside. That was the hardest part, I told myself. Once I was inside, once I was behind the wards, I'd be safe. Yeah, the wards could be broken, but it would take a lot of power and time and that time would let me get to the weapons I'd stashed in various places. I hadn't taken *everything* with me when I'd packed up. I couldn't…there was a small cache of weapons that was safer *here* than anywhere else, protected by the strongest, most expensive spells I'd been able to purchase from Green Road.

I could feel their power, subtle…so subtle. Wrapping protectively around those dark, dangerous weapons. Yeah, I had enough firepower in there to take down almost anything that might come gunning for me.

Maybe if I'd had one of those weapons with me…

Bile churned its way up my throat.

No maybes. No ifs. It's already done, Kit.

Something rolled across my skin, hot, prickling power—

A gasp lodged in my throat and although I did *not* run inside the house, I damn sure moved fast.

Drawing the Desert Eagle, I kept it in my hand, along my thigh where it wasn't going to be easily seen as I crossed the sidewalk. The sun was still a brilliant glow in the sky and I didn't *see* anybody, but I damn sure *felt* him.

Who was it?

Didn't matter. Unfamiliar magic…on my property.

That meant one thing. Not welcome.

I reached the door and slammed my hand against it, letting the ward take me in. By the time I'd managed to disengage all of them, I was shaking. Once I was inside, I was sweating so hard, I'd soaked through my shirt and my breaths came in ragged stops and starts.

But I was inside.

Inside—

The wards—had to engage them. Once I did that, I'd be safe. I was almost hysterical by the time I managed to do just that and then, boneless, I slid to the floor, clutching the Desert Eagle and trying to keep from hyperventilating. Passing out. Bad. Very. Very. Bad.

I breathed in through my nose. Held it. Blew it out, then did again, forcing the chaos in my head to settle.

When I sucked in another breath, an odd scent teased my senses. Warning sounded in my head and just as slowly, I blew the breath out, took another one.

Evergreen.

For some reason, my house smelled of evergreen…pine. Not that chemical pine scent, either.

But real, honest to God *pine* trees.

I took another breath and pretended to relax, letting my head fall back against the door so I could look around better. The lights were out, but that didn't matter. My night sight was keen and I could see the darkened room just fine.

And something wasn't right. A shape in the corner—

I focused, reached out.

There wasn't a soul alive *inside* the house. But there had been people in there recently. I could scent something familiar. Staring at that odd shape that didn't belong in my house, I pieced this strange puzzle together.

My heart started to race and I surged to my feet, hitting the panel for the lights. There was no way I was seeing things right.

Immediately, my breath caught, once more.

Over in the corner, dominating almost a third of my small living room, was a Christmas tree. The lights had come on the second I'd hit the light panel and now I could see the soft white glow flickering all around the tree.

On top of the tree was a star—it wasn't the typical star, though. A laugh that was almost hysterical bubbled out of me as I realized what it was. It had the gleam of pure silver and the eight-tipped throwing star should have looked utterly ridiculous, but I didn't think I'd ever seen anything more beautiful.

A Christmas tree.

It was the end of January.

But there was a Christmas tree in my house.

I took a step closer, eying the ornaments. Some of them were typical ornaments, but others weren't. More throwing stars. A set of throwing knives. Something coiled around one of the branches caught my eye. A silver garrote. Exactly like the ones I had woven into my collar and belt.

I covered my face with my hands as another laugh ripped out of me. It turned into a sob.

"Don't go getting all carried away. We wouldn't know normal if it bit us. But it might be nice to have something…well, nice."

"Yeah." Sleep was actually closer than I thought, I realized, but I forced my eyes opened, stared outside. "Nice… what's nice and normal."

"Christmas…you ever do Christmas, Kit?" His hand stroked my nape.

I snorted. "Hell, no. The aunts and Grandmother celebrated the solstice and I'd helped in the house, but I don't think that's the same as doing Christmas." I rolled my head to peer up at him through my lashes. "What about you?"

"Yeah." He stroked a finger along my cheek. "Me and the kid always did it, just me and him. Will be different this year, but…" His hand slid into my hair and tangled. "You're going to do Christmas this year. With me."

I lifted up a little to look at him. "I am, huh?"

"Yeah." He lifted up onto one elbow and pressed his mouth to

mine. "Nice, normal…it doesn't get much more nice and normal than that."

"Christmas, huh?" I lay my head back on his chest, smiling a little. "We going to get a tree?"

"Damn straight a tree. I'll buy you presents. You can buy something, too. I think something red and slinky, like all those lingerie things you look at and never buy."

The memories cut off abruptly as somebody knocked. "Kit. It's me."

Colleen…

I glanced over at the Christmas tree and then turned toward the door. I'd think about the tree, Damon, all of that in a few minutes. That son of a bitch.

I'd *told* him I needed time.

"He put it up the week after we brought you back."

I stared at her over a cup of tea. I didn't want to talk about the tree. Or Damon. Or anything.

But…

I shot the tree a dark look. "Christmas was more than a month ago…I've been back longer than that. There's no way that tree has been sitting there that long." It was a real tree, too.

"It's a living tree. It will need to be transplanted soon, but…" Colleen shrugged. "He's here every week to water it. That's what he says, anyway. I could water the damn thing. But when I show up here on Fridays to charge your wards, he's sitting outside waiting."

She ran a finger around the outside of the mug of tea. "Should I have maybe sent him away?"

I shoved back from the table and rose. Edgy, restless energy filled me and there was just no way to purge it. I turned and stared at the tree. That delightful and deadly tree, decorated with ornaments and weapons.

I doubted many women would feel their heart flip over in their chests, but I certainly had. Even now, staring at it for probably the tenth time, I still felt a weird little catch. "I don't know how to answer that, Colleen."

Then I looked over at her. "What does it matter to you, anyway? You don't much like him. You never really did."

She'd never said as much. But I knew my friend.

Colleen made a face at me. "Like him?" She shrugged. "It's not a question of whether or not I *like* him. He's not exactly the guy I would have pictured you with. That would have been Justin."

"I don't love Justin," I said, crossing my arms over my chest and looking back at the tree.

"Why do you love *him*?"

The words slashed at me. *Why*…not *do you*, but *why*.

She didn't even have to ask. But then again, Colleen wouldn't need to. With her empathy, she'd probably known before I had. "I'm not sure if I can explain that or not," I said, my voice wooden. "And I don't even know if it matters. Not now. If I can't put myself together, it won't matter. I can't be with him when I'm like…this."

"You'll get there, Kit," Colleen said, her voice gentle. "You're not giving yourself enough time. And you still haven't answered me."

Turning, I faced her. "What does it matter?"

"I'm just trying to understand." She shrugged and plucked at a loose thread on her shirt.

"I don't want to talk about this." How could I talk about it when I didn't understand it myself?

I grabbed the mug of tea off the table and headed down the hall. But as I passed by the living room, I caught sight of something I hadn't seen before. The tree had been partially hidden behind the couch and now I saw all of it…including all the gaily wrapped boxes on the floor.

Presents. More than I could count. And that ache lingering deep in my chest rose higher, threatening to rip out of me.

"He bought me presents," I said and my voice sounded ragged even to my own ears. Passing a hand down my face, I turned and looked at her. "I'm twenty-five years old and nobody's ever bought me a damn Christmas present."

Colleen shifted her attention past my shoulder, staring at the tree. "Actually…you're twenty-six."

I started, and then laughed sourly. Yeah. I was twenty-six. My birthday had come and gone and I hadn't even noticed. "Twenty-six, and not a single Christmas present." I didn't exactly celebrate it, but then again, I'd never had too many people give me gifts, period. Colleen had sometimes given me things on my birthday, and Justin had done the same when we were together, but beyond that?

Colleen didn't celebrate Christmas. My relationship with Justin had been one of the crazy, sporadic things and we'd always been on our *off* stages when the holidays rolled around. My family…nothing from them.

Gazing at all the gifts under the tree, I rubbed my hand over my chest and wished I could make the ache there go away. "Why did he have to do this?"

"Because he loves you," Colleen said, her voice matter of fact.

I looked over at her, barely seeing her through the tears. I tried to fight them, but it was getting harder and harder to hold them back.

Colleen reached up and touched my cheek. "And you know, I'd really *like* to tell you a different answer, Kit," she murmured, shaking her head. "I wish I could tell you there was nothing but guilt motivating him. That he just felt responsible and thought maybe this was a way to make it all better. Maybe that would piss you off and you could kick him to the curb. I'd love to say he's doing it for any other reason than the truth, but that son-of-a-bitch does love you…and you love him."

I turned away from her and pressed the heels of my hands against my eyes, waiting until that burning sting passed. I sucked in one breath after another and waited until I thought I could speak without my voice giving me away.

"Kit—"

"Stop," I said. I swallowed and shook my head. "Just…just give me a minute, okay?"

She wasn't helping. I wanted things to be easier. Not harder.

I couldn't even count all the presents under the tree. Technically, all those weapons glinting off the pine boughs were gifts, too. Sidestepping around the wrapped packages, I made my way over to the tree and touched one of the stars hanging from a seemingly delicate thread of silver. I watched as it spun in the light and then pulled it down. The balance of it, the weight of it in my hand was perfect. I touched the tip of it with my finger lightly and then looked over at Colleen.

"I don't understand it either, you know. It's just…when I look at him, something inside me feels whole. And before….well, you know…I even felt peace. It wasn't really that I felt *safe* with him—I *do* feel safe, and I like that. It should be *okay* to enjoy that. Although…hell. I don't *need* to be safe. He made me happy, just being next to him, and he made me *whole*. It was like I had something empty inside me and didn't even realize it until I met him…he filled that part of me."

Happy…whole.

And now look at me.

I laughed bitterly. I wasn't ever going to feel *whole* again, though. And happiness felt just as out of reach.

"You'll be happy again, Kit."

Closing my eyes, I pressed the heels of my hands against my eye sockets. "Coll, please stay out of my head, my emotions. I've had…*me*…invaded enough."

"I…I'm sorry. Damn it, I'm sorry. But it's just right there and it's hard for me not to see it."

Hearing the soft brush of her shoes against the floor, I turned and looked at her.

"I *can't* and I *won't* tell you that you're going to *get over this*," she said, watching me with sad eyes. "I know better. But I also know *you*. You'll pick yourself up…you're already doing it."

Was I?

Her fingers brushed my arm.

I reached up and caught her hand in mine. Then I looked

back at the tree. "What kind a crazy bastard decorates a tree with weapons?"

"I have to admit, I wondered the same thing when I was watching him. But when he was done, I couldn't think of anything that would have suited *you* more."

Tentatively, she slid an arm around me and I sighed, rested my head against her shoulder. She was taller than me, curvier and I felt like a little girl standing in the embrace of her bigger, wiser sister. Maybe it wasn't a bad thing. We both eyed the presents strewn across the floor.

"You going to open them?"

"No." I wasn't ready to do that.

No yet.

I didn't know if I ever *would* be. Not any time soon, at least.

I'll wait…

One gift hadn't been wrapped.

I didn't see it until after Colleen had left.

She'd offered to stay. And I'd been so tempted to let her. Instead, I'd just asked her to charge the wards, maybe give them an extra kick, then, before I could give in to temptation, I'd told her goodnight and locked the door behind her.

Unable to stay in the living room, staring at the tree, I fled down the hall to my room and that was where I found the other gift.

A blade.

His metal gleamed in the soft light falling in from over my shoulder, dancing along the length of steel, along the grip. I recognized the design right away, but what I couldn't figure out…how had this blade gone from something I'd only half-worked on for a few minutes one day to this?

I'd been sketching it while I talked to him one day. Doyle had been there. Then Doyle had taken off with the sketch. I hadn't realized it until later.

Well. I guess that explained the *why*.

Swallowing around the knot that had decided to take up permanent residence in my throat, I moved into my room and sank to my knees in front of my bed. My fingers shook as I reached out to touch it. Silence roared in my head as my fingers brushed the grip. I'd stopped expecting to hear any music, so it didn't tear into my heart, although I'd be lying if I tried to pretend I wasn't disappointed.

But still…the blade. Man. He was beautiful.

His length had the odd gleam unique to silver. It wasn't pure silver—I already knew that. Silver wasn't a good metal for swords or knives, not on its own. It's too soft. But a talented swordsmith can forge a blade with enough silver in it to make it suitable…deadly.

Damon had apparently found a very, very talented swordsmith.

I closed my hand around the grip and lifted it and despite everything, I couldn't stop from swinging him once, just once. A smile spread across my face at the sound he made, slicing through the air. Maybe I couldn't hear the music anymore, but this blade made his own song.

The weight of him was different in my hand, the balance something I'd have to get used to. But maybe if I was going to adjust to life without the music of my blades, it would be easier at first if I did it this way.

A new blade. Something that didn't carry all the memories of the past.

I glanced around and it wasn't a surprise to see the scabbard lying near the foot of my bed. He'd wanted me to see the blade first, but he'd made sure he had the right tools for me to carry it, too.

"Damn you, Damon," I whispered, stroking my finger up the blade. I caught the end and bent it, watching it bow just a little and then go back to its sleek, straight length the second I let go. Perfectly balanced. Perfectly forged.

I sheathed him and left the blade lying on the bed. A few months ago, that's the very spot where Damon would have been.

Instead of the man, I had a piece of forged steel and

silver.

The irony wasn't lost on me.

CHAPTER TWELVE

I wasn't surprised to see Justin loitering outside my office when I pulled in.

I was actually *more* surprised by my presence than his.

As the car door opened, I met his gaze across the busted pavement and tried to pretend life was normal. Things were normal. Everything was fine.

Justin did the same and flashed me a wide, wicked smile. It didn't have the same effect it used to, but I was able to smile back. I pulled the blade from the back seat and slid it into place, acutely aware of the fact that he was watching.

"That's a new piece," he said, his voice neutral as he crossed over to stand near the front of the car. He leaned one hip against the banged-up hood and studied the sword for a moment before looking up at me.

"Yeah." I shrugged restlessly and stroked a finger down the pommel. "It's new. My other one is still back in Wolf Haven and this…" I finished on another shrug. I wasn't ready to pick up my old sword until I could hold her without feeling like I was dying inside. I didn't have to explain that to him, either. He'd know. "I could use some practice with it, though. I'm not as up to speed on fighting with a blade like this as I ought to be. If I can get you a similar one, wanna go a round or two?"

His brow lifted up. "If that's your way of getting some

blood out of me, I guess it's the least I can do."

"Ha-ha." I hauled my bag out of the back. "I called TJ. She's sending somebody with my gear so I'll have some sort of practice blade for you later on. You can come back by when you feel like it or I can call."

He shrugged. "I was sort of thinking about hanging around. If any work comes in, I can help you with it." His shoulders moved in a restless shrug and he added, "Not going to be doing anything with Banner for a while. Maybe never. Dunno yet. So I'm at loose ends."

I studied him from under my lashes. "Just what sort of disciplinary action is this, Justin?"

A mean grin curled his lips. "The best kind." Then he shrugged and looked away. "Don't worry about it, Kit. They aren't coming after me and I made my point clear. All's well and good. I'm just sort of…jobless."

"Well." I turned and stared at the empty parking lot. "As you can see, I don't exactly have a bunch of people storming down my door, Justin. I can't really see how hanging out here is going to improve your job prospects."

"Oh, things will turn around for you, Kitty." He watched me. "They always do."

"Whether things turn around for me or not, that doesn't mean I'm looking to take on a partner."

"Not even for old time's sake?"

I gave him a baleful look as I started up toward the door to my office. Halfway up the walk, I felt the shimmer of something skitter along my flesh. I recognized the odd presence —strong and female, full of magic. I'd felt this person before. It was the same woman I'd sensed last night, only I hadn't fully keyed into the fact that she was female.

I'd been in too much of a panic to realize it then.

It wasn't the were I'd been sensing off and on, either.

One glance at Justin told me that he'd felt it, too. "Any idea who that is?" I asked.

"Nope." He smiled. "Hey, this is your place of business. I'm just here to…"

"Look pretty?" I offered.

"Well, until you want to me to do something else, I guess that will work." He pretended to smooth down his jacket. "She's female…I can tell that much."

I lifted a brow. "*I* can tell that much, Romeo." I went about unlocking the doors and something about the familiarity of it soothed the jangled mess of nerves inside me. I was at my office. A smart-assed friend was with me. Somebody with magical blood was loitering far too close for comfort. This was all familiar territory. And it was daylight. I was safe as long as there was daylight.

But Jude can come out in the day—

Stop it, I told myself, shoving that fear down deep inside, so deep, so far, I couldn't even feel it, couldn't sense it. If I couldn't, maybe Justin *wouldn't.*

The wards whispered away under my touch and I moved inside, stepping away from the door long enough for Justin to move in behind me before I shut the door. I reactivated the wards before doing anything else.

I wasn't sitting defenseless in my office with some sort of magic thing out there.

"You can't exactly expect her to come in if you have the wards up," Justin said, a wry smile on his face.

Absently, I stroked my sword, staring outside, trying to find whoever it was. She hadn't come close for me to be able to see her yet. Not in the parking lot. Not on the street beyond. "I…"

"Kit. This isn't how you work," Justin said quietly.

I turned and stared at him. "I know how I work," I snapped, jerking my chin up at him. If I wanted to stay in the office with the wards up, then…then…

Shouldering past him, I locked myself in the bathroom and pressed my back to the door. I could do this. I could. I was *here*, right? I'd come in here, I had a blade on me. I'd left Wolf Haven. I'd done a job already and I'd faced Damon.

Damon's not the problem.

Of course you're carrying a blade…you go grabbing at them in the night like a scared pussy.

You left Wolf Haven to shut TJ up. You didn't do it because you wanted *to.*

That voice kept nattering over and over in my head. Fisting my hands, I drilled them against my temples in an attempt to drown it out. *Shut up shut up shutupshutupshut*UP!

A moment of silence passed.

Then…a whisper… *You're stronger than this…we* made *you stronger…go out there and prove it.*

An icy shiver raced down my spine and I dropped my hands. Shoving away from the door, I looked around. Okay. That…that wasn't right.

We *made you stronger*?

If *I* was stronger than this, then I was that way because *I* had made myself that way. Granted, I didn't feel very strong right now.

Groaning, I tugged at my hair and shoved off the door. Maybe I was closer to losing it than I thought.

A few minutes later, I slipped out of the bathroom.

Without looking at Justin, I deactivated the wards.

Without looking at Justin, I settled behind my desk.

Without looking at Justin, I reached for the pile of mail that had built up.

Normal. I'd just pretend to be nice and normal and do nice and normal things. That's the ticket.

That's…

The shimmer of magic hit me stronger.

Rubbing my fingers together, I glanced up toward the window and mentally braced myself. "I don't like this already."

Justin had settled down on the busted-up couch and out of the corner of my eye, I saw him pull out his tattered deck of cards. "A job's a job, right, Kitty?"

Grunting, I pulled out a knife and starting opening mail. Most bills had gone electronic decades ago, but the United States Postal Service wasn't totally defunct. A lot of high magic users didn't totally trust E-shit of any kind so they stuck to traditional methods, like mail or courier—that wasn't a bad thing. Courier work had kept me fed for quite a while.

Another business enterprise that still relied on the USPS? Junk mail. A couple of flyers, a request for my presence at a very important seminar for small business types. Junk, junk and more junk.

Then something that burned when I touched it.

High magic in the mail wasn't an unusual thing. Since you had to be human to work in most government jobs outside of Banner, sending stuff like this wouldn't even catch the attention of a postal worker, but it seemed a little weird to waste a spell of this caliber when a courier would have gotten it to me quicker and made the spell unnecessary.

"What's that?"

Justin had caught the magic coming off it already, moving my way as I leaned back to study it. The envelope looked like something out of another century—like two or three of them past. The handwriting was a broad, elegant scroll and totally unfamiliar. Tapping the edge of it against my desk, I met his gaze.

"It would appear to be an envelope," I said.

"Ha-ha." He held out a hand.

"I know how to handle my own mail." I reached inside a drawer and pulled out a thin strip of leather. On it were a series of beads. It was one of the charms I'd bought from Green Road over the years and like most of the inactive spells, it didn't do anything until it sensed my touch. Magic lasted longer when it wasn't constantly wasting its energies. Colleen crafted most of the spells and charms I used and she keyed them all to my touch. Once I touched it, the magic in it hummed to life.

"Too much magic in that thing to rely on a charm," Justin said.

I shot him a look. "Justin…this isn't how I work…letting you do the job for me." I waited until he backed off before I did anything else.

If I was getting a bad vibe from it, I'd let him handle it, but I wasn't.

There was plenty of power pulsing from the thing, but it was neither malevolent nor harmless. It just…*was*. Odd as it seemed, the thing just pulsed with power, like it wanted nothing more than to get my attention.

I placed the charm over it and waited.

The beads on it glowed as the magic within flared. Finally, the beads flashed green, signaling it should be safe to proceed. If magic of the nasty, dark kind had been sensed, the beads would have gone black. Scooping up the charm, I dumped it back in the drawer and reached for the envelope.

Justin stood close by and I could feel the tension crawling off him. "Tone it down," I muttered. He was freaking *me* out and wasn't I messed up enough already?

Slipping my knife under the top edge, I broke the seal. Then waited.

Nothing but that steady pulse of magic. Okay. I sliced it open and set my knife aside, blowing out a breath. "I feel like an—" I started to say as I reached inside to pull out the document inside.

I never managed to finish the sentence because magic shrieked, splitting the relative quiet of the morning with a wail like a dying banshee.

Hurling the thing down, I shoved back from my desk and braced myself. Magic built around us, harder, higher, hotter. *Tighter*—somehow, the feel of the magic grew *tighter*, wrapping around us like a bubble. Oh, hell, I hope that bubble didn't pop with us inside.

I put myself at Justin's side, noting yet again that the silver on his sleeves had started to spark. His dreads whipped around in an unseen wind. "What the hell is this?" I asked, but my voice was lost in the magic maelstrom.

"Old magic," he shouted. "Not felt anything like it in a while. Just stay by me."

I felt the odd, static warmth of his magic wrap around me—it had a strange, metallic sort of feel and made me think of blades clashing, shields flashing in the morning sun.

The two magics built and built—that foreign presence that I didn't like at *all* and Justin's familiar magic, like a giant warrior mantling over us, shield lifted and ready.

And then, as abruptly as it had started, it died. It didn't *fade*; it just *ended.*

Justin cut a dark look my way and snapped, "Next time I tell you there's too much magic to trust to a charm, will you *listen*? You know blades. *I* know magic and—"

I put a hand on his arm.

Somebody was coming.

I could hear her.

Felt each footstep like an echo on my soul.

"Not now," I said, keeping my voice low as I shifted my attention to the door.

As one, as though we'd rehearsed it a hundred times, we moved back to where we'd been. Justin's protections didn't lower, though—that strange, mantling sort of shield stayed up and ready and I was damn thankful as I settled behind my desk and pretended to study the sheet of parchment in front of me.

The note on it was simple. It filled me with an odd sort of revulsion and curiosity.

Glad to see you're still open for business. I'll be there shortly to discuss a job.

I.

That was all.

I.

Okay.

Who is *I.*?

The door opened and I looked up. Guess it was time to find out.

CHAPTER THIRTEEN

The woman standing there was nobody I'd ever met before and the power I'd sensed in her wasn't even the tip of the iceberg. If she'd turned around and walked right out, I would have been just fine with that, too. She made my teeth ache.

Plucking up the piece of parchment, I held it aloft and met her gaze. "Your handiwork?"

"It is." She glanced around and lifted a hand, touching it the door jam. "May I enter?"

The question bothered me. She wasn't a vampire, but most people didn't ask to enter a place of business...not if they weren't vamp or vamp-affiliated.

Leaning back, I kept my hands on the arms of the chair, trying to get a better read on her. I couldn't. All I could get was *old* and *powerful.* "You got a name...something other than *I*?"

A smile flirted with the corners of her mouth as she continued to stand there, just outside the door. "I do. You can call me Isidore."

Her accent was strange. Okay, *everything* about her was strange. My gut was twitchy, tight. It wasn't exactly screaming, *Don't do this job*, but I was definitely getting the *proceed with all caution* flag.

"Well, Isidore," I said slowly, keeping my eyes on her.

"If you want to talk business, I guess you'd do better coming inside."

The smile on her face widened and she slipped inside, closing the door at her back.

Her gaze moved to Justin.

I could see him from the corner of my eye. He was sitting on the couch, that worn-out deck of cards in his hands. Never play cards with a witch. Especially Justin. The card tricks are just the least of it. He flipped one into the air and it spun around, hovering lazily in the air for a good twenty seconds before drifting down and settling into place. Solitaire. His version of it. I'd seen him use similar tricks to cheat at poker and any other game. Nobody ever beat Justin.

He looked over at me, his gaze bouncing off Isidore as if she wasn't there. With a sly wink, he nodded and then went back to his game.

"Is this a…business associate?" she asked, looking at me and canting her head to the side.

"Of a sort." I pushed my chair back from the desk a little more and slouched a bit, lacing my hands over my belly. The pose might have looked lazy and careless, but it put my hands in very close proximity to the gun and K-bar I'd strapped into place earlier. I liked having them in very close proximity. Especially when she sauntered closer, her movements just a little too graceful to be human. The typical human didn't move like that. They just weren't that comfortable in their skin.

I wondered if the silver-charged ammo in the Eagle would be enough to hurt her. Silver wouldn't kill a witch, but since I didn't know what this woman was…

"Do you always study those who wish to hire you like that?"

I blinked. "Like what?"

"As though you're trying to decide if you can kill them or not?" An amused smile curved her lips.

Surprised, and unsettled, I straightened in my chair, taking her in with even more caution. I was good at summing people up without them realizing it. I'd been doing it for years, but she'd just made me in two seconds flat. Was I *that* much off my game? Or was she just that good?

I managed a casual shrug. "Considering the kind of work I do, and the kind of clients I've had to handle sometimes, it's a good idea to know whether or not I can kill them."

"Hmmm." She settled in the chair across from my desk and crossed her legs. She wore a long, brightly colored skirt—it made me think of gypsies and fires and dancing in the night. As she laced her fingers over her knee, she continued to study me. "I am not immortal."

Why offer that piece of information up? Unless she was just trying to keep me off-balance. Not that it took much these days.

"Very few creatures are," I said after a few seconds. I gave her a lazy smile. "Some are just a hell of a lot harder to kill than others."

She laughed. It was a warm sound, the kind that invited you to laugh with her, share in her humor. I didn't feel inclined to do that. She was creeping me out. "Oh, I think I like you, Kit." She leaned forward and winked at me. "I'm a *lot* harder to kill than others."

"Yeah?"

My palm itched. It was reflex. Knowing I couldn't call my blade made it that much worse.

She reached down and pulled something from the intricate leather belt she wore.

I held myself ready and didn't even breathe as she moved.

A heavy thud echoed through my office as she dropped a pouch on my desk. "A deposit on the job," she said.

I eyed it narrowly and didn't move. "Perhaps we should discuss the job before any sort of payment."

"Don't you want to see what it is?" Her eyes were wide, avidly locked on my face. She had a way of looking at me, talking to me like my every word mattered so very much.

"Considering the noise it made as you dumped it on the desk, I'm going to guess it's money…in coin. I got to say, I haven't ever had somebody try to pay me in coins before.

Wouldn't bills be easier to carry around?"

Justin came off the couch.

She looked at him.

I didn't.

When he reached out and grabbed the bag, she said, "I'm not hiring *you*, boy."

"Boy?" I grinned.

"Trust me…when you've seen as many years as I have? Everybody seems like a boy…or a silly girl." Her gaze slid my way.

Her meaning was clear.

Lifting a brow, I shrugged. "If I'm a silly girl, why are you here in my office asking me to do a job? Wouldn't it be more effective for you to do it?"

"I…can't. For complicated reasons." She glanced at Justin again as he untied the pouch.

He whistled out a breath. "Yow. Nice deposit."

Glancing over at him, I waited. When he showed me what was in the bag, I almost swallowed my tongue. Blinking, I leaned closer to study the coins and had to fight the urge to rub at my eyes. "Is that *real*?"

"Of course it's real," Isidore said, her tone bored.

I wasn't about to take *her* word.

Justin reached in and took out one of the coins, tossing it up and catching it in mid-air, studying it with a jaded eye. "It's real," he said, his voice tight. "And there's easily fifty coins in here. Silver and gold. A fucking fortune. And this is just the deposit?"

Easily fifty? I wondered how he'd eyeballed the coins and come out with that number, wondered how he was so certain it was real. But if Justin was certain, then I was good with that.

Shifting my eyes to Isidore, I ran my tongue over my teeth. A fortune in silver and gold.

There weren't too many jobs that paid *that* well.

"Just who do you want me to kill?"

And she laughed. "Oh, darling Kit…if I just wanted somebody *dead*, I could do that myself."

Thirty minutes later, she left.

I kind of wished she'd been there about a hit.

Staring at the pouch full of silver and gold, all tucked away, I decided it might have been better if I *hadn't* lowered my wards.

Justin continued to play with the gold piece he'd pulled from the bag and even after her presence had faded, we remained silent.

Finally, after nearly fifteen minutes, Justin blew out a breath. "I think the last time I felt that much magic off somebody, it was when I was sent with a team to take down a Druid over in Europe."

"A Druid?"

He grunted. "Long story. His wife had finally died…which was the end of him. They need each other to survive, stay sane. He started going crazy."

"How old was he?"

Justin shot me a look. "We found relics in his home dating back to the Iron Age."

I blinked. "Whoa."

"Yeah." He looked at the bag of coins on my desk. "I think she's older."

"Shit."

"Yeah."

He tossed the coin in the air and I watched as it did the same thing his cards had done, spinning lazily around in the air, powered by his magic. It was an old piece of gold, the edges worn and smooth, handled by so many hands.

"When you say a fortune, just how much of a fortune are you talking about?" I asked.

He shrugged and held out his hand. The bit of gold settled into his palm and he closed his fingers around it. "I've seen pieces like this selling for twelve grand, Kit. And it's not in prime condition. Other pieces in the bag might be."

"Prime condition…meaning?"

"If I'm right…" He uncurled his fingers and I leaned, eying the faded and worn image depicted on one side. "And I probably am, this is Alexander the Great—"

I held up a hand. "Stop. Alexander the Great…as in *the* Alexander?" I might not know coins, but I knew fighters—even after more than two millennia, the name Alexander the Great was still known to men.

"Yeah." Justin rubbed a thumb over the image and grinned at me. "*That* Alexander. Coins that old are pretty rare. It's not the worth of the *gold*…it's the collectable value of the coin. And Kit…it's a pretty damn collectable coin."

I frowned and reached out, plucking the coin out of his hand. "You're telling me this is over two thousand years old?"

"Yep."

Not quite certain I bought it, I studied the coin. Yeah, it looked old, but *that* old? "I never knew you were that big into coins."

"Hey, it's metal." He shrugged. "A man's got to have a hobby…metal is mine. And it's possible I'm wrong about *who* is on the coin, but I'm not wrong about the age. That's old, Kit. And it's genuine. I can feel the age on it. That makes it pretty damn valuable."

I tossed it back at him. He snagged it out of the air and as I settled back down at the desk, he went back to his little game of tossing it in the air and making it float.

"Where did she get that kind of money?"

He studied me. "Well, *she* is old."

"You really think she's two thousand years old?"

"Yeah." He dropped down on the couch , balancing the coin on his fingertip. "Actually, I think it's entirely possible she's even older. You going to find this vase for her?"

I looked down at the picture she'd drawn for me.

She was going to pay me that money…*a fortune in gold*…to find a vase.

Find my vase for me, Kit…return it to me.

That was what she wanted me to do.

I touched the sketch and pondered it. "There's got to be

more to it than this. Who would pay that much money for a vase?"

"That's a question I'd want an answer to…along with others."

I looked up at him, lifting a brow.

"The name."

Reaching up, I ran my hand through my hair, groaning as I tried to work his meaning around in my head. It wasn't happening. "Maybe I've been out of this too long, Justin. I'm not following."

"Give it time," he said easily. "You had your mind on other things…like whether or not you just wanted to kick her out. But didn't you notice? When you asked her name…how did she answer?"

I blinked and then closed my eyes, replaying that bit through my mind.

"You got a name…something other than I?"

"I do. You can call me Isidore."

"You can call me Isidore," I murmured. I looked over at Justin. "She never said that was her name."

"Which meant she never outright lied to you. You probably would have picked up on the lie. You usually do. If you hadn't, *I* would have. She avoided that trap pretty neatly. So the question is…is her name really Isidore, and if it's not, why did she lie about it?"

"I've had plenty of people come to me and not give me their real name when I'm doing a job."

He shrugged. "True enough. But over something like this? If you're really just locating a vase, what's the big deal about her name?"

"Hell, Justin. You're a witch, you know that answer better than anybody. There's power in a name. But…that's not the answer, really." I bent forward and studied the image Isidore had drawn. She had a talent for it. I rubbed my finger over the line of the vase as a knot of discomfort shifted and swelled inside me. "This is more than a vase…more than just some family heirloom. I think it would have to be, if she's willing to pay *that* kind of money for it."

He shrugged. "You're hung up on how much she's paying. If she's loaded, that may not even be that much money to her."

"I don't think that's the case." I shook my head. "A lot of the older ones are stingy…they might spend it on something they *want*, but they aren't going to throw it away so easily either."

I went back to studying the vase, the curves and lines of it, the images depicted on the side. There was a story in them; I just had to figure out what it was. "No, this thing is important to her. Otherwise, she wouldn't have come to me."

"You're taking the case, aren't you?"

I looked over at him. Unless something absolutely screamed for me *not* to…I blew out a breath. "I probably am." Running my tongue over my teeth, I eyed the way he was running the coin back and forth across his fingers. "You seem pretty fond of that ol' Alexander there. You want it?"

"I thought you didn't want a partner."

I curled my lip at him as I settled down behind my desk and booted up the computer. I needed to figure out the importance of this vase, first and foremost. "If I'm going to be dealing with high magic, makes sense to have somebody who knows high magic at my back. You in or not?"

"Absolutely." He grabbed the sack of coins and hefted it in his hand. "Fifty-fifty split?"

"Seventy-thirty."

"Kit…come on, now."

I grabbed the drawing from the desk and put it face-down on the micro-scanner. "Hey, I've got business expenses. What do you need to take care of…buying yourself more sparkly jackets?"

"I'll be the one dealing with the rough shit if the high magic gets ugly," he pointed out. "I'm also jobless and probably going to be that way for a while. I need the cash. Sixty-forty."

"Hey, it's not my fault you and discipline don't see eye to eye. Take your joblessness up with Banner." I shrugged and pretended to ponder the sixty-forty split, but since that was what I'd planned on offering, I didn't ponder long. "Fine. Sixty-forty, but any expenses you rack up come out of your share of the money."

He grinned and tossed the coin into the air. "I can handle that. Just let me cash this baby in and do some restocking."

I rolled my eyes and focused my attention back on the computer. Isidore was going to be back this time tomorrow. I wanted to know more about the vase by then. Just in case.

It was almost eight.

I hadn't unearthed *anything*.

At least not anything useful.

Tons of information about the name *Isidore* and *vases*, but most of it was all connected to France and museums and my client was not French, and I was absolutely positive the design on that vase wasn't from the 1800s. I was no historian, but it looked a hell of a lot older.

I ended up hitting a historical site, going back through the ages and studying various designs until I found something that *might* be the same basic design. Plus, it was also Greek. Since the coins she'd paid us in were Greek, maybe…

I stopped and reached for the bag, pulling out a handful to study them. Were all of them Greek?

It didn't take me more than a few seconds to make that call—no. Maybe I didn't have the hobby that Justin did, but the coin in my hand now definitely wasn't Greek.

It was in rough shape, too, but I could make out what looked to be a face, a crown…probably a king of some sort. On the back there was a cross. This wasn't Greek. Something about the cross made me think of early England, although I didn't know why. Quite a few of the coins in the bag looked like that, although there were a number of coins from Asia.

One thing was clear—these were from different cultures, different periods. I couldn't count on those to help me narrow my search down. Still, when I turned back to the computer, I focused on *Greek vases.*

The search for *famous Greek vases* didn't do much but confirm my hunch. The vase Isidore had sketched out definitely looked like one of these; the style of hers matched the Greek ones, right down the silhouette-like figures decorating the sides.

While most of the ones I came across during my search featured battles, the one Isidore wanted me to find depicted a woman.

I went back and studied that image, turning my head and studying it from every conceivable angle. I don't know what I expected to find.

The woman painted on the side held a vase in *her* hands and you could almost make out the echo of *another* woman on *that* vase…

She was surrounded by mountains, a streak of lightning coming down to shatter them. She'd drawn another angle of it and the view showed animals, lying down. Yet another view showed people—caught in embraces that weren't exactly…appealing. It made the skin on my neck burn and the scars hidden by the tattoos started to ache with a deep, deep cold.

Flames danced all around each of the pictures. Not a calming sort of image, really.

No, the entire thing made me think of power. Death. Chaos. Destruction.

I swallowed as something worked free in my memory. The very idea was enough to turn my gut to ice, but…come on. That was myth, right?

But even as I tried to tell myself that, a cold sweat slicked my back as I bent over the keyboard.

"It's just a myth, Kit," I told myself. But I had to be smart, and check.

I clenched my jaw and then typed in another search.

The search engine didn't even waste time on *that* search. It immediately brought up the very last thing I wanted to see; in *theory,* it was supposed to be a box, right?

I'd hoped I'd see a corrected search.

But what I saw were images, artistic renderings…and many of them depicted a woman.

The bottom of my stomach dropped out as I saw the heading of the very first text result, followed by the neat little summary underneath.

Pandora's Box wasn't actually a box, but a vase…

CHAPTER FOURTEEN

Justin walked in the next morning and stopped dead in his tracks.

"Wow. You look like shit. Did you *sleep*?"

I shot him a dark, ugly look and flipped him off. "Did you sell that coin yet?"

"Ah…I've got a couple of buyers lined up. Why?"

"We may not be taking this job," I said grimly.

He didn't even bat an eyelash. "Okay…" He drawled out the word slow and steady as he shut the door behind him. "You want to tell me why?"

I crooked a finger at him and waited for him to come around and join me. I hadn't slept. I hadn't left my office. I'd ended up calling for Chinese to be delivered and I'd eaten maybe a quarter of the orange chicken before I dumped it. My shower lasted all of thirty seconds because I was terrified to be where I couldn't see the front door.

To top it all off, that damn were had hovered around most of the night, too, and there had been one point when I'd almost gone out there and picked a fight with whoever it was.

But the second I'd started to do that, sanity intruded and I'd retreated back behind my desk and focused on the job. What did it matter if there was a were skulking about when I had an ancient evil showing back up in my office trying to pay me a fortune in gold to find her lost relic?

I knew too much about ancient relics—I even *owned* a few of them—and the more powerful ones were better off being either destroyed or in very, very careful hands. I questioned whether or not *my* hands met those qualifications.

Fights and distractions would have to wait. I needed to be ready. Knowing *my* luck, Isidore would come back early.

Congratulations, TJ. You wanted me back kicking and screaming in this world… I'm back. And I'd really like to scream at you. Kicking something might help, too.

I eyed the clock. We had an hour. One hour for me to decide. What was the lesser evil? Keeping the vase from her? Or risk letting somebody else keep it?

Justin crouched next to me, his gaze darting from one sheet of paper to another, taking in the notes, the pictures I'd printed out. Of course, there *was* no picture of Pandora's vase…mankind believed it to be a legend, but I'd gone through as many of those grains of sand as I could, looking for any shred of the truth.

Instead of trying to explain it all, I said, "Computer, on."

The screen flared to life and I turned so I could watch Justin's face as he read.

The skin around his eyes tightened and his mouth went flat.

"*Pandora*? As in the chick who unleashed all the evils into the world?"

"If my gut is right, that's the one." I sighed and looked back at the computer, wishing the story on the screen would change. I didn't think it would, though.

"You can't take the job," he said, shoving upright. He pulled the coin from his pocket and flung it on the desk. "We wait until she gets here, tell her we can't do it. I'll alert Banner and—"

"I don't think it's that simple," I said softly, reaching out and catching his wrist when he would have spun away.

His skin felt hot under mine and his eyes glittered intense and bright. "Want to explain why not?"

"It's *hers*, for one. What if she's the only one who is *meant* to have it? What if it was stolen and having it in the wrong hands is even worse than having her open it? For *that* matter, what if being out of her hands is the thing that *opens* it? History gets things wrong all the time."

Justin squeezed his eyes shut. I watched as he shoved the heel of one hand against his eye socket. He probably felt like gouging his brain out. I'd felt like that more than once throughout the night as I thought this through. None of the prospects sounded all that pleasant, but then again, we were operating in the dark. That was never good.

"Besides…" I crooked a grin at him. "*If* the legend about the box has any basis in truth, then she already opened it…the evils of the world, death, greed, old age…all of that is already in the world. The only thing that *should* be left in it is hope. Right?"

He lowered his hand and glared at me. "Ha, ha. You want me to bet on a legend written by *humans*?"

I shrugged. "We don't have much else to go by at this point."

"Shit." He spun away and paced the floor, a blur of magic and silver as the threads in his sleeves started to spark.

"Why do they do that?"

He frowned and then glanced down at his sleeves. "Metal."

I lifted a brow at him. "Meaning…?"

He sighed and rubbed his hands over his face. "Kit, is this the time?"

"Well, I never seem to think about asking you at any other time," I pointed out.

He lowered his hands and stared at me. And then, before I could so much as brace myself, strands of silver were flying at me. *Dozens* and *dozens*…like I was caught in a web of them. I held still, trusting in one very simple thing—Justin wouldn't hurt me. That much, I could count on.

But it was damn hard not to panic as I found myself all but caged in silver—there had been a lot more of it worked into his jacket than I'd realized and now, all of it was stretched out between the two of us, wrapping around the arms of my chair, the back of it. Not touching *me*, but still, a very effective binding, since I was sort of sitting in the chair.

"Metallurgy," he said, his voice low.

Slowly, the silver uncurled and retreated, pulling back in a graceful swirl and winding back around his arms.

My breath lodged in my throat and I still couldn't breathe.

Memory flashed through my mind.

Silver…something silver had grabbed me when I tried to throw myself over the cliff. "You…" I forced the words out. "You're the one who stopped me from jumping."

He jerked his head in a nod.

"Remember how my magic seemed to be getting out of control the last year before Banner called me in?"

Eying all that silver, I whispered, "Yes."

"Apparently I had a new talent working its way free and I didn't recognize it. Seeing as how the two of us carried a hell of a lot of metal and it calls to me, it split my concentration," he said. The silver was back in place on his arms, sparking in that odd, erratic little way. "I couldn't control the magic until I learned to control the metal better. Banner didn't just come looking to *recruit* me."

My gut went tight.

"Justin…"

He turned away and moved to stare out the window. "If they didn't get me under control, I would have been exterminated."

I closed my eyes. "How long have you known about this?"

"Since the beginning." His shoulders strained against the jacket as he crossed his arms over his chest. I couldn't see his face, but the resignation in his voice hit me, hard. Right in my heart. "I didn't go willingly. Not at first. I made everybody think I did because if I didn't…well…"

He shrugged.

"You didn't want your friends coming after you and getting in trouble with Banner."

"I didn't want *you* coming after me." He looked over his

shoulder at me. "The one person who had a decent chance at tracking me down and getting me out of there was you. And they knew that. They made it clear if I tried to cut loose before I had a grasp on the metal magic and my old gifts, they were going to put me down. Anybody who helped me would suffer, too."

"Put you *down*?" I echoed, rising from behind my desk. I had to fight the urge to scream, to tear into something. *Anything.* "You're not a sick dog or a lame horse."

Dull green eyes met mine. "Try telling that to the higher-ups at Banner. Anybody who presents a threat is a sick animal in their eyes."

I clenched my hand into a fist. "Yet you worked for them."

"I owed them five years—that was the *cost* of them training me, teaching me how to use the metallurgic magic. It's apparently pretty damn rare…and they weren't lying about that. In the past five years, ever since I learned what it was, I've only met two other witches who had even a trace of it. Only one had a handle on it." He turned around, resting his hips against the window sill. Head bowed, he focused on the floor beneath his feet as he continued to speak. "That one was my instructor. Said he could teach me to use it, but teaching me came with a cost and an oath—the cost was my service. I had to give them five years and if I didn't agree, they were going to just kill me so they didn't have to worry about the new talent driving me crazy."

"They can't just *kill* somebody who hasn't presented a threat." I was so damned pissed, I could hardly see straight.

"Kitty…this is Banner." His words were thick with derision. "They can do whatever in the hell they want."

"So you just *agreed*?"

He lifted his head and met my eyes. "Not at first."

The look in his eyes made my gut go tight. Part of me didn't want to hear what he had to say. But it was too late to close this door now. *Kind of like Pandora's Box…*

His lashes dipped low, shielding the vivid green of his eyes and he sighed, his shoulders rising and falling under the sturdy black cloth of his jacket. "They took me to this…I guess you can call it a hospital, but it's more like a jail. That's where I met the other witch who had a gift for metallurgy. He was strong…I could feel him from miles away. You've met those kind before. Like a storm coming on."

"Like you."

"I hope not." The words came out of him in a ragged rush and he spun away, braced one hand against the wall. "The closer we got, the worse it felt. He wasn't the *only* one…just the worst of the lot. The hospital is private—it's one of those places where rich humans send their family members when they are looking for a *cure*."

My lip quivered and I clenched my fist out of habit. I was caught off guard when I felt a hilt in my hand, but when I looked down, I saw the knife. I'd forgotten I was holding it. For a second…I pushed the thought away. Hopes like that were painful. Almost like ripping my heart out. "Cures."

Justin was silent, but I suspected his thoughts had gone down the same path mine had. I didn't particularly *like* taking contract killings, but I'd do it. One of the few contracts I'd taken had been for a man who claimed he could *cure* NH kids…for a price. Justin and I had taken him down, a team approach. It had needed to be a team, because the man had been a high-level witch, even though he'd hidden that fact from the world.

Only idiots go after the high-levels without the right kind of weapons.

My weapon had been another high-level witch and the two of us had killed that son-of-a-bitch, but not before he'd tortured and killed nearly fifteen NH kids. The families who'd sent their kids to him for the *cure* had signed waivers absolving him of all responsibility for the *risky* cure…and he'd murdered them, knowing he couldn't cure *anybody*. And they'd paid him to do it.

Killing him had been fun.

I'd pissed blood for a week after it because he'd tried to smash my organs while Justin and I fought through the magics he flung at us, but in the end, we'd won. He'd died.

Four months later, Justin had told me he had been offered a job with Banner: *They'll let me kill things. Lots and lots of things. And I get to play with lots of cool weapons…you never let me play with yours, Kitty-kitty.*

"Tell me about this hospital," I said after the silence had stretched on too long.

"It's privately owned." He remained where he was, one hand clenched into a fist, braced against the wall. His entire body was rigid, his spine so straight, I thought it might crack from the strain. "Most people send their families there looking to *cure* them…they sign releases without really reading the fine print. And that says: *Patients to be released with doctor's orders only…or upon successful remission of their condition.* Once they go in, the family can't get them out."

"That can't be legal." I could barely force the words out.

Justin's laugh was hollow, echoing through my office and sending a chill down my spine. "Legal, Kit? We're talking about NH rights, here. You and I both know those pretty much exist on paper and that's about it. If humans get the advantage and decide to take it? We're screwed. In that place? They have the advantage."

I whirled around and flung my blade, watching as it buried itself in the wall. It quivered there and I stared at the handle, struggling to calm the racing of my heart, the rage I felt beating inside me. *Trapped…no one is coming…*

I knew what it was like to be held prisoner.

"You can't tell me that they could have a werewolf in there, or a werecat, and that NH will still quietly sit and let them do…whatever. That they just *take* it."

"You'd be surprised at what a were will do when it's being pumped full of *Night.* Most of them are barely more than zombies." Justin shoved off the wall, skimming a hand back over his dreads. "The witches are just as bad…they've got their own little army casting spells twenty-four seven, holding everybody under magical lock and key. Magic is either locked inside them or they trap them in a confinement spell so any magic they cast is slammed back at the user. Even the pacifists are treated like war criminals."

The more I heard, the sicker I got.

"Where is this?"

He slid me a look, and then slowly shook his head. "Going there right now is insane, Kit. The two of us would never make it out alive."

"So we just leave people trapped like that?"

A muscle twitched in his jaw. "For the time being, we have to. We've got another problem on the table. But…I'm working on it. I'd planned…" He shrugged. "I'm working on it. Right now, some of us are doing what we can…*quietly*…to spread the word about the dangers there. Hopefully it will save some people before we can figure out a better approach."

The silver on his sleeves flared so bright, it almost blinded me. "But we have to be careful…anything we do will take time, and whether I like it or not, some of the people there *can't* be let out."

"What's that mean?"

He lifted a hand and I watched as the silver threads winding around his arm spread out. They were sliver-thin—twined together and twisting around to make that dense, odd design. I had absolutely no idea how much silver he had worked into that thing. A hell of a lot, though. The threads separated completely and I realized then that nothing but his magic held that silver to his sleeves.

It formed a circle in the air above our heads and I lifted my gaze to stare at it.

"The metallurgist there…his magic is stronger than mine," Justin said, his voice quiet and soft. "I could feel him from miles off and he made my teeth hurt. They don't kill him because he's a useful lab rat…plus, he's hard to kill. They told me the Banner cops have tried to kill him four times, always using iron bullets. Each time, he shattered the metal before it could touch him."

"Why did they try to kill him?"

"They first time was because Banner had been tracking him for over six months. When they finally caught up with him, he was using a human girl for a pin cushion." Justin turned the silver threads into rain. I flinched as all those threads separated into pieces no longer into my pinkie and came hurtling down around us. It didn't touch me or him, but I could hear it slamming into everything around, my desk, the carpet floor, the table, the couch. "He was using metal shards, no bigger than this to penetrate that girl's body, over and over. She was still alive when they first arrived. She bled out before they could take him down."

My eyes felt hot and my gut had long since got raw and nasty. "Is this place a hospital or a prison for the criminally insane?"

"Take your pick." Justin bared his teeth at me. "But you could walk in there completely sane, and completely harmless. It won't matter to them, as long as you're not human. They'll take you; they'll break you and they'll keep you until you die. Some of the people can't ever leave, though—no other place could hold them and killing them isn't…easy. Might not even be possible. Some of them have to be contained, like the metallurgist—he was born evil, I think. The magic just made him crazier. The metal made him meaner, fed his need for blood."

"Did you worry that would happen to you?"

Justin stared at the silver littering the floor around us and then he looked up. I felt the soft, sighing whisper of his power dance through the air and then the silver gathered itself back up, winding into that graceful chain and returning to his sleeves. "I was already mean, Kit," he said, smiling half-heartedly. "Maybe not homicidal, but I had a knack for killing things. And they were ready to leave me there if I didn't agree to get trained. The metal was calling to me, taunting me…teasing me. If I didn't say yes…"

Something sick crossed his face and he turned away. "I didn't want to take the chance. I said yes. I gave the oath and they took it from me in blood. If I tried to leave before I fulfilled that commitment, I would have died. No second chances. No bargaining."

Now *I* felt sick.

"And now?"

He shrugged and flicked a look at me. "Time was up right before the job went down with you and your…Damon. I was about to turn my shield in when I heard the rumblings, so I decided I'd stay and make sure things were clear there. Banner isn't *all* a sick monster, Kit. The sickness is in the higher-ups and I figured if there were problems, I'd rather be in a place where I could get you help if you needed it." He grimaced. "Sometimes I can't decide if I regret that choice or not…if I hadn't stayed, I wouldn't have been around to rope you into that job. But if I had left Banner…"

I swallowed and turned away. "If you'd left, you couldn't have brought Banner down on Jude. He was going to grab me at some point anyway, right?"

Justin didn't say anything. But I suspected he saw it the same way I did. Jude was an opportunistic snake and he'd waited for his moment. He'd have made his move sooner or later.

Rubbing the heel of my hand over my chest, I stared at my weapons wall. During the evening hours last night, TJ's wolves had dropped off more of my gear and I'd spent an hour putting them back up. It no longer felt so naked and I felt some measure of calm just looking at the familiar lines of each blade, the staff, the bow. Pulling one of my knives from the wall, I started to toss it, concentrating on that—just that—as I waited for my nerves to settle.

I wasn't quite back up to my old speed, but I was getting there. And this time, I didn't drop the blade. As it spun above my hand, I forced myself to think. "And now? What now, Justin? You're clear with them?"

"Very."

I didn't look at him. "And safe?"

"Yeah."

The edge I heard in his voice caught my attention and I grabbed the blade's handle before I turned my head to look at him.

A mean smile slanted his lips. "I spent the past few years gathering every dark, dirty secret I could on the higher-ups, Kit. And there are a lot of them. Unless I do something that violates the charter, they can't—and *won't*—bother me now." Then he shrugged. "There's no reason for them to, really. They're cold-blooded assholes, but they are efficient. They only focus on problems. I'm not a problem anymore."

Maybe Justin wasn't, but I sure as hell felt like being one.

What I was feeling must have shown on my face because he said softly, "Don't."

I just stared at him. Banner had made my life *hell*. And now to learn this?

"They're too big for just a couple of us to take on right now," Justin said quietly. "The entire system is fucked up, but once we get the poison out of it, it will work again."

"And how do we get the poison out of it?"

A faint smile curled his lips. "Lots of ways to handle poison, Kit. But we've got bigger problems..."

His gaze moved past me to linger on the desk, the drawings, the pictures.

"Like Pandora's Box."

I needed to breathe.

I needed to move.

I needed to think.

But I couldn't leave the office until I knew what was going to come of the job.

I couldn't know *that* until I talked to Pandora.

Isidore.

Whatever she called herself.

After the unsettling discussion with Justin, I tucked myself away behind my desk and tried to focus back on the job. *Possible* job. Possible nightmare. Disaster in the making. Apparently, that was the sort of job I courted these days.

Pandora's box, for the love of all things holy…

I went to start doing another search, trying not to think about Justin standing at the window and brooding, but before I could think about what to look for, a revelation came to me.

A moment, one of those random memories that come to

you out of the blue.

I'd gone to a friend's months ago. Right before my life had exploded and careened straight to hell. One of the Speakers Damon had been investigating had been a friend of mine…of ours, I guess. Her name was Es, and she was one of the strongest witches I knew. Stronger even than Justin, although her power was a different sort. Justin was a warrior; Es was a healer.

Banner *did* serve a purpose in our world—they hunted the NH problems that managed to slip past our notice, not that it happened often. Damon had come to their attention after several Assembly members had died and Banner worried the new Alpha was about ready to make a big power play—*if* that had been his intent, it could have been a dangerous situation. Damon had hundreds of werecats in his clan and he was smart, sneaky as hell.

Justin had come to me to clear Damon before they decided to execute him. It turned out that all of it had happened because of *me*. Damon had been killing Assembly members, all right. He'd been killing people who had spoken to my grandmother. All hail the evilest bitch in the world.

She'd been looking for information on me and those who had seemed at all *agreeable* to giving any information had shortly ended up dead by Damon's hand.

Es had been the first one he'd spoken with—she'd told my grandmother to get fucked.

When I'd found all of this out, I'd almost been sick.

Pandora's box…

The memory tried to work free and my gut churned as I tried to avoid thinking about everything *else* that happened as a result of that case.

"They wanted you simply because they believe you can show them Aneris Hall."

"None but our blood can find it. It's like the fabled Fountain of Youth or Pandora's Box."

"Well, those aren't quite so fabled…"

Not quite so fabled.

Narrowing my eyes, I hunched over my computer. It had

been months since I'd seen or spoken to Es. But she'd sounded pretty damn certain when she'd said that.

Pandora's Box wasn't so fabled.

Did that mean she knew something about the box? About the bearer?

I typed up a message and sent it, keeping it short and sweet, hoping she'd do the same.

My head was a mess and I felt like I was walking on the razor's edge here. I didn't need to have anything else thrown at me, even if it was under the guise of well-meaning concern.

In case that didn't pan out, I went ahead and sent Colleen a message, too, another short and sweet note.

Do you know anything about Pandora's Box? Legit info, not myth or legend. Thanks, K.

That was it.

After I'd sent the message to her, I shot Justin a look. He had his head dipped, chin resting on his chest, posture deceptively relaxed. I knew better. There was so much tension, the air felt like it was going to crack. I hoped he'd be able to level off before our lovely new friend showed up. I was counting on *him* to be the steady one here. Me and steady hadn't had a passing acquaintance in months.

I went to turn back to the computer but I hadn't so much as thought about what to do next before Justin said, "Stop worrying, Kit."

I looked up at him.

He was still in the same position, head down, eyes closed, slumped with his shoulder resting against the wall by the window.

"What?"

He shrugged lazily. "You're worrying. It's all but eating you up. You got enough to handle without worrying about me. I'm good."

"You don't look good."

He slid me a faint smile then. "Not yet, but I will be. Just give me a few."

I blew a slow, careful breath. "I can do that, but you need to understand…we can't just leave things the way they are."

"I know." He nodded slowly, shifting his attention to stare back out at the dismal little square that made up my parking lot. "It's just too big a job, too big a prospect for you and me to handle alone. And we'd have to be careful about who we trusted to help us if we take this on."

I processed that. Okay, I could see where he was coming from there.

"You worry about this…figure out whether or not we should do this thing for…Isidore," he said.

"You going to let me call the shots on that one?"

"Yep." Once more, he closed his eyes and settled back into that deceptive, lazy slump. "Your gut knows more than the two of us combined. I'll trust what you think is best."

CHAPTER FIFTEEN

I felt her coming.

The air got heavy and tense.

The magic crackled; Justin's responded to the energy dancing in the air and I thought I might choke on how much power was in the air.

It climbed higher and higher, seconds ticking away into minutes as her presence drew closer. She must be strolling along at a snail's pace, letting us think and worry and brood, I thought.

Something on my computer chimed and I looked over, thankful for the distraction, but it wasn't much of one. The message from Colleen was short and sweet.

No. Didn't think it was anything more than a legend. If it's real, I'd say don't open the box.

I grimaced and deleted the message, making sure it was gone from both my inbox and the drive.

No response from Es yet.

Just in case she decided to reply while Isidore was in the office, I shut the computer down and put my phone on silent. Wasn't taking that chance.

"We going to let her know we're aware of what's up?" Justin asked.

I'd been wondering just that. Now, as I caught sight of her coming across the parking lot, I nodded slowly. "I don't think there's any way around it. I can't do this, or even decide, without more info."

Justin flexed a hand and laid it on the wall.

I heard him murmuring and my skin started to crawl as his magic flooded the air. Power ripped out of the very earth as he strengthened the wards. No way she was going to miss—

Oh. *Oh*...something more subtle whispered just under *those* wards. Something quieter. Much quieter. For a split second, black dots swarmed my vision as the death ward danced in between the wards I already had wrapped around my place.

I recognized it only because he'd used it once.

It was the ward he'd used when he'd gone after the child killer—if things went bad in here, that ward would trigger. "Think it's going to get that ugly?"

He flicked me a look. "You want to risk it?"

"No."

His eyes practically glowed from the magic—it always made him a little crazy. "I left you an exit. Take it fast."

I just stared at him. He knew that wouldn't happen.

Hopefully it wouldn't be necessary. One word from him was all it would take to trigger that sucker.

One word...or...you know, his unexpected death.

A moment later, the door swung open and there she was, in her spooky, ancient splendor. That same smile curved her lips up. "May I enter?"

Show time...

Leaning back, I rested my hand on the Desert Eagle. I had to research more and figure out what might kill the really, really ancient. If she was my kind, I'd go with copper. If she was a witch, iron. She almost felt like a cross between the two...maybe I should try for both.

"You know, generally in a place of business, you don't have to ask permission," I pointed out. "People run businesses to make money. That's pretty much an open invite."

The woman shrugged. It was an easy, elegant gesture that

sent the pretty, jewel-laden necklace around her neck shimmering. The necklace was silver. If she had silver against her skin, I could bet silver wouldn't do her in. Mark that one out.

"I don't always know…or care…about modern rules," she told me. "May I enter?"

Now that was a shocker—an old creature who didn't get or care for modern rules, whether they were spoken or not. It told me something about her, though. She was a creature of habit, *her* habits, and she had an odd thing for courtesy, it seemed. "Yeah, you can enter. I've got questions for you and you'll need to answer them before I can make a decision on this job."

A smile flirted with the corners of her lips. "Questions…isn't the money enough of an answer?"

"Money doesn't answer questions." I plucked one of the coins up, the one bearing the depiction of Alexander the Great. It was pure chance that it was the one that my fingers had found out of the mess, but seeing his face made me itch inside. So old. Had she known him?

Spinning the coin around, I showed her the image of Alexander. "Some of these coins are more than two thousand years old."

She arched a brow. "That only increases the worth, I would think."

"True." I tossed the coin into the air and caught it, a restless, absent gesture. Abruptly, I tossed it at her, hurling it as fast as I could. She caught it, snake-quick and without flinching. "Any idea who is on that coin?"

She glanced down, bored. "Alexander the Great." She threw it back at me and I caught it. *Ouch*—she had one hell of a throwing arm. Another thing to keep in mind. She was strong. Stronger than me. But who in the hell wasn't?

"Huh."

"Are these the questions you want to ask me?"

"Nah. I'm actually more curious about your…vase."

Something sharpened in her eyes. Lust. Need. Longing. "Yes…let's talk about my vase, Kit."

"Is the picture you drew accurate?"

"Yes." A line formed between her eyes. "It's mine. I know it better than any other on earth ever could."

"How long have you owned it?"

"Always." Avid greed lit her eyes, something almost fanatical. "It's mine…it has always been mine."

Okay, then. "I've been researching it, but I'm not having much luck finding any information on a vase like it."

That scary gleam left her eyes and she arched her brows. "What information do you need?"

"Oh, anything. Everything." I lifted one of the pictures I'd printed off, skimmed the legend over, placed it back, facedown, on my desk. "Does it possess any unusual powers? Is it enchanted? Spelled?"

She rubbed her fingers against her palm, leaning back to study me with curious eyes. "It has…certain powers, yes. But they are useless to all but me."

That was truth, my gut told me. I felt a little bit better knowing that.

"Whoever took it, do they know that?"

A coy smile curved her lips. "That…I cannot say. It's possible they think it possesses its own…magic. If that's what they think, they are wrong."

"Hmmm." No answer there. Mentally, I shrugged. "What powers does it have when *you* come into the picture? Death? Destruction? The plague?"

Something flashed in her eyes and she leaned forward. "Come on, Kit…don't play games. Ask what you really want to know."

Okay. Might as well go for broke. "What happened when you opened the box, Pandora?"

She started to laugh.

I've read books where people were described as having a 'bell-like' laugh. Isidore's… Pandora's… whoever she was, her laugh came pretty close. But it didn't put me in the mind of anything light or happy.

No, it made me think of something sinister.

For whom the bell tolls…

Yeah, it was enough to send a shiver down my spine.

As her laugh faded away, she propped her elbow on the arm of the chair and rested her chin on her upraised fist, studying me with amusement in her eyes. "You're a clever one, aren't you, Kit?"

"Not clever enough…I haven't figured out the answer to that question yet." Behind the shield of my desk, I curled my hand around the grip of the leaf-blade Damon had given me and waited.

"If you had to name the evils of the world, what would you say they are?"

Jude's face flashed through my mind and I tightened my grip on the blade. I wasn't going to break down. Not here. Not in front of her. I couldn't. But if I had to name an evil, I'd name him.

Instead of giving voice to that, I shrugged. "I don't buy into the myth as it's written. Death, sickness…man is going to get sick and die. In this life, at least. I don't buy that you opened the box and suddenly man lost his immortality."

"Hmmm. Again, clever girl." She leaned forward now, her eyes practically glowing. "But how does that answer my question?"

"If I answer yours, are you going to answer *mine*?"

A smile tugged at the corners of her mouth. "I'll be more inclined."

More inclined. I held her gaze. "I'm not working this job blind. If you want me to take it, you'll have to give me more information." Then I shifted my attention away from her, staring at the pages littering my desk. "The evils of the world…greed is one, I guess. It's not a bad thing to like money, but if you love it above all else, it leads to bad things. Addiction…en—"

"You're not being honest," she chided. Lacing her fingers together, she cocked her head to the side and smiled at me. "Kit, you can read a lie on a person as easily as you can read a book. And you've already…noticed a similarity between us. Don't tell me you haven't. If *you* can read a lie, what makes you think I can't?"

"I'm not lying." I looked at her, clenching my jaw. "Those are evil things."

"Evil, maybe…but that's not what you think of when you first think of evil." Then she settled back in the chair, her smile taking on a catlike satisfaction. "It might make it a little more interesting if I tell you the legend was tampered with…and it's far older than what people think. Even the oldest scholar doesn't understand how old the myth of the vase is."

My breath seemed to lodge in my throat. "And what about the evils you let out? Ever thought about putting them back in?"

Pandora shrugged. "You would have to know more about those evils before the answer would make sense. Death…sickness…just what did I loose when I opened the box?"

And the words she spoke next made the oxygen inside my lungs seem to dwindle down into nothing.

I was still trying to process it as she left.

No matter what happened, I needed to find the vase. Once I did that, I'd figure out the next step.

"That were is back out there," Justin said, his voice calm, like we hadn't just had a monster walk out of the office.

"I know." I swallowed and focused on the coins she'd given me the other day. I'd wanted to throw them at her. But I hadn't.

"Any idea what he wants?"

"No." Slumping in my seat, I closed my eyes and tried to breathe, although my throat was really, really tight. It was almost impossible, sucking air in now. "Bigger problems at the moment, right?"

"Yep." His voice was closer and I cracked open an eye, watched as he came over and settled in the chair across from me. His green eyes were unreadable and his magic was a steady, soothing presence.

No matter what I chose to do, he was going to back me up. And if I made the wrong choice and ended up dead, so would he. It wasn't a comforting thought.

"You're taking the job, aren't you?" He leaned back in the chair and pulled out his tattered deck of cards. Our gazes met as he shuffled them and I watched him flip one into the air.

"I think I have to," I said. I thought about all the legends behind the box…vase. Yeah. Vase. It was hers. It had always been hers—*that* was one thing I was certain about. It was meant to be hers. Whether she should have opened it—if that was what happened—I don't know, but it was hers and it needed to stay that way. Something told me that thing came with power and objects of power were best left alone. If she wasn't the one in possession of it, that just added up to bad things in my book.

"After what she just told us." He nodded slowly and then asked, "Why?"

I rose, my hand still curled around the grip of my new sword. Apparently, it had become my security blanket. I laid it down across the surface of my desk and moved to the wall holding my weapons. I started to pull down the ones I needed, tucking them away, threading the garrote into my collar, another into my belt, knives into their various places in my vest, along my waist and two in each boot.

"Because it's hers. Not matter how many times I spin this, it always comes back to that. It's a relic, and something tells me it's got power in it—even if it's power only she can manipulate, they go together. Objects of power don't belong in the hands of those who don't understand that power." I knew that all too well. I'd ended up with a few of those objects of power and they still creeped me out. Crouching in front of the trunk, I opened it and studied the contents inside. There was a strap holding a pair of fingerless gloves in place. I grabbed them and pulled them on. They were black and heavy as hell, thanks to a webbing of silver and iron mesh between sturdy layers of cotton and leather. If I got into a knock-down-drag-out, I'd do more damage with those than with my bare fists. "Even if the vase only responds to her, if it has power, then it needs to be with the person best suited to care for it, not just some thieves who made off with it."

"What if she's not *meant* to have it—maybe *that* is why it was stolen."

"Already thought of that." I rose and looked back at him. "And if I get a bad vibe at any time, I'll reevaluate. Right now, we focus on finding it. Then we cross the next bridge when we come to it." I didn't want to ask, but I better do it now. "That is, assuming you're still *with* me on this."

The scowl on his face almost made me smile. "Like I'm going to let you do it alone."

CHAPTER SIXTEEN

The following morning, I was supposed to meet with Es. She'd emailed me back late yesterday—her reply had consisted of four simple words.

Come see me, Kitasa.

That was it.

Well, I'd wanted short and simple. Be careful what you wish for.

Seems like I'd spent most of yesterday spinning my wheels—technically, I could call it *research* although I hadn't learned anything. Justin had gone off to do his witchy shit, although he hadn't unearthed anything, either. If he had, he would have called me.

Now I had to drive across half of Florida. Wasting my time. I felt like there was a clock ticking away in my ear. I was getting ready to go when Justin called.

"I've got a consult."

"Yeah?" I checked the mirror and had to fight the urge to reach for a pair of scissors. I needed to get my bangs out of my face and most of my hair was just about down to my collar. "I've got one, too."

"Who and where?"

"Es. Her place." I put the phone on the counter. "Go to speaker."

His voice filled the bathroom around me as I reached for

a comb and combed my hair into sections. "Who are you meeting with?"

"A couple of witch historians. I want more info on Pandora, or whoever she claims to be. They won't meet me at your place. I won't meet them at their place. We found some neutral ground a few miles from the Lair, of all places. Meet's at ten."

"Historians?"

"Yeah." I heard him sigh, heard the frustration in his voice as he said, "We got to start somewhere, right? Why the meeting with Es?"

"Something she said once. I think she might know something about the vase. Or I could be off on a wild goose chase."

"It's a start, especially seeing as how the bitch didn't give us any idea where to start." He paused and then asked, "You think it's true? That shit she said?"

My gut twisted a little. "I don't know. I need to go. Don't want to keep Es waiting. Let me know how your meet goes."

"Will do."

The line went dead and I finished braiding my hair. Two short braids framed my face, baring the tattoos. If it wasn't for those, and the look in my eyes, I probably would have looked about twelve years old. As it was, I might have passed for twenty.

No help for it. I needed a haircut. I needed to get on the road.

I needed to find a better line of work.

"You smell of old magic. It's not pleasant." The look on Es's face was one of complete distaste. And unless I'd really lost my touch, I thought I saw something in her eyes that looked like fear. Resigned fear, as though something she had dreaded for a long time was finally coming to pass.

It wasn't reassuring.

But instead of saying anything about that, I just forced myself to smile at her. "Wow, Es. Yes, it has been a long time. Good to see you, though. Please...don't hover. It drives me nuts."

A low chuckle escaped her. "I'm sorry, Kit. That was rude of me." She rose from her perch on the stoop and came to stand in front of me, her pale, colorless eyes resting on my face. "You look rather well."

"And you're a better liar than I thought," I said sourly. "I look like a horrid, broken waste."

"That is your grandmother talking." Es gave me a disapproving look. "You look like a woman who is pulling herself out of hell. Again. You did it once." She reached up to touch my cheek and I didn't let myself flinch away. "I hate the fact that you have to do it again. But you will. You will be stronger, wiser, sadder for it. But never doubt you'll do it."

As she spoke, she watched me with an intensity that left me uncomfortable. It was like she was trying to tell me something but I didn't know what.

Licking my lips, I decided to focus on the matter on hand. "I need to know about Pandora, Es. You know, the stinky, old magic smell. Just what does old magic smell like anyway?"

She smiled at me and it was a familiar one, full of humor, wisdom and patience. "That just depends on the magic, dear Kitasa. This smell...it's old blood, malice and cruelty."

That didn't make me feel better. And I hadn't exactly felt warm and cuddly to begin with. Out of habit, I flexed my hand. Es lowered her gaze and watched.

Something in the back of my mind burned. "Please stay out of my head, Es."

"Even magical injuries can be healed...if you'll allow it," she said gently.

"It's not an injury." Nobody understood the bond with my blade. I knew how it felt and it was like somebody had cut an arm off. Once a person lost a limb, no amount of healing would regrow it.

She sighed. "So very stubborn."

Like she was anybody to talk. But I didn't point that out to her. Judging by the smile in her eyes, she knew exactly what I was thinking, though. Drove me nuts, the way witches could do that.

"Would you feel better if I told you that you are just as frustrating to me?" Es stroked a hand down my arm and squeezed. "Just as frustrating…just as endearing."

I swallowed and looked away.

"Now I've made you uncomfortable. I'm sorry. I just…well, I wanted you to know. I've missed seeing you. Speaking with you."

I looked back at her, forcing myself to speak past the discomfort. Affection always left me…out of place. I just didn't know how to handle it. "I missed you, too," I said, and it was like I had to drag each word out. But I said it. "I can't say I'm sorry I didn't visit. It's hard enough even now."

"I understand."

Coming from her, I could accept that. It didn't sound like a trite platitude. Es didn't use those. If she said she understood, you simply *believed* that. Gazing into her pale eyes was too hard, though. If she understood how hard it was…I blinked, my eyes burning.

Clearing my throat, I focused on the job.

"Can you help me with this Pandora thing or not?"

"Can I help?" she murmured, echoing my words. She walked away, the white garments she wore fluttering around her. She took the mug of tea she'd left on the stoop and lifted it to her lips. "When it comes to that one, the wisest thing anybody could do is stay away. Very far away."

Her pale eyes met mine. "But that's not an option, is it?"

"Doesn't seem to be." Turning away, I stared off into the brilliant blue sky. Clouds dotted the horizon and the sun played hide-and-seek, turning the edges of one fat puff to silver. I stared at it until my eyes stared to burn. "My gut tells me that walking away from this only makes it worse."

"Worse for whom?"

The question was soft, and under the gentle tone of Es's voice, I heard a world of worry.

Turning, I studied her. To my light-dazzled eyes, she looked strange. Bright lights didn't affect me the way they would had I been fully human. I didn't have trouble focusing on her, but light seemed to cling to her. It was an…odd sight. Odd, and unnerving.

Finally, I shrugged. "I can't answer that. I just don't know. The only thing I do know is that it doesn't feel right to have something called Pandora's Box in somebody else's hands. Especially *unknown* hands. It would be like..." I faltered for the words. "Hell, putting my sword in the hands of my enemy."

"So it's the lesser of two evils in your mind." Tucking a strand of hair behind her ear, she sipped from her mug. "Were I in your shoes, I might agree."

"I get the feeling you disagree. What do *you* think I should do with the damn thing?"

She smiled, a faint curve of her lips. "Find the deepest, dark hole in the ocean and cast it down into it. Is that viable?"

The idea had merit. Then I shrugged. "I'd have to find the damn thing first. And I need more info to do that. Do you know anything about it? She…" I swallowed the nasty, coppery taste of fear crowding my throat and forced myself to ask the question. "She told me…" I paused. My throat was dry. Even *thinking* this was almost impossible. "She told me something that's almost impossible to believe. I have no way to confirm it."

"Don't you?"

"Es." I spun around, ready to hit something. I didn't have time for this enigmatic shit. "Look, can you help me or not? I need *more* than what she told me. I don't even know enough to know what I should do with the damn thing when I find it. I'm operating blind and I hate it."

"Yes. I imagine you do." She turned away and crossed back to the stoop, settling there with her arms wrapped around her knees. "What I know may or may not be of any use. In the end, you need to trust your gut on this."

"I can't just go by what she says. And research is

pointless. There's next to *nothing* about Pandora in the mortal world."

"Please." Es closed her eyes. "Stop saying her name." Then she sighed. "There was never much known outside of those legends…only a handful of scholars, only a select few ever knew more."

I narrowed my eyes. "A select few?"

She rubbed a finger down the hem of her sleeve. It held silver and green embroidery. Very pretty...upon closer inspection, I realized it was the pattern used in the crest for Green Road, the house Es belonged to. There were four houses in the order of witches. Green Road was the largest, the oldest, the most powerful. "Do you know the written history of Green Road is almost as old as the written history of the *aneira*?"

"I don't much care about *aneira* history," I said. The *aneira* might have bred me, raised me, trained me, but they had also tortured me, beaten me, starved me. They hadn't bothered to share their history with me. Why should they? I was a useless, mongrel half-breed, not fit to even breathe their air, according to my grandmother.

"You should care. It's more important than you realize." She stared at me and yet again, I had that odd, uneasy feeling that she was trying to tell me something. "Sometime soon there will be things about them that you *need* to know. And your resources are…limited."

I bit back the taste of bile and fear. "My grandmother won't give up. I know that. I'll deal with it." *Somehow…*

"Oh, she's not what I was talking about. Not *all* things related to your people are bad, Kit. After all…" She reached up and touched my hair. "You're not. But you're right. She'll continue to seek you. Prepare for it. However…it's not the *history* I was referring to. It's the age. We are old. Very old. All of us are—*aneira,* witch, were, vampire. The offshoot races…some of them came later…our scholars think they happened when our kind interbred with mortals and the genes mutated. Some of the offshoots might have happened as a weird sort of evolution when the population was unique…merfolks, for example, are often found in areas where the livelihood is dominated by water. Not just oceans, but rivers, and lakes. Witches interbreeding with humans, say in Ireland and Scotland. And that's where we often see selkie and the *mer*. Our scholars think our DNA caused the mutation a millennia ago that gradually led to those changes—an adaption."

She was getting scientific on me. Wonderful. I shoved a hand through my hair and gave it a hard jerk. "Es...where are you going with this?"

"You have absolutely no patience." This time, the expression on her face was nothing but pure indulgence. It was the look a mother might have given a child. But it had been a long time since I had been a child, and my memories of my mother were very dim. Echoes of her singing...and I thought that maybe she had loved me.

"We are *old*, Kit. Very old. Vampires like to talk like they are the oldest of us…even older than mortals."

My gut knotted in fear and I already knew I wasn't going to like how this conversation ended. "That's stupid thinking," I said. "They feed off others. If humans weren't here to feed them, how did they come into existence? And how did they make the new ones?"

"Stupid thinking," she agreed. "At our core, we were all human once."

I twitched. "The *aneira* weren't. Witches weren't."

"You think not?" Her head tipped back and she gazed up at the sky as the wind tangled in her hair. "We are the closest to human even now. Genetically, we are just a few short strands away. A manipulation here. A mutation there. Although we are born genetically different, we are more human than any of the others. We even possess more humanity than they do."

I snorted. "Oh, you're wrong there. My grandmother has the humanity of a cesspit."

"Well, there are humans who lack any sort of humanity, aren't there?" She lowered her head and her gaze met mine. "A vampire bites a human and initiates the blood exchange.

Within days, the human either dies or becomes a vampire. Within a few years, the soul begins to die and with it, the humanity. When a human is bitten by a were, the chances of him dying run about seventy-five percent. The few who survive will change. And they are no longer remotely human. We who were never human have no concept of what it is to crave blood. To look at another and see only prey...to have to fight the very instincts within us."

She was making me nervous. Not just with what she was talking about, but the way she was acting.

She sighed and brushed her hair away, fisting it in her hand to hold it back from her face. "Our history tells us that for centuries, we hid in plain sight. Wise women, wise men...people might have suspected what we were, but they trusted us, let us aid them, and that was what we did. Because that was why we were created."

"Created?" I had to force the word out.

She fingered the embroidery on her sleeve. "Yes. Just as your kind was created...with a purpose. We would protect mankind, while your kind hunted the monsters she had loosed."

The monsters…

"Pandora," I whispered.

It was true.

She slid me a look, mild disapproval in her gaze. I could hardly care at that point.

It was all true, then.

"All the legends about the box…death, sickness…?"

"She did loose death and sickness…vampires *are* known as the undead, even now. It's an odd sort of death, and their hungers *bring* death. The were? How many die when they are infected?"

Death…sickness…

Swiping my damp hands down my pants, I tried to think.

"Think about it," Es continued. "True death, sickness. They've always existed. But she brought about a *new* kind of death. A new kind of sickness…and with them came destruction. Those were her evils. Not all that rubbish in the legend."

Blood roared, pounded in my head so hard, I thought I might be sick. My hand itched, and I closed it into a fist. There was no comforting whisper, nothing I could do to ease the fear I felt. Except face it and deal with it. My voice was surprisingly steady as I made myself ask, "Is this for real? You all actually know this to be fact?"

"It's as close to real as any of the old legends." Es tipped her head back, a small smile on her face.

"She made us."

"No." There was a pause, so brief it was almost not even there. She lifted her lashes to stare at me. "She made *them*. We were made to hunt them down, heal the poison from the blood...preserve the human race. But nature has a way of deciding what will win out. And nature decided she liked having all of us around."

The array of thoughts running around in my head was dizzying.

Pandora created them…weres, vampires.

And we were created too. My mind screamed out in denial at the very idea.

I slammed my fist against my temple in attempt to slow that wave of thought, but it didn't work.

"Es, I think you need to start at the beginning."

"That...would be a very long story."

CHAPTER SEVENTEEN

"There are some...or were some, at least, who believed she was Lilith."

I blinked.

Lilith. Bent over the mug of tea Es had pushed on me, I wondered just how many more surprises she had in store for today. Huddling over the table, I tried to pretend like I was drinking that tea I hated as I processed what she'd just told me.

Processing…and still not taking it in. I could only think *one* Lilith of real importance.

"Lilith. As in the first wife some people think Adam had before Eve?"

Human theology was a little outside my scope, but I knew the basics. Mostly because there were scores of bad things tied into human theology and sometimes those bad things collided with my world.

My world. I was already doing it...thinking of myself back in this world. Damn it all to hell. I wasn't ready for this. And it didn't matter. If I wasn't ready, I'd better make myself ready.

"The very same. I don't know if there is any truth to it. If there is, it makes a poetic sort of sense. She created races that would disseminate Adam's descendants...taking her vengeance, angry still, after all these years." She paused, shrugging. "The truths I know are the truths as they were passed down through my line. Vampires and weres were the world's first monsters…and the ones who survive the change are predominantly male…and here we are, both of our races...created from man, and our races are predominantly female. Created and bred to drive those monsters to extinction."

"And exactly how are we to do that?" Unable to sit there drinking tea, I stood up and started to pace. Pulling a blade from my vest, I made it dance in the air over my hand as I waited for her answer.

It turned to a blur of silver and black as she watched me.

"Kit...you are a very talented killer," Es said, her voice dispassionate. "You do not even enjoy doing it. You kill only when you have no choice or when you believe the person truly needs to die. But no matter what anybody thinks, you are a talented killer. You know your targets and you take them out with a minimal amount of fuss and despite the fact that you often hunt prey much stronger than you, you manage to remain alive."

Catching my knife out of the air, I tapped the flat of the blade against my palm. She knew so much about me, so much about how my kills affected me. I think she knew more about my race than *I* did. Which wasn't surprising.

I run my tongue across my teeth and moved forward, choosing the words with care. "Hypothetically speaking, if I were to kill, I'd think it would be wisest to do it with a minimum amount of fuss. And ideally, it would be best to go with a decent gameplan, so I *can* stay alive. Because being dead would probably suck."

She smiled. "I'm pleased to know you think so. I've worried about that."

I flushed and looked away. Actually, it was a surprise to realize I even *thought* being dead would suck. Most mornings, it was a struggle just to think about getting up. Why wouldn't dead be better?

"Kit...if you ever need to talk, I'm here."

"I've heard that line. A lot." As shame and misery

twisted me into knots, I tuned away. "Talking solves nothing. It undoes nothing. I still have the memories and I still carry the marks of what happened. There is no point is talking about it."

"Do you think you're the only one who has survived such horror, Kit?"

"No." I closed my eyes. "But I don't want to hear what helped somebody else heal, and I don't want to share what he did to me. He made me into a thing, Es. Just a thing. I don't want to share that and relive it. I want to remake myself. That's all I want. Now can we get back to Pandora?"

There was a heavy, uncomfortable silence, something I wasn't used to with her. But then Es averted her gaze and the strange, terrible moment passed. A sigh escaped her and she started to speak.

"You already know you come from a long line of talented killers. There are rumors, legends mostly, that both our races have been…watered down. We're our own offshoots. There are those who believe we used to be much, much stronger. Much deadlier."

I stroked my finger down the edge of my blade. Yes. I'd heard stories of such, back in Aneris Hall. I'd brushed them off. That old *reclaiming the glory days* shit.

Es, either unaware of my distraction or ignoring it, continued to speak. "Once, the were population and vampires numbered much smaller than they do now. And if my kind had done what they were charged with doing, eventually yours would have wiped out the stragglers and there would be no more vampires, no more weres. Nothing but humans."

"Charged with…"

The look on Es's face turned haunted. "Charged with. We can heal the body, mend broken bones, ease the pain of childbirth, but to understand how to do that, one must understand the human body. We were the healers of the world, Kitasa…and nobody knows more about how to destroy the body than the ones who also heal it."

Unblinking, her eyes stared into mine. "Do you

understand what I'm telling you?"

I gave a short, tight nod.

"Babes were murdered in their mother's wombs. Women died while carrying. When they'd realize what we were up to, we'd flee…and they'd chase us. And your kind would wait."

"Vampires bear no young."

Es lowered her head. "No." She shook her head and rose from the table, carrying the mug of tea over to the sink and placing it inside. Her hands rested on the edge and she stared out the window. "Vampires bear no young. But they did take mates, leave behind families. They even loved…for a time. Until their souls withered and faded. It's a slow process, Kit. One that takes years. The longer you *believe* you can cling to your humanity, the longer some thread of it will try to linger on. If you wanted to get to one of them, just get to their families. The witches got to many of the families."

Fuck…

I didn't realize I'd spoken aloud until Es turned her head and looked at me. "That sums it up nicely, doesn't it? We were bred to exterminate one race, and safeguard another. And you…" She flexed her hands. "You were bred to hunt. To kill."

"Apparently none of that took very well. Witches are pacifists now. I'm more than just a hired killer—my family? They stay in their halls and play war games and talk about the good old days of honor and battle. We're…"

Nothing, I realized abruptly. The fabled *aneira* race were bunch of fools, gathering around and clinging to a time when they'd been something *more*.

I looked at Es. "They're nothing now."

"*They* are. You, however, are far more."

I didn't agree with that. Shrugging uncomfortably, I looked away. "The point is that grand plan obviously failed. What kind of hunters are the *aneira* now? Aside from the warrior born, witches don't lift a hand to defend themselves, even under threat of death. And the vamps and weres are still here."

"Yes." She nodded. "Nothing went according to plan, it

seemed. But that's all for the best."

Something small and ugly inside me wondered. *Was* it for the best that creatures like Jude still existed?

Damon, no; I didn't want werekind annihilated, but vampires…

"You can't have one without the other," Es murmured. "With one breed of monsters, you have the other. They are their own check and balance system—they fight over territories and perceived insults. They cull the population of the other. And…" She looked down, staring at something I suspect only she saw. "There was a belief that we were next."

My heart froze. "What?"

"If we'd accomplished what we were meant to do, we would have been next, Kit." She turned around and rested against the counter, arms crossed over her chest as she watched me. "Those who made us believed that mankind was the race intended to rule this earth. As long as there was any creature that could be perceived as a threat, then mankind could never truly be the dominant force."

"Are you saying..." The words trapped themselves in my throat.

"We were made to fix the problem, Kit. Then we would become a problem ourselves. But we would be much easier dealt with than immortal creatures like vampires or weres. Easier to kill, really."

"So we would have been next," I said softly.

"That was the fear." She watched me. "We are far from immortal, Kit. As you well know. We're harder to kill than humans, but we can definitely die."

Closing my eyes, I processed that. How much of this did I believe? How much did I *need* to believe?

"You choose to believe what is needed for you to get your job done…and you'll know what that is."

I shot her a dark look. "I hate it when you do that."

"I'm sorry." She shrugged a little. "It's not intentional." She sipped her tea and turned her head, staring out the window at the rolling green fields that surrounded the house.

Blowing out a breath, I glanced down, saw I still held my

blade. Tucking it away, I focused on the matter at hand. On Pandora. I'd come looking for information.

That was still true.

"I don't know how much of this I believe to be fact. I know *my* order believes it to be true. That much I know. Whether that means it is true…?"

"What happened to throw this great plan out of order?"

"It was called the Great Purging," she said, lowering her mug to the table. She spread her hands flat on the table, her gaze locked on something I couldn't see. "The name alone brings up terribly warm feelings, doesn't it?"

"Positively cheery." I wanted to throw up a little, just thinking about what sort of things *that* brought to mind. "I don't suppose I can assume a happy end, right? I mean, our races were created—that tells me something with a lot of power was in play. Any chance you all rose up and destroyed whoever it was?"

She blew out a breath. "There was an uprising, yes. But not the kind you hope for. The tide had turned…few weres left in the world and most vampires lived in hiding, creeping out only to try and increase their numbers. That wasn't going well, either."

"So what happened to change things?"

"Her name is lost to time. She is our Nameless one. Our founder of the Green Road. Legend says she'd gone to a village, seeking out a were who lived there in secret." Es stared off into nothing, her voice soft and distant, as she recounted a story she must have heard a hundred times. "On her way, she was attacked. A vampire, one of the older ones who had built up a tolerance to daylight. He recognized her as a witch. She was one of the purgers—a killer of unborn babes, a woman who rendered women childless in her quest to rid the world of the plague of monsters." Her tone was thick with anger, scathing and dark and her eyes flashed with pure rage. "The plague…that was what they were told to think. How they were raised, what they were *created* for. Brainwashing…all of it."

She surged up from the table and I caught a hint of her

magic—the first time it had ever slipped out of control. It slammed against my shields and I caught a hint of something that made me think of wind and air—but nothing light or soft. These were no spring breezes.

It was like a hurricane—a cold one, tinged with ice, and deadly with it.

Slowly, I shifted my gaze up and met her eyes. Something flickered in her eyes and that magic—the winds and ice and chaos—was cut off.

Es turned away from me and moved to stare out the window. "The Nameless One had a knack for fire and managed to burn him and as she tried to flee, a man appeared. He saved her life."

Over her shoulder, she glanced at me, a small smile on her face.

"She'd been injured, and as she lay there, she watched this man shift into a giant monster…the kind she'd been taught to fear, to hate. To destroy. He saved her from another monster. The stories say she was certain he'd turn on her and kill her."

"That's not how the story goes, though, is it?"

"No." She sighed and lifted a hand to press against the glass. "No change happens overnight, though. She was killed, years later, by her own, still trying to convince others. It was her daughter who finally made others see. The girl had the gift of sight. She saw what was coming. Discontent had been brewing between your kind and mine—I think whoever created us had hoped we'd turn on each other and handle that problem for them when the time was necessary, but along the way, the Nameless One had managed to convince enough witches, and even a few of the *aneira* that something wasn't as it should be. We began to see what we had done, what we'd let ourselves become. Murderers. Killers of innocents. It broke something inside us. And that is when the tide turned. We withdrew from the …*battlefield*. We withdrew, but the very essence of what we were had become damaged. So we changed what we were…that is why only the warrior born among us fight. Even now."

I realized, as those words faded away into the silence of the room, she did believe the legend. Maybe not all of it, but enough. "Things aren't the same now. You all can let yourself off that leash…so many witches have died because they wouldn't defend themselves."

"It's not *wouldn't*, Kit," Es murmured. She turned and looked back at me. "It's *couldn't*. Centuries, perhaps even millennia after this…war ended and we still carry it inside us, racial scars that will never fully heal. The vast majority don't even understand it but try to force a pacifist to fight and see what it does to her, to him. It tears them apart."

Them… I blinked, staring at her. "You're warrior born?"

"I am the mother of this house." Her gaze locked with mine, those pale eyes clear and direct. "I am all that stands between them and those who would harm them, in the end."

"You have warriors here," I said, trying to wrap my mind around that. *Es*, calm and gentle *Es* was a warrior.

"And I am the strongest. It's my place."

Groaning, I pressed the heels of my hands to my eyes and tried to process everything. All of this information, everything about Es, about Pandora's Box. I rolled it all through my head and tried to figure out the next step.

"This…legend…story, *whatever*. You got any idea how far back this goes? How old any of us are? How old she is?" *The older she is, the harder it will be to kill her…*

"Green Road has existed for millennia. She is far older."

Millennia. My brain ached just thinking about it and an icy sweat broke out along my spine. My grandmother was old…old, not ancient. She'd seen a couple of centuries come to pass and she probably had another one left in her before the world would be rid of her. Not soon enough—age brought strength.

"She's strong."

Curling my lip, I muttered, "I'd already figured that out."

"She's not infallible."

"Nothing is infallible. Even the supposedly immortal have weaknesses," I said, shrugging restlessly. Knowing that didn't make me feel any better. "But that woman has walked the earth for *how* long?"

"She's been around for millennia." A far-off look entered her eyes and then she sighed, a deep, wracking sound that seemed to come from her very soul. "But she hasn't walked the earth all that time. She sleeps, and awakens as she chooses…and sometimes, her body weakens and she takes another."

"*Takes* another?" Those words froze something in the very pit of my stomach. As the heat gathered in my hand, I clenched it into a tight fist and tried to ignore it. It was easier that time around because I had something to think about. Something that maybe I could hate. Slowly, I turned and stared at Es. "Just what does *that* mean? It's not like she can just pick one up at the grocery store."

"No. Any woman of her bloodline who is with child will suffice for her."

Her eyes, nearly colorless, practically burned into mine.

Any woman of her bloodline…

Blood crashed in my ears, all but roared while rage and horror tore into me, leaving nasty, gaping holes behind. "You say she does this when she wakes…what causes this? Why does she sleep anyway?"

"It's her cycle. You know everything works in a cycle, Kit." Es rubbed the spot between her eyes, a weary expression on her face. "From the records we have, she'll glut herself…on power, chaos, the things that drive her. Then she falls into a rest. When she wakens, she's weaker, tired. And it's time for her to cast off the old body and find a new one."

She came toward me, the weariness on her face fading. Her eyes gleamed, all but glowing with intensity. "We kept it safe, you know. The Order of Witches, for centuries, we kept it safe. And then it was stolen."

We kept it safe—

"Oh, fuck *me*," I snarled. I spun away and drove a fisted hand into the wall as the understanding hit me. The vase…the *witches* had hidden the vase. From Pandora.

I felt like I'd been punched in the chest.

And Es just continued to talk, merrily chatting away.

"We kept her hidden, where she couldn't sense any of the outside world. If she'd just *stayed* where we'd hidden her, tucked away inside…"

"Tucked away…" Hand throbbing, I turned to look at her. I'd donned the mesh-lined gloves again and when I'd slammed my fist into the wall, the weighted mesh had dug into my skin. My knuckles were already complaining and it was a nice distraction, one I didn't have time for. "Just what do you mean, *tucked away*?"

Es lifted a brow. "The vase is a portal…and a world. *Her* world. Her home. Her prison. She's been trapped inside for more than eight hundred years. The witch Brighid of the Blue Sky locked her in and all the houses found a way to spell the vase so that she wasn't able to sense anything happening outside the world. It drained her of her ability to rouse herself. It kept her…quiescent. But the vase was stolen. Outside of our protections, we can't maintain the spells. She's awake now. Awake and aware."

And ready to play Invasion of the Body Snatcher.

Sucking in a breath, I turned away. *One thing at a time. One thing at a time.*

My mind was still stuck on the pregnant bit. A pregnant woman of her bloodline. Why?

I eased that to the side until my brain was a little more ready to think it through. A minute. I just needed a minute. The more concrete problem was one that needed an answer , too.

"Who stole it?"

Es stroked a finger down the embroidery of her sleeve. "They believe it was the work of several people. A witch we had to cast from our house and he was working with a witch unknown to us. Vampires are also involved—we caught their…reek…on the grounds."

"The witches?"

"The one we'd cast out is dead. I believe his conspirators saw him as a means to an end—Adjo was always weak. He was used and once his usefulness was at an end? They disposed of him."

"I need to know more about him…Adjo."

"I'll make sure the information is provided, but nothing about him will help you, Kit. He was just a pawn."

I was starting to feel the same way about myself. Rotating my head one direction, then the other, I thought about the rest of what she'd said. "And the unknown?" I squinted and rubbed at my neck—it didn't help. The unknown…that didn't add up. For her to *be* unknown, she'd have to be from outside the houses. "An independent."

"That's the thought. Our magic can be traced. We know it. Feel it. Sense it. But Adjo wasn't working alone—there were powerful magics involved and his skills were only average. An independent is the only answer that fits."

I nodded slowly. "Why a vampire? Any evidence?"

"Just what was sensed at the place we hid her."

That wasn't much help. At all. Rubbing the tip of my finger down my brow, I forced myself to ask the next question—the one that left my gut clenching and knotting. "You think she's locked on the trail of one of…what, her descendants?"

"Yes. And more…I believe she's already found her. That's why she is still *here*." Another one of those eerie, intense looks. "You've met her."

Sucking in a breath, I spun away and shoved my hands through my hair, thinking of that young, innocent face. That poor, scared girl.

"Clara," I said softly.

"Is that her name?" Es's voice was sad. "I've always wondered what her name would be. I'd hoped I'd find out. Before…"

"Before what? Shit, Es. What's up with you?" I asked.

"Many, many things." She reached out and caught my hands. "Listen. There's not much time left."

She spoke and it was like the words she had to say were pushed *inside* me, forced inside me—entire conversations crammed into my head in the span of seconds, all from a touch.

The Blooding…remember.

A power exchange…

You can't let it happen—

And then, abruptly, the contact severed.

Es's hands fell away and I stumbled back, my head spinning, whirling from the knowledge she'd crammed inside it. "The Blooding?" *What the hell?* "Es, what does some ancient urban legend have to do with any of this?"

"How many urban legends have their basis in truth, Kit?"

Before I could figure that odd little phrase out, something attacked the wards.

CHAPTER EIGHTEEN

Four of the warriors barred the way.

One of them was Tate.

Her hair had grown out since I'd seen her last. The strength of her magic burned hot as I moved into the hall.

She shot me a look. "This isn't a fight for half-human dollies."

We got along really well.

"Not a fight for stupid witches who have their heads up their asses, either." I gave her a sweet smile. "Hard to see that way."

I drew the gun from my hip and wondered if the ammo in it would do much good against whatever was tearing up the wards. They were shuddering from the impact and I could feel their distress.

Whatever…why was I trying to fool myself? I already knew who was out there. I could feel the weight of her years, her magic crawling along my skin.

Pandora had come to play.

I had silver-wrapped ammo in the Eagle and the bullets were charged, but how did you take down a…what in the hell was she? Hell-spawn? Es had made the implication she was something far older than us. And something that could actually *create* other races was far stronger than any creature I'd ever come up against. Witches could do some mad powerful things and weres, vamps could make others of their own kind, but to actually create *another race* was a new power entirely.

Hell-spawn seemed to cover it pretty damn well. Especially if what Es had said was true, and she *was* Lilith.

The lights flickered over our heads as something slammed into the wards and the heat in the hall built as Tate's power gathered around us.

"Tone it down," one of the witches said, her voice soft. "If you cook us before you blast her, it doesn't matter if we fight or not

"We don't fight."

Es moved up at the hall and as she passed by, a wind kicked up, causing the heat to dissipate and a cool welcoming brush of air that left the sweat on my flesh drying. It wasn't entirely comforting, though. The look in her eyes, on her face, was one I knew.

Es stopped by Tate and rested a hand on her shoulder.

The two shared a look and then Tate shook her head. "No. Es, no."

"Go on, now," Es murmured. Then she turned and looked at the warriors gathered behind her, and the witches standing in a knot behind them. "Take them all to the healing hall. Tate, you stand guard. If you have to, take the whole building down before you lock yourself inside. But that's *all* I want you to do. Your word on it."

"*Fuck* that," Tate said, her voice breaking.

"You do this, or they all die." Es looked to the door. "You've been given orders, my dear ones. I'm still head of this house. You'll obey that order…or I'll force you to obey."

Silence fell, heavy and oppressive.

One of the warriors flung herself at Es. I didn't know her name. Unable to watch such a private moment, I looked away as the woman, nearly six feet tall, clung to Es and sobbed like a child. It lasted seconds and then, as abruptly as it had happened, the woman pulled away. In a voice that boomed loud as a cannon, she called out, "To the inner hall!"

Listening to their feet, I shouldered through the moving flow of bodies. I brushed against Tate and felt the contact like a burn against my flesh.

Another thunderous crack slammed against the wards. It echoed somewhere deep in my heart. It certainly felt like it; something had just claimed another massive chunk out of me, I knew it.

Gripping the butt of my gun, I placed myself shoulder to shoulder with the witch. Her pale, silvery hair was drifting gently around her, moved by an unseen current and her eyes were glowing. She was throwing power off in waves, yet it never touched me. Gathering it, readying it.

For what?

I wasn't entirely certain I wanted that answer.

"I'm not locking myself away and hiding," I said sourly. Drawing the short sword from the sheath at my back, I stared at the door. Death in battle was one I could deal with. Death at the side of a friend, I'd almost welcome.

"You can't die today," Es said softly. She turned her head and stared at me. "If you die, the girl doesn't have a chance. Nobody else can stand against her."

I gaped at her. "I've *met* that foul bitch. She can squash me like a bug."

As if to reiterate that, that massive power outside slammed into the wards and one of them exploded, collapsing with a shriek around us. The lights flickered, and this time, they died. Gentle green lights rose to life around, powered by magic, hovering just a few inches from the ceiling. In that eerie light, I stared at Es, convinced she'd lost her mind.

"It takes more than power to defeat certain things, child. Don't you know that by now?" She lifted a hand and placed it square on my chest. I flinched at the contact, forcing myself not to jerk back. "Very often, it takes heart."

Swallowing the bile that crawled up my throat, I shook

my head. "Pretty words. Empty ones. But pretty. She'll toss me around like a rag doll when the time comes."

"In a fight, yes. But you don't *fight* her." She leaned in, grabbing my shoulders as she pressed her lips to my ear. Her voice was low, almost too low for me to make out. "You're a trained killer…not a fighter. A *born* killer. She can die. Her body is mortal and right now, it's the weakest it will ever be. Soon, she'll be even weaker. What would *kill* that body? She doesn't know this world…doesn't understand it. And she doesn't understand *you* or how you fight."

She leaned back and dropped a glance.

My heart skittered to a stop as her gaze landed on my gun. "The vessel needs to be destroyed, but so must she."

Her hand touched my face and yet again, that roaring chaotic rush of knowledge came slamming into me.

The words all blurred together, but then, abruptly, everything slowed. Es's gaze locked and held with mine.

"She has power over vamps and weres", she murmured into my mind, her voice calm and steady.

Power over them…even the thought of that turned my stomach and filled me with terror.

"The very controls that were bred into us make it difficult for us to strike out at her. You don't have that problem. You're the most capable for this, in more ways than one."

And then the connection ended and Es shoved me back, her voice filled with command and terror as she shouted, *"Go!"*

There was another crash against the wards and I felt it echo in my gut as I stumbled into the wall. My ears rang at the intensity of it and something wet trickled down my neck.

"Go!" Es shouted again. But apparently she didn't trust me to move fast enough.

Something slammed against my chest and I went flying down the hall.

As I struggled to get up to my feet, arms came around me and lifted me. "Put me down," I snarled, driving back with my elbow.

"Leave her."

I sagged, recognizing the voice. It was the woman who'd sobbed as she hugged Es only moments ago.

"She's going to get herself killed."

"I know." Her voice was a husky murmur and I thought she might be crying. "She's known this was coming since she was a kid. She told me it would happen. We can't stop it and if we try, just about everybody here will die. So what do we do? At least if Es makes her stand, she'll weaken the bitch."

Her breath shuddered out of her. "She has to be weakened, otherwise none of us stand a chance against her."

Back when I ran away from home, I lived on the streets. When I first came to the States, I spent a summer in the Midwest and it's an experience I don't ever want to repeat. I'd been living in an old barn and had done just fine for a while. Food was easy to find and the weather didn't suck.

But then the storms started.

A tornado almost a quarter-mile wide ripped through the area where I was staying, and I cowered against the ground while that twister pummeled everything around me. I'd been convinced that would be my last night on the earth—I didn't want to die, huddling in the dirt.

I hadn't died.

When I finally crawled out of the pile of timber, hay and debris, I'd never been so glad to see a night end and I left the Midwest that very day, stealing a car from a dealership that had somehow managed to go mostly untouched a few towns over.

That was right before I landed in Orlando.

For a while, that tornado had haunted my dreams.

Wild, uncontrollable power that decimated everything around it.

I had a feeling tonight would surpass that night—power for raw power.

The witch who'd hauled me to the hall had disappeared inside to watch over the rest of her charges; her name was

Serene. It didn't seem to fit her, not at first glance. She was definitely a warrior through and through from the top of her violently red hair, cut in a short, spiked style, down to her battered leather boots. But her voice was low and soothing and her eyes were kind.

When I'd said I'd stand watch at the door, she'd eyed me with a look that said she wanted to just club me over the head and be done with it. I'd been braced to take whatever she had to dish out. It would *hurt* but I could take it.

It hadn't been necessary. Tate had just sneered at the both of us. "Let the little dolly get her ass kicked if that's what she wants."

Serene had just sighed and disappeared inside.

Now the two of us stood and watched. Waited.

The wards were all but gone.

The roof was broken, bits and pieces of it missing. It might have given way altogether, but apparently Pandora had thought fire was the best way to do it and Tate thought otherwise. She could toss it around, and she could also kill it. Every time a fireball had exploded out of the night, Tate had lifted a hand; I could feel the heat coming off her as she sucked the magic inside her and the air around us was almost unbearably hot.

"How much of that can you take in before you have to let it out?"

Tate's gaze slid my way. Her gaze burned like molten copper and a mean smile curved her lips even as she gave me an appraising look. *Yeah, witch. I know how you work. The little dolly isn't stupid.*

Tate looked like she wanted to laugh. Or fry my ass. But she only shrugged. "Plenty more. Of course, something is going to melt when I finally let all of this out."

Witches couldn't suck in that kind of magic indefinitely. Sooner or later, it had to come out or it would kill her. And probably anybody within a thirty foot radius of her when she went supernova.

"You want to take off running now?" Her eyes laughed at me.

"Nah. I figure Es wouldn't have put you on guard if she didn't trust you." I crossed my arms over my chest, gripping the Eagle and staring up at the ruins of the roof for a long moment. My ears popped as the atmosphere did a weird little pitch and shift. Here we go again.

The ground rumbled under our feet. Bracing a hand against the wall, I squinted through the remnant magic, trying to see—

Something exploded through the night.

A hand closed around my arm. I swallowed back a gasp. Tate's touch was hot as a brand. "You need to get ready to go through," she said, all laughter gone from her voice. "That was the final ward. Whoever is at the door is coming in."

I heard a low, soft laugh.

It drifted through the night. Wrapped around me.

Music and bells…

"Why are you doing this, witch?"

Pandora.

"Little fool."

I tensed as her voice sounded in the back of my mind.

I tried to close my head against her, but it wasn't as easy as it should be. Closing her out shouldn't be that hard, but I felt like I was trying to slam a door against a coming flood—*impossible.*

"*There was no reason for this. All you had to do was find my vase. Just do your job…no questions asked.*" Pain, hot and burning, sliced through me, like it was trying to split me in two. But not *physically;* I felt like she was trying separate me, body and soul.

The agony ripped through me and I slammed the butt of my gun against my temple. Flesh ripped and blood dripped down my skin.

I heard a rush of voice. Felt that scorching touch that was Tate's hands on me. She was grabbing my face, shouting at me.

Stupid little dolly—

Yeah. Stupid—

"Get out of my head…"

"You'll do your job," Pandora whispered. I felt another one of those jabs and something inside me splintered. Sensory memory, sharp and clear, exploded and I felt her laugh as a ghostly touch feathered over the skin of my neck, tracing the lines of my tattoos. *"I'd wondered about these. Do you know what I do to those who disobey me, Kit? I'll take you into the dark. And you'll relive all your worst fears…"*

Panic crowded inside my chest and blackness whirled around me. It threatened to drag me under as she poked, prodded at another memory. Whether it was desperation or terror, I don't know, but this time, when she tried to slide past the barrier of my memories, I shoved back, and I shoved hard.

I felt her surprise as I managed to take my mind back and before she could push her way inside again, I bolstered my shields, terror and adrenaline lending me much needed strength.

I didn't have time for anything else before hands closed over my arms.

"Now." The voice, the command, didn't register. "Tate, do it."

The *heat* did.

Heat, magic, the very world seemed to explode as I fell backward. Pandora struck out at me again, trying to shove inside my mind, but I managed to keep her out once more.

Over the explosion of power, I heard her scream.

CHAPTER NINETEEN

There was nothing left.

And even though I couldn't see any sign of the battle that had waged over the past hour, I knew Es was gone.

Near where the door had once stood, there was a small crater maybe six feet across and I crouched there, smoothed my hand across it. *Why, Es?*

But there weren't any answers. Looking around, I blinked back the tears rising inside and stared at the witches milling around like lost children. They'd just now come out of the healing hall. In a few minutes, they'd find their center and focus, but just then, I imagined they were even more shell-shocked than I was.

Es had been their everything.

And she was dead because of a monster I'd led to their door.

Standing in the remains of what had been the door, I stared at the lone room that had survived the destruction. The healing hall. The outer walls probably looked like a bunker would, had it come through a battle. Fire-scorched, battered. But whole. The spells Es had laid on it all those years ago had protected it, just as she'd said they would. Everybody inside that hall had survived. Had she been readying for just this moment? Had she spent her entire life preparing for just this?

I swallowed the ache in my throat and looked away from the healing hall, staring at the devastation outside.

Beyond the hall, nothing, and nobody, had made it. The home itself was charred bits of wood and melted metal. Colorful bits of glass, also melted, broke under my boots as I moved through the destruction.

Tate stood at the far edge, staring over it all with an unreadable look on her face.

"She's gone."

I stopped and looked over at Serene.

There was no point in asking who she was talking about. Averting my gaze, I stared out at my car, felt the urge to run to it, take off...disappear. If I ran, maybe Pandora would follow me.

If I ran, maybe I could escape all of this.

I never should have stayed here.

If I hadn't, I wouldn't have had that first run-in with Jude.

I wouldn't have met Es, so I couldn't have endangered her.

Pandora would have never been able to seek me out.

All of this could have been avoided.

Hindsight was such a bitch.

Crossing my arms over my chest, I focused on the charred ground and said, "I shouldn't have come down here."

"Don't."

Serene's voice was gentle and sad. And...oddly, Es-like.

It made the ache in my chest spread.

"She's dead because I came here." Shaking my head, I strode away.

Serene followed.

"She's dead because some ancient bitch with a grudge decided to come knocking," she said, her voice flat. "An ancient bitch who decides to make an appearance every few centuries and when she does, a whole bunch of mortals die. When *that* happens, your kind and mine gets jerked around, the weres get all primitive-like and regress for a century or two and the vamps get even more cold-blooded. She tries to send us all back to the dark ages where everybody jumped at shadows and where *we* were supposed to play exterminator, something that was driving us insane. Es did the same damn thing any of us would do—she stood up to her. And you want to play martyr? Fuck that."

I glared at her. "You think I want to play martyr?"

"I think you want to bury your head in the sand and feel bad—I don't blame you. *I* would feel bad—hell, I *do* feel bad. I was her guard. I was the one who was supposed to take the hits for her, but I was also charged with keeping her house safe." Serene scrubbed her hands over her face and then abruptly, she sank down onto the ground, looping her arms around her long legs, staring at the house. "I can't protect the house if I'm dead next to her. And the bottom line is this—none of us were going to survive this fight. Not today."

Tired, grieving, furious, I sat down next to her. "I can't believe that Es was just *supposed* to die, Serene."

With one hand fisted in her hair, Serene stared at the house. Her voice came in slow, uneasy, broken bits as she said, "But sometimes that's how it is. Things happen…because they were meant to." With a jerky nod, she looked at Tate. "Like her. That mouthy, mean bitch. Sometimes I hate her, you know. And we aren't supposed to hate. But I do. I hate her. But her ability for fire is almost unmatched. I felt the fire that bitch was casting around. If she'd been slamming that full force into the healing hall from the get-go, she might have managed to break through. Tate was the only one who could have neutralized that much fire coming at us. Not even Es could have taken that kind of heat in her."

I slid a look toward the witch in question.

Tate was still standing in the exact same spot she'd occupied earlier, her expression stony, her gold eyes glittering.

"And…" Serene closed her eyes and a spasm wracked her body. Then she looked over at me and her eyes were glassy. "Es's protection over this house passed to me on her death. I'm the mother now. It works that way. I was keyed into what was happening as she passed and I was witness to what was going on as that…thing…picked herself up off the floor and dragged her sorry ass off. She's hurt now. Between what Es did to her, and the damage she took when Tate's fire tore through her, she's hurt. And pissed…and maybe a little worried, because she knows she can *be* hurt."

Licking my lips, I picked through those words. Serene. She was the mother now. A warrior of the house? Okay, that's not the important piece. She'd witnessed Es's passing—my heart broke a little more and if I could have, I would have tried to comfort her. But I was too broken myself.

"Pan—"

"No." Serene's hand, quick as a blink and strong as the earth itself, shot out, closing over my wrist. "Don't say the name. There's power in a name. You know this. Don't speak it."

I curled my lip. "*Not* speaking a name feeds fear."

"This isn't a demon, Kit. She might *love* that you're afraid, but your fear or lack of it doesn't change her power in any way." Serene shook her head. "If she'd been forgotten, her name lost in the sands of time, perhaps we wouldn't be dealing with this plague now."

Crossing my legs in front of me, I shook my head. "No. A creature like her doesn't cease to exist just because she's forgotten."

"That's a debate for a different time." Serene sighed and rose to her feet. "I have to gather my house. Prepare for Es's wake. And you…" She held out a hand.

Although I didn't need it, I accepted it and let her pull me to my feet.

Our eyes met and I felt that oddly familiar calm settle around me. Yes. Warrior or not, I could see her as mother to this house. "You have a job to finish."

I don't think I'm equipped to handle this job…not the one I'd taken on from Pandora and not the one that both Es and Serene seemed to think I was taking on now.

"There's nobody else who *can*," Serene said quietly.

"She's too much like a witch for any of us to confront. She's like…umber-primeval witch, or something. But she knows magic. What she *doesn't* know is weapons. She doesn't know *you*, or your kind or how you think. You already know vamps and weres are going to be useless against her. So who is going to step up? Your useless family? Humans?"

Clenching my jaw, I looked past her to the ruin around us.

"The time to stop her is *now*…before she takes over that new body. Before she kills a child. Not just because of those two innocent lives, either."

"That's reason enough, isn't it?" I rubbed the back of my hand over my mouth and tried to breath. Between the ache in my heart and the fear, it was almost impossible.

"Oh, it's reason enough. But just think about how much worse it's going to get, Kit. I know what Es told you. You really want to see what the mortals are going to do if the Blooding starts all over again? They've got the technology now to do us a lot of damage. You were born *after* the wars, Kit. If she has her way, though, the wars will start back up…and they'll be worse. A lot worse."

My heart turned to ice as I realized what she was saying.

Oh. Fuck.

"Yeah." Serene's gaze was far more direct and her attitude was far more blunt than Es's. "We'll be looking at another interspecies war…and we might just manage to do what we didn't all those centuries ago—push the vamps and weres into extinction. But who knows if any of us will survive."

"I get the point." I turned away and strode to my car, weaving my way through the rubble, ruin and drifting eddies of smoke. The devastation stopped somewhere between the house and the area where most of the people parked, so many of cars had come through unscathed, including mine. I had just laid my hand on the door when Serene said my name.

I paused and looked back.

"Do me a favor. Make that bitch wish she'd never come looking for you."

I wasn't even a mile away when the call came.

The Imperial March was the tone I'd been using for Justin for years and I wasn't surprised that he was calling. "Call to speaker," I said, glancing in the mirror. A speed-freight was roaring up behind me and I crossed over into the other lane. Those things moved at almost two hundred miles an hour and half the time, they didn't care if you got out of the way or not.

"What's happened?" Justin's voice cut out of the phone, sharp as a blade.

"Es is dead."

The words were like a slap and I had to pull over as the grief hit me, hard and fast.

"*What?*"

"Es is dead. Pa—" I remembered Serene's warning and as stupid as it seemed, that house had provided me protection too many times. Es had died doing it. I'd respect their concerns. "*She* knew I was there. Es had information about her. She wanted me to come down. So I did. *She* showed up—I don't know if she followed me or what, but she came down and picked one hell of a fight. Es is dead."

"Son of a *bitch*."

Over the phone, I heard a strange crackling noise. If I wasn't familiar with magic, I might have thought the connection was acting up, but it was Justin's magic, chaotic and turbulent, spilling out of him and seeking release. The grief in his voice tugged me. "You knew her?" I asked.

Seconds ticked by. Numerous vehicles, including several of the speed freights sped by, rocking my battered old car as I sat parked on the side of the highway.

Finally, he answered. "Yeah. She…ah. She was one of my earliest teachers when I went to work for Banner. That's how I figured out something was wrong. Word started spreading fast; she was big in our world. People are going to want blood for this. Not just the witches, but Banner, too.

They tried to call me back in."

"What?"

"They want me back. I told them to get fucked with a battering ram."

"You have such a poetic way with words."

"I learned it from you." He blew out a sigh. Voice thick, he whispered, "I can't believe she's dead. Shit. How many others?"

"Just Es." I passed a hand over my face. "I don't want to talk about this now. I'm parked on the side of the road. I've got information but I don't want to discuss it until I'm there and…" It hit me, then, what I had to do. "We're going to have to go to the Lair, Justin."

A snarl trembled in his voice. "*What?*"

"Don't." I checked my mirrors and pulled back out onto the road. "Don't give me grief and don't hassle me. But we're going to have to work with them—there's information they *have* to know and if you have an issue with it, just go back to Banner. My head is already spinning from what I had thrown at me. I don't need to deal with this."

"Why do we need to work with the shifters, Kit?"

"Because it's necessary. And if *I* can handle working with them…" Working with *Damon…* "So can you. Suck it up, buttercup."

I hung up on him and focused on driving.

Memory swarmed up, taunting me, as I stared at the blade on my bed.

Call me, I am here…

I gasped for breath as the largest one drove his fist into my stomach. Doubled over, trying to breathe, I thought, Please…just let me die…*That was all I'd wanted to anyway. That was what had led to this.*

I caught the flash of something silver tucked into the guard's boot. His name Visran. One of my grandmother's favored guards. If he was here, doing this, it was with her approval. Perhaps she'd even given them leave to kill me. I can only hope—

I snagged the blade and swung out, clumsy from the cold, from hunger. The hot, wet splash of his blood on my hand was a shock and instead of keeping my hand around the blade, I lost my grip.

Seconds later, I was face down in the dirt and panic assailed me. Not again, not again!

"Little whore!"

Vicious pulls destroyed what remained of my clothes. The shirt hung in rags around me. I twisted and fought to get away from them, but it was pointless. Me, against two hardened royal guards.

Call me, I am here—

That voice. *I was going mad.* If I'm losing my mind, can it happen already so I don't have to *be here!*

Hard hands wrenched the shreds my pants away and I screamed, twisting. Just barely, I managed to get my feet up and as Visran tried to grab me, I got my legs between us and kicked. He went flying back.

"Stupid cunt—"

The other one, Tolan, laughed. "I like it when they fight—"

Call me!

This time, it was a strident command that all but leveled me and the heat building in my hand left me screaming.

And then—

I knew the weight of a weapon in my hand.

Even at sixteen, broken, battered and bloodied. I knew what it was to hold a weapon and realize that I had to fight or be destroyed.

Those last moments were nothing but a blur, but it was a blur of silver and blade and blood.

I left Visran and Tolan dead in the snow, taking their packs and fleeing into the night, certain my grandmother would seek me out. And all the while as I ran, the blade had whispered to me. *I am here now. I am here…*

Reaching out, I touched her hilt and drew her from the sheath and stared at the gleaming, liquid length of silver.

"You're not here *now.*"

If ever there had been a time when I needed her, it had been when I was trapped up on that mountain. Broken, desperate.

But she hadn't answered my call.

And she couldn't come to my hand now, either.

Stroking my fingers down the blade, I closed my eyes…and wished.

Then I turned back to my weapons trunk and went about getting myself ready.

Just what did you take to the party when you were dealing with some ancient, psychotic evil who unleashed holy hell just for the fun of it?

CHAPTER TWENTY

The Lair was a massive building built decades ago that sprawled across an entire city block. Once it had belonged to the mortals. It had been a government building, although it was hard to see any sign of that now.

The cat clan of Florida had taken it over sometime during the war.

When we'd…come out…so to speak, it had been a thing of necessity. A couple of stupid, young weres had been caught—*on camera*—shifting as they fought and the video went viral. Then there was another sighting, and another…

Discovery was inevitable, it seemed.

The Assembly—our governing council—had thought if we controlled how we made our presence known to the mortals, we'd have the upper hand. In a way, they were right.

In a way, they were wrong, because nobody, and nothing, can predict how fear will dictate a situation. Things had gone…mostly okay, for the first few months, despite the numerous suggestions that we all be *contained* until more about the *threat* was understood.

It didn't matter that we'd been living among them all this time. Humans are nosy creatures and they think testing and research and all that shit will solve everything. Or maybe mass extermination had been their endgame.

In the end, it hadn't mattered.

The smarter mortals had already figured out that we were too many. Even if our population was only a fraction of the mortal population, creatures like weres and vamps, or people like witches held too big an advantage to assume numbers alone would be the deciding factor. They wanted cool, rational thinking to prevail.

But others were less than impressed by that logic.

Attacks broke out, most of them staged by fanatical humans looking to brand the NHs as animals. The attacks led to mistrust on both sides. That led to an interspecies war that lasted almost a decade and had resulted in the death of millions. It had taken wisdom on both sides to realize that in order for us to co-exist in this world, something had to be done.

The Assembly offered a treaty.

Human governments fought over this point and that, but after two years of bickering and negotiations and even more deaths, an uneasy peace was found. The more advanced countries were the first to accept the treaty. Third-world countries still have struggles breaking out even now—there were a few places where either one species or the other pretty much ruled. Me? There are a few countries I won't ever visit—the hospitality to the NH population leaves a lot to be desired.

By treaty law, places like East Orlando—any place heavily populated by NHs—remained under NH control.

NHs had agreed, naturally, not to encroach on human territory.

Whatever in the hell that meant.

If you were licensed, like I was, you could move back and forth between the segregated areas without much trouble, and humans could come looking for a wild time on NH turf—or *claim* that's what they'd done. But heaven forbid any shapeshifter try to grab a meal at restaurant on human-regulated land. They could, would, and did refuse to give service to any *non-human*. And if they decided to make a call to the cops, the NH could be arrested for so much as breathing. Banner would pick your ass up and you better be prepared to make a good argument or you might find yourself doing hard labor or maybe even spending a few months in a box.

It was the younger ones that always ended up in the worst trouble.

After you'd been around a few years, you learned to either stay on your own territory or travel with enough people so you had witnesses.

Guys like Damon were wise to steer clear of mortals. They oozed menace and even though he could play mortal when he wanted to, he usually didn't bother.

Few of them did.

Right now, the Alpha was currently striding my way and the look on his face had hot little darts zinging through my belly.

It hadn't been that long since I'd seen him.

A couple of days?

It seemed like longer.

There was a subtle difference inside me and whether it was because I'd forced myself back into my life, or something else, I didn't know. I wished I had time to think about it, time to do more than think…

In the back of my mind, I heard his voice. *I'll wait…*

His gaze locked with mine as I closed the distance between us and I wracked my brain thinking of what to say, how to say it. There wasn't an easy way to do this.

"Kit."

His voice, low and rough, stroked over me and for that brief, brief moment, some of the tension melted away and I let myself just…*feel.* The need to move closer to him was strong, so very strong. I could close those few inches, slip my arms around his waist…

Then his gaze dropped to the tattoos on my neck, left exposed by my braids and I tensed.

Just that quickly, his eyes jerked back to my face and I had to fight the urge to tug at my collar, loosen the braids. Anything to hide—

You already covered the scars, I reminded myself. *Your way.*

Maybe there wasn't as much of a difference inside me as I'd thought.

"Damon." My voice came out steady. *Go, me! I am aneira…*

The words drifted through my mind and even though I didn't know if it was right of me to lay claim to that anymore, just the *words* soothed me. It was so messed up, because the *aneira* had never done much of anything for me. But it was my…

My birthright.

Damn it.

I *was aneira.*

Broken or not.

Steadying my shoulders, I lifted my head and met Damon's gaze.

My sword arm is mighty.

Something glimmered in his eyes. It might have been a smile. Might. It was gone too fast and I didn't let myself think about what might have caused it. *Yeah, look…scared little Kit is ready to try and kick ass again.*

Setting my jaw, I looked around. Too many people. We couldn't have this discussion here.

"We need to talk. It's important. And it involves the whole damn clan."

A black brow arched and then, without saying a word, he stepped aside, letting me precede him into the Lair.

"Now, Dair."

Over the phone, I heard them talking.

He had no idea what was going on. His grey eyes hadn't left my face for longer than a minute or two. I'd told Damon it involved all the shifters and it would be easier to explain it all at once.

He'd taken me at my word and hadn't wasted any time getting the Alpha of the Wolf Pack on the phone.

Alisdair MacDonald was balking.

Politely. Of course he was being polite; wolves were *always* like that. It drove me nuts. But he was still balking.

Damon's lip curled in a sneer and he said, "I don't care if you have a piano recital and a date with the President of the Fucking States of America. I said you're needed. It's shifter business and you're the Alpha. Unless you want to let your second handle it. You wanna send Megan over here to play with me?"

Dair's response was almost icily polite, but there was an undercurrent of something snide and sly. It didn't matter. As far as shifter politics went, *might* made *right*. The cat clan outnumbered the wolf pack by a huge number. The rats trickling back into the area had to align with somebody since none of them had stepped up to lead, so Damon was also speaking for them.

That meant unless MacDonald wanted two factions pissed at him, he'd do what the Cat Alpha wanted.

After another twenty seconds, I heard the other man's consent, his voice flat and displeased as he said, "I'll need an hour."

"Try to make it sooner." Then Damon hung up and looked my way. His gaze raked over me, lingering on the Kel-tech strapped to my thigh, the Eagle, the sword. I had no doubt he was aware of the garrote and other various weapons, too. I hadn't even broken out the big guns yet, either. Those were at home. "You look like you're loaded for bear, kitten."

I stroked my hand down the hilt of my sword and turned away. Moving to the bar tucked up against one wall, I dug out a tube of water. The bar was more for decoration anything else—it held water and there was a bottle of Redcat there. It hadn't been opened. Twisting my water open, I guzzled it, wished there was something other than the whiskey, but that shit would put me on my ass and anything weaker would be like water for Damon and his metabolism.

Better off probably. I needed to be thinking for this. Throat dry, I took another drink and within a minute, I'd emptied the tube. Dumping it in the recycler, I looked up.

Damon was exactly where he'd been when he ended the phone call.

Big hands, those beautiful, golden hands hung at his sides. A black T-shirt stretched over a wide chest and the battered jeans he wore looked like they'd seen better days. Annette, the previous Alpha, had dressed in designer silks—she'd been completely lovely and completely evil.

Damon looked like somebody's worst nightmare and more than once, he'd proven to be just that. He'd been Annette's favorite soldier before he killed her—she said *kill* and he said *who*.

Now he was Alpha and he was staring at me like he thought any small move might terrify me.

I glared at him.

Once more, that smile flickered in the back of his eyes and I hated how it made heat flutter inside me.

"You look like you're ready to go fight the world, baby girl."

His voice could still send shivers down my spine. Giving him a narrow look, I stroked a finger down my sword's hilt. I wasn't ready to carry her yet. I knew that and until I could carry her without her being a burden, it was foolish to try. I removed her, left her in her sheath near the bar and then turned back to Damon.

A headache pounded behind my eyes, pulsed at my temples, strong enough to make me almost physically ill.

As the silence stretched out, I shrugged out of my jacket and tossed it on the back of the nearest chair. His gaze zoomed in and I went still.

He'd seen the new blade.

Blowing out a breath, I rotated my shoulders. "You're an odd man, decorating a tree with throwing stars and daggers, Damon."

"Well, I didn't think you'd have much use for snowmen and rosy-cheeked angels." He prowled around, head cocked as he studied the blade. "I take it the blade suits you?"

"Like it was made for me." That sounded lame. It *had*

been made for me. Turning away, I rubbed my hands over my face. I didn't have time to talk about the tree, the gifts…us. I had to tell him about…*me.* Get it all out before anybody showed up.

Others didn't know what I could do with the sword. He did, and he'd understand how much this crippled me.

And…

Es.

Closing my eyes, I closed one hand into a fist while her words echoed in the back of my head.

Even magical injuries can be healed...if you'll allow it…

So much of me wished that was the case. That this was just a magical injury that had some mystical cure. But life didn't work like that. There were no easy answers. No magical cures.

Sometimes shit happened and you had to deal with it.

Sometimes shit happened and you had to hurt over it.

"Es is dead," I said softly.

A harsh intake of breath was the only sound he made.

Turning, I stared at him and saw a strange, overly bright glimmer in his eyes.

Two seconds later, he was standing in front of me. Head bent, he stared into my eyes. "*What?*" he demanded.

"She's dead." I met his eyes, saw the pain I felt echoed in his gaze. "She..."

I shook my head.

Pandora's Box is open…and the monster killed her.

He spun away and a harsh breath wracked him.

Unable to stay still, I lifted a hand, painfully aware of the knot that tried to choke me.

The second my hand touched him, he spun back to me and then I was caught up in his arms, pressed against that wide, warm chest, one hand cradling the back of my neck.

Tears burned my eyes.

I let them come.

It wasn't a weakness to cry for a friend. I knew that.

Damon buried his face against my neck, and although I knew there was no way he'd ever allow himself to weep, he'd cared for her, too. He didn't care for many, but somehow along the way, Es had forced past the strong, solid walls he kept locked around himself.

Maybe I was crying for both of us.

I wished we could have stayed there.

Just like that. I needed more time. More time with him. More time to grieve. But there were other things that needed to be said before we were no longer alone.

Slowly, I eased back and the second I did, his arms loosened.

One big hand, rough and hard, came up, gentle as a spring rain to wipe the tears from my face. "Tell me the bitch who did it is dead," he said, his voice flat and level.

"I wish I could." I closed one hand around his wrist, staring into his eyes.

He blew out a breath and stared past my shoulder. "Okay. Then we go after whoever it is together. Can we do that?"

"That's…part of why I'm here. I'll get to that once MacDonald gets here. But first…" I made myself pull away, turning to stare at my blade. How did I say this?

I squeezed my eyes shut.

"Do you remember that day?" I said slowly, forcing each word out. "The day you went to kill Marlowe…and I was working with a cloaker?"

His voice came out, rusty and jagged. "Yes."

"The man's name was Xavier. He…" I flexed my hands, rubbing at my palm, at the heat that gathered there. It was some remnant instinct, I supposed. Left over from all those years when my body had taken comfort in that bond—a bond now broken. "He was a witch—you already know that. But he was one of Jude's. Enslaved to him somehow. I don't know how. Don't know what that fucker had on him, did to him. But he was the one who grabbed me and Xavier was there when I…"

My chest locked up on me, made it harder to get the words out as terror tried to wrap me in a tight, confining shroud.

A warm hand brushed down my cheek and I looked up, found Damon watching me. The stormclouds in his eyes whispered of things like regret, rage…need. I felt all those things, and more. But instead of going to him, I turned away.

"I woke up. He was there. I called my blade…and it was the last time I ever managed to do it."

The very air seemed to freeze around us. I stared at the huge ornate clock on the wall, watched as each second slowly dragged by.

The air currents seemed to shift and I turned, watching as Damon took one step, then another, staring at me, his gaze burning. "What?"

"I called my blade. And Xavier did something…I don't know what. But he managed to break the bond with my blade. I can't call her anymore."

He shook his head. "That…"

"People tell me there's a fix. That it's just an injury that needs to be *healed*." I shrugged and turned away. "I know my body. If I had a broken rib, I could tell you which one. If a bone was broken, I'd know where and what kind of break. This isn't an injury. It's something else—I felt the magic he shoved inside me, and I felt it wrench me apart. He broke the bond. The blade's not mine."

"That's fucking shit."

I flinched at the harsh sound of his voice. Anger flickered, stirred. Slowly, I made myself face him, trying to keep a grip on the anger, but it was so hard. "No. It's not. *I* know what the bond feels like. Nobody else does—"

"You're more than just your bond with a sword, Kit. And you don't just *own* a weapon because you magically call it to you." He shot out a hand and fisted it in my shirt. "Even if *you* think a bond is gone, that doesn't make it so." He reached up a hand and traced his fingers over the bite he'd put on my neck. "Trust me. I know."

I went to knock his hand away. Once more, I found myself caught in his gaze and instead of moving away, I just stared at him. "That's different."

"Maybe it's not a magical connection," he murmured,

shifting his hand to my face. He stroked his thumb over my lip. "But it's still there. This isn't about us, though. It's about you and your sword. It's yours—*she* is yours. She came to you and until she chooses another bearer, she remains yours. You didn't *magically* learn to use her, did you?"

I curled my lip at him.

He pressed his thumb against my mouth.

"If you did, maybe that means *I* can kick your ass if we went a round."

"You wish." I sneered at him.

Lids drooping over his eyes, he continued to watch me. "She's still yours. Unless you decide to give her up."

He might have said something else, but there was a polite knock at the door.

I broke away from him, turning to stare at my sword. *Still mine.*

Part of me wanted to believe that. Just as part of me wanted to believe what Es had said.

But I didn't have the time think about this, along with Pandora…and Es.

Something would have to wait until later.

And sadly, that would have to be my blade.

CHAPTER TWENTY-ONE

Alisdair had finally arrived along with his second, Megan. She wasn't happy to see me.

Chang and Doyle were also there, along with several of Damon's top men.

We sat around at the table, a nice, big happy family.

Not.

Megan seemed to think I'd lost my mind.

Chang's face was unreadable. Damon hadn't lifted his gaze from the table.

And Doyle was juggling knives. Literally. His hands moved in a blur and I smelled the sharp scent of blood in the air—he'd cut himself a time or two, but he hadn't stopped. He was either worried or nervous, I suspected and he wouldn't put the knives down.

I had other things to worry about, but the blur of silver in front of him was distracting.

"You're serious."

Shifting my attention from Doyle to Megan, I met her eyes. "Do you think I'd be sitting here if I wasn't? Trust me, I got other things I'd like to be doing."

"Yes." Alisdair smiled, his voice cool and smooth. "I hear you're enjoying a change of pace down in Wolf Haven.

Serving drinks. Must be a little less stressful."

The silence that fell across the room was keen, sharp as a blade. It seemed everybody in the room was waiting. Even Doyle had gone still. His eyes glittered as he stared at the back of Alisdair's head.

"I don't know that I'd call it less stressful," I said. Asshole. I let that thought show in my eyes as I stared at him. I was fed up with playing the diplomat and I was tired of being nice.

I'd walked that line—yeah, I had always been a mouthy little bitch and I didn't do their territorial bullshit well, but I'd played by their rules.

I'd been *good.* I did what I was supposed and I tried to stay out of trouble…for the most part.

And look where it had gotten me.

Alisdair's eyes narrowed on mine and I just glared at him. "After all, I was dealing with all the mongrels who ran to get away from your pack and I can tell you, some of them are even more annoying to deal with than *you* are."

A growl trickled out of Megan's throat and she rose slowly. She was a tall woman and she managed to look even bigger even though she hadn't really done anything.

I was used to having people loom over me.

Flicking her a bored look, I shifted my attention back to Alisdair. He was her Alpha. She might be pissed over the insult, but she wouldn't dare attack, not here. Not unless *he* told her to.

"If I'm so annoying, Ms. Colbana, I'd be happy to leave." His smile was bland but his eyes were pure ice as he rose, smoothing down his oh-so-perfect three-piece suit. "I assure you, we won't bother Colbana—"

"MacDonald, you need to sit down," Chang said, his voice polite.

Megan looked at him. "Be quiet."

Chang glided forward, ignoring Megan. "There's a threat of some magnitude and the wolves will be affected. You need to be here. Or you need to leave Orlando. Immediately."

Damon had yet to look up.

Megan went to block Chang, shoving a hand against his chest. She was about three inches taller than him. He stilled as she laid a hand against him, his gaze landing on her hand where it butted up against him. He was leanly built. Elegant, I'd always thought. And he one was scary-ass motherfucker.

Megan didn't seem impressed.

"Excuse me?"

"You'll have to leave. You're outnumbered. You'll either be a help or a hindrance in what we're dealing with and we will not tolerate a hindrance," Chang said, his voice neutral. He glanced down at her hand again and his eyes flashed, from dark brown to an eerie, flickering light green . "You should move your hand, Megan."

"You think you scare me, Chang?"

The words hadn't even died on the air before she went flying. I didn't even see Chang move, but Megan was on the floor, landing at Doyle's feet. He looked like a kid in a candy store; she was surging to her feet but Doyle kicked them out from under her and flipped her over, one of the blades he carried pressed to her neck.

"Right there," he said, his voice sounding just a little too smug as he dropped his weight down. "You know if I cut you *right there* with a silver blade, you are going to have a damn awful recovery period. Spinal cord… you might even lose some mobility."

"He sounds like you," Damon said, shooting me a look.

I scowled and stood up, staring at Doyle. He had the knife at the right spot. But Megan was older. Probably better trained…

Neither Chang or Damon looked worried, though.

Alisdair was on his feet, staring at Damon. "Call him off."

"Not doing that." Damon shook his head. "She's stupid enough to get in my lieutenant's face, she can stay where she is or fight her way out of that mess." He shrugged. "Doyle's just a kid. She can probably take him. If she gets his knives away. Tell me something, Dair…you train your wolves to fight with weapons? She got any idea *how*?"

You're not helping.

A muscle pulsed in Alisdair's cheek. "She'll apologize."

I moved around the table, taking the smart route—the one away from Alisdair. This thing was turning into a clusterfuck. I didn't know if we needed the wolves with us on this or not. But we *didn't* need to make enemies of them and that was what would happen if we sent them scurrying away from Orlando with their tails between their legs.

"Doyle."

He didn't look up at me but I knew he was listening.

"I think she gets the point," I said, watching as blood ran along the blade. "No point in putting her in a bed for the next few weeks while the nerves regenerate. We're going to need all the help we can get on this, right?"

He sighed. Then, before she could move, he was up and by me.

"I don't need some stupid half-human helping me," she snarled as she stood. Muscles knotted and flowed under her flesh.

"Yeah? You sure about that? You haven't even heard the really good parts about my special new friend yet, Lassie."

She lunged and then stopped.

I don't know who was more surprised, her or me, but the short sword Damon had given me was between us, just that fast, his tip pressed to her neck. He felt good in my hand. *Damn* good. I held her gaze.

"Now listen," I said softly. "I'm not going to toy with you like Doyle did. I'm not a cat. If you keep this up, I'll just take your damn head off and fuck the consequences."

"Enough."

Megan tensed at the low, guttural growl. The tension spiking through the air seemed to hit her harder than me. Her shoulders bowed forward, but then she jerked them back, pride glinting in her eyes. She shoved past me, jamming her elbow into my stomach.

I ignored it.

I didn't have time for her attitude.

I went back to my seat, settling down.

"I have some questions, starting with…just how do you *know* this woman is Pandora?" MacDonald's eyes, coppery gold, rested on my face.

"Because when I asked, she didn't lie." I met those eyes dead on. "And because I'm good at what I do. Very good. You should be aware of that after all this time."

Megan opened her mouth. MacDonald silenced her with a look. "Ms. Colbana, if she is who you claim, then I believe you. As you said, you are very good at what you do. What I want to know is this…why does it involve me? Or even any of us?"

There we go. Time to get down to it.

Alisdair just wanted the facts.

"Have you heard of the Blooding?"

None of them moved. None of them changed their expressions. But those words had an impact—I could feel it.

All the knowledge Es had crammed into my head had finally settled into place and I could pick through it, understand it. It made sense in an odd, awful sort of way.

MacDonald continued to watch me, but he hadn't said a damn thing.

"Well? Have you heard of it or not?" I asked. I damn well knew the answer.

"Who hasn't?" He gave me a condescending smile, one that was just a little too superior, a little too smug. It settled me, though. Odd how a smirk can make you feel a little more secure. Or maybe it's just me. "Naturally I know of the Blooding. I received the standard education fitting for the leader of my kind, after all."

You're a reject, Kit. We might not say it out loud in polite company—or around Damon—but you weren't good enough. I am. He didn't say those words. But I saw them echoed in the back of his eyes.

Trying to piss me off? I just stared at him. It would take more than a clever little potshot to do it.

The tension in the room was enough to choke me. It was going to get worse, I suspected.

"How many wolves were created during the Blooding?"

"Who knows? It was ages ago and the facts have been lost to—"

"Ballpark figure is two-hundred thousand in Europe and Asia alone," Damon said, his voice flinty and he gave MacDonald a look that said, *Say anything. I dare you.*

MacDonald's face turned to stone.

"That's just the figure for wolves." Chang sipped from his water. I looked over at him but he was also watching MacDonald. "Asia is almost equal, as far as cats and wolves go, but it's estimated perhaps one-hundred-fifty thousand cats were made. History says the shifters had to start spreading further out—migrating to Africa, Asia…even America."

Okay now *that* was interesting, but I didn't have time to mess with history lessons.

I watched MacDonald. "Do you know anything about the vamp population during that time?"

His lip curled. "Why ever would I care?"

There was no love lost between shifters and vamps. That was nothing new. Still, I suspected he did know the figure. He was a smart guy and smart people tended to cling to that old saw: *know your enemy.*

"I've heard the figure was pretty damn high. They say vampire numbers skyrocketed. If you increased by a few hundred thousand, I guess it's safe to say vampires increased by even more." I watched his eyes as I spoke, saw the minute tightening. Yeah, he knew the numbers, alright. "It's estimated that anywhere from seventy million to two hundred million humans could have died during the Black Plague. Of course with werewolves, you stand a better chance of surviving it if you're healthy. If you have a disease, your chances go from about five percent to maybe…what, *half* a percent, even less?"

"I'm not a statistician or a doctor, Ms. Colbana. I don't know."

I saw the knowledge burning in his eyes, though.

"You still added a hell of a lot of people." Leaning forward, I murmured, "Seventy-five million, MacDonald. If even one percent of that number had a chance at surviving the plague and one of your kind, or a vampire showed up in the night…? Panic must have been running high then. You think they made a million new vampires? Two million?"

"It was easily a million."

I slid Chang a look. He didn't look at me as he rose from the table. "Vampires all but decimated Europe during the Blooding," he said quietly, moving to stare outside. "Shifters keep an excellent written history, second only to the historians of the Green Road. We remember our enemies very well. The Black Plague wasn't solely responsible for all those deaths, Kit. It was vampires ravaging so much of Europe. But they didn't want the sickly people—those who would die. They wanted a healthier sort for their dungeons. For feeding, for sex. As the plague ravaged the mortal population, they looked to a healthier sort and started targeting weres. I believe the Order of Witches even has data about how their number decreased during those years."

I stared at him. "Witches would have been able to handle the plague better than mortals. Heal it themselves or be healed by their houses."

"The plague wasn't the predator," he said, looking at me, his liquid eyes full of ugly truths.

It was no wonder most of the world over hated vamps. "They hunted witches, then."

"I don't have factual references of that." He inclined his head. "But we do have a written history going back about our kind. Yes, our numbers increased…they had to, if we wanted to make a defense against the leeches who were trying to enslave any warm-blooded creature they could get their hands on."

"So it was forced on able-bodied mortals, then."

Chang stared at me. "I don't know how they were selected. But if somebody hadn't stood against the vampires who were killing thousands by the night, then they had to do something. The plague killed *millions*…but it's suspected that many deaths attributed to the plague were actually people who were killed by vampires. It was just more expedient to blame it on the plague rather than bloodsuckers."

"This is all very interesting."

Megan delivered that statement with complete sincerity. The smile on her pretty face was one hundred percent believable. And as I swung my head around to look at her, even though I didn't see it in her eyes, I knew exactly what she was thinking.

Just get this over with.

"But again, what does any of this have to do with Pandora…and what does *she* have to do with us?"

I shifted in my chair and debated just what I should say.

Not all that long ago, Es had told me to trust myself. Even thinking of her left a hollow emptiness in my heart. "Pandora took her last body during the Black Plague…and I think you guys got a power charge off it."

I had their attention now.

CHAPTER TWENTY-TWO

I didn't *quite* get around to telling them that they might be susceptible to whatever weird magics Pandora possessed.

I managed to fill them in on what Es had said happened when she took over a body and they somehow caught the leftover power—maybe it made it easier for the shifters to change sick people, for vampires to successfully bring more humans over, I don't know. The atmosphere in the room as I finished *that* explanation wasn't a cheery one.

And it would only get worse. But as I moved onto to tell them about Clara, the sweet, pretty, pregnant girl who was about to become a target—might already *be* a target—a roar echoed from somewhere off in the Lair.

A split second later, there was a cat's scream, defiant and enraged.

That might not have bothered me.

But I felt the prickle of magic and Damon was already climbing to his feet, a dark, angry look on his face.

Closing my eyes, I rubbed the spot between my brows and stood up, looking over at Damon. "Tell them to stand down."

A storm gathered in his gaze as he swung his head around to look at me.

"Tell them to stand down, Damon, or you're not going to like what he does," I said softly.

Justin wasn't close to us, not yet. I would have sensed him before now if he was, but I knew the man's magic.

When Damon didn't answer me, I said softly, "He will end up killing whoever gets in his way if they aren't very, very good, Damon. How many cats have you got that can stand up to high magic?"

There was another roar. It was deeper this time—a different were had attacked. The roar went on and on and on—and then, abruptly, it ended. I didn't like that.

Since he hadn't answered me, I decided to help him out. "You can do it. Chang could." I flicked a glance at Doyle. "In time, the kid can. Your enforcers and probably a handful of your more elite fighters can do it. But he'll cut through as many of them as he has to, just because he feels like it. What's the point?"

"If he needs to see me, he can make an appointment," Damon said, his voice flat.

"He's not here for you. He's here for me." I moved away from the table and grabbed my sword as I headed for the door. "I don't face high magic on my own. He's working with me."

I felt his shock, his fury. At the door, I paused and looked back at him. "Didn't you hear the word *partner* earlier? If I'm back in, I work the jobs with the tools I've got at my disposal. Justin's a damn good tool."

The ground under my feet trembled. Closing my hand around the door knob, I said, "And that tool just might make the place come down around your ears if you don't tell your people to stand down."

I wasn't surprised when they joined me.

Damon pushed in front of me and I read the rage in every part of his body. Oh, well.

I followed my gut, which usually didn't steer me wrong, yet somehow managed to get me in a lot of trouble. This time, it led me to the courtyard. It hadn't even been a year since I'd had my first confrontation with Damon in this very place. It looked different now and not just because Justin had thrown up a barrier ward. They'd done some decent landscaping and it looked lush and welcoming—not like a place only a queen would be allowed.

Not that it was terribly welcoming right now.

The barrier ward shimmered and I wondered if they could see it.

A cat came streaking out of the Lair and lunged for Justin.

He hit the ward, crashing into it with a whine low in his throat.

That answered my question.

"Tell Harry Potter if he fucks up my cats any more, I'm going to rip him apart," Damon said, his voice just barely above a growl. He crossed his arms over his chest and stood there, legs spread, menace all but pouring from him.

"I'm not your messenger girl, Damon."

Still holding my blade, I approached the ward, taking in the feel of it. Strong, yeah. Designed to stand against those who presented a threat. Okay. That left me wiggle room. I wasn't going to threaten Justin, and I wasn't a threat to the sleek little creature crouched across from him—she wasn't hurt. At all. Probably went in after the injured one and that was why the barrier hadn't hurt her. She was a delicate little thing. Judging by her coloring and body type, she looked like a serval. I'd seen a few of them before.

The serval opened her mouth and screamed at Justin but didn't move. I frowned as I noticed the big golden cat she was standing guard over.

His blood pooled around her feet.

I tapped the tip of my blade against the ward.

Justin didn't look at me.

"Heya, Kit." A wild, reckless grin split his face. Magic danced in the air and his dreads were drifting around him, caught in that field of energy. I wanted to tell him to suck it in, but that wasn't smart. Not here. Not now. "I have news for you. Just wanted to talk to you and these asses weren't letting me in the door."

"I see." I nodded and looked around the barrier. So far, the only injured party was the unconscious cat the female was guarding. "So what did you do?"

"Since they wouldn't let me through the door, I made my own."

Feeling the heat along my spine, I dodged forward. The ward didn't fight me. I felt it sting my flesh and that lasted about twenty seconds, but I tolerated it and glanced back at Damon in time to see him curl his hand into a fist, staring at me through the ward's glimmering presence. I suspected he could see some echo of it. Some shifters were more sensitive to magic than others. Damon was one of them. He didn't like it, but he could still pick up on it.

For a second, he just stared at me and then he laid a hand just above where the ward began. "It's going to hurt," I warned him.

Then I gave him my back.

Telling him not to try and muscle in would be a waste of breath.

The ward started to spark.

Justin's grin took on a meaner slant as he slid me a look. "I wasn't going to cause any problems, but they were in my way."

"Did it occur to you to call?"

"I did." He shrugged. A grim look entered his eyes as his gaze lingered on my face. "You didn't answer."

Then he looked away, but not before I caught an echo coming from him. A twist of nightmare and darkness—memories. I knew him too well not to understand. The last time he'd tried to call me and hadn't gotten a hold of me, I'd disappeared and he'd had to help track me across a continent. Swallowing, I looked away. This wasn't the time or place for either of us to have those sorts of bad moments.

Magic groaned, screamed and I shifted my attention upward, staring at the domed ceiling of the ward as it sparked again. There was an ominous little shriek, something jagged and biting, like claws drawing down metal.

I reached into my pocket for my phone only to stop as I realized I didn't have it with me. Well, hell. "I think I left it in the car."

"Yeah." Justin didn't look worried about the ward, but there was still a world of tension gathered inside him. If we didn't get him leveled out soon, somebody would get hurt. "You're out of practice, Kitty-kitty."

"Tell me about it." I eyed the two cats, the fallen one and the female serval standing guard over him.

"He's fine. Just a headache." Justin looked past my shoulder and that wicked light in his eyes made him look almost demonic. "Your boy over there is sweating a bit, Kit."

I looked back.

Damon was indeed sweating, a fine sheen of it breaking out along his forehead as he continued to push against the ward. "You think it's going to do you any good to have him break through? He doesn't want to come in and discuss the weather or the stock market. He's pissed—you hurt one of his cats."

"No."

Arching my brows, I swung my head back around and waited.

"I hurt *three* of them." Justin shrugged. "The other two are out on the grounds. Don't worry. They'll all be fine." He rolled his head back and forth, cracking his neck and I saw the shimmer of silver dancing over his sleeves as he readied the magic. "And I didn't hurt the little serval over there either. I just fucked up the ones who got my way."

"That's typical." This could get so ugly, so fast. "Will you behave, please?"

I had visions in my head of him wrapping all that silver around Damon—he could shred the flesh from a shifter's bones with that much. He and Damon might be a match in a fight, I didn't know. But I didn't want to see this.

"You take all the fun out of my life, Kit." Then he sighed. "As long as no more of them come gunning for me, I'm fine. I'm here on official business, after all."

I frowned and glanced at him. He smiled and tapped the badge he'd affixed to the pocket of his jeans.

Perfect.

He had his Assembly ID with him. He'd kept up his

investigator status—either that, or it was one hell of a forgery. Damon's people really hadn't had any excuse to deny him the right to speak with me. Maybe they didn't have to show him inside, but they could have used the phone.

And I could have mine with me, I thought sourly.

"Let the damn ward down."

He sighed. A split second later, my ears and my skin buzzed as he sucked all that magic back inside him.

The angry, crawling presence of a dozen shifters made my head ache. "He's on official business." I turned to face Damon, folding my arms over my chest and putting on the best bitch face I could muster. "Any reason why he was turned away when he asked to speak with me?"

"You going to hide behind that fucking budge?" Damon asked, his voice silky, his gaze locked on Justin.

"Nah." Justin tugged it off and tossed it in the air, spinning it with his magic. "I'd be happy to toss in the dirt and go a round with you. But…well. Priorities and shit."

Then he looked at me, his grass-green eyes glowing. "I got news on the vase, Kit."

"What?"

He leaned in, his voice low. It didn't matter. Everybody there would hear, even if he spoke in a whisper. "It was stolen by a couple of witches teamed up with a vampire house. Most of them are dead now." He glanced past me, his gaze landing on Damon for just a fraction of a second. "But the vase was in the possession of Samuel Allerton before he died. He had it in under lock and key. When he died, it passed to the next in line of his house. A vamp by the name Amadeus."

"Amadeus." Closing my eyes, I tried to focus on something other than the fact that I now had to contend with vampires, not just crazy ancient magic hell-beasts. "A vampire named Amadeus."

My gut cramped. Fear started to scream inside my head.

A hand, hard and brutal, closed around my arm. Dimly, as Justin's magic jolted through me, I heard deep, guttural growls coming from all around. Not from Damon, though.

He was silent as stone. I feel his gaze boring into us, although I didn't dare look at him.

"Maybe we'll find a Beethoven, too," I said, forcing the words out of my tight throat.

Justin stared at me. Then, because he probably knew I needed it, he said, "If ya want, we'll round up a whole damn symphony of them. They can play us a dirge while we fry their asses."

Damon's quarters seemed a hell of a lot smaller now.

Doyle persistently remained at my side, although he kept giving Justin the evil eye.

Justin ignored him. Sitting in the chair across from mine, he had his deck of cards out and he played one of his crazy games of Solitaire while he answered some of the same questions that I'd had to. Alisdair looked more worried with each passing minute.

Chang didn't look too happy.

Doyle stared at the cards like he was half-mesmerized.

And Damon looked like he wanted to start ripping Justin apart, piece by piece.

Yeah, that would be an easy feat.

"And what's *your* take on this…*Pandora*?" Alisdair said. He had a look in his eyes like he wanted Justin to say anything but what I'd said.

Justin shrugged and flipped the ace of spades into the air. It hung there, spinning around and around as he met Alisdair's eyes. "MacDonold, my take is that is she's crazy old, crazy powerful and she has more high magic in her than I've seen in a while. The last time I felt anything even *close* to her was when I had to help go after a two-thousand-year-old Druid."

The card slammed down, arrowing itself into place with unerring accuracy. Justin continued to look at Alisdair. "It took twenty witches to take him down…and he *wanted* to die."

"Enough," Damon said, knocking his knuckles on the table. "Pandora. Got it. Big problem. Let's move on. What else do we need to know?"

"What, other than the fact that if she snaps her fingers, you all might go and hump her leg?" Justin grinned. "I think that about covers it."

Silence dropped down like an anvil and for a second, nobody moved, nobody breathed. They all stared at Justin and then, one by one, their attention shifted to me.

"You couldn't have found a better way to put that, could you?" I said sourly.

Well, if nothing else, Justin had cut through to the heart of the matter.

She'll make you her furry little bitches, boys, whether you want it or not…oh, and she's going to go after one of your babies. Fun, right?

A manic glint had lit his eyes as he delivered that coup de grâce and after we'd managed to calm the sheer chaos down, everybody had leaped into action. Even Alisdair finally got on board.

Megan was rounding up all the females and trying to figure out who could or couldn't be pregnant. I didn't tell her that I already knew who the chosen target was, because if Pandora failed with Clara, she might try to find another one. Getting them all safe would be ideal.

Alisdair had called his warriors into action and anybody who had experience with high magic was being put on alert. Some had a natural affinity for resisting high magic—Damon was one of them. It was how he had managed to kill the witches months ago, and anybody else who had those abilities would be the ones best equipped to face off with a crazy ancient bitch.

They hoped.

My gut said they were right.

But my gut also said it wouldn't be enough.

She'd cut them all down if they got in her way and she

wouldn't bat an eyelash. Why would she? She lacked the empathy, I suspected to feel anything if she killed one of them, or a dozen,or a hundred. The entire clan wouldn't even bother her.

She could just create more.

The only thing that would affect her would be if she couldn't find her next host.

What we needed to do was protect that baby. Keep the baby alive. Keep Clara away from Pandora.

That was the goal.

Why not kill the girl?

That voice murmured in the back of my mind and sent a shiver down my spine. Cool, cold and practical.

I had no idea where that thought had come from, but *no.*

The cats could protect Clara for the short term. Long term, get Clara to Green Road and let them figure out the best option. They'd handled Pandora once, maybe they could figure out the best route if I failed.

When I failed.

Not that I'd include that bit when I told Damon. I'd just suggest that Clara might be best protected by people who could hide who and what she was. I had to head out, but before I did, I needed to pass that info on to Damon first—I already knew he'd follow me out to my car. I'd give him the info, get out of here and get my gear. Meet up with Justin.

And get ready to get my ass kicked.

Probably killed.

But there was no way I was going to kill some poor girl just because she had the bad luck to be born with the wrong blood.

I knew what that was like.

Heading out, I tried to ignore the weight that rested on my shoulders. And Damon's dark, brooding presence, hot at my back.

"Is he serious?"

I met Damon's eyes over the roof of my car.

"I think so."

A muscle pulsed in his jaw. "So…she can, what? Control us? Enslave us?"

"You're asking me questions I can't answer."

"Try." His voice was rigid.

Justin had left twenty minutes earlier, out to round up some *unsavory types*, as he'd called them. I suspected he was reaching out to various Banner contacts and independents. I had no idea how deep his network went now, but I suspected it was pretty extensive.

Edgy tension came off Damon in waves. I'd thought he might settle once Justin had left. Clearly, I was expecting too much. I opened the door and blew out a breath, trying to think through what to say.

There was still a *lot* to say. And oddly, only half of it related to Pandora. That was all we had time for, though.

Tucking my sword behind the seat, I thought through this possible explanation, that possible scenario…

"You realize that I don't *know* what I'm talking about, right?" I finally said, turning to look at him.

Dark turbulent eyes met mine.

"You never seem to know, and you always end up almost right on target." He crossed his arms over his chest. The muscles under his shirt bulged and the tattoos on his right arm, just barely visible under the sleeve, caught my eye. Memories of the times I'd stroked my fingers across those thick, dark lines of ink rolled through my mind…along with so many others.

I pushed it all aside.

"You familiar with the coercion spells some of the independents use?" I asked him, dragging my attention away from the mesmerizing lines and swirls of those tattoos.

A black brow rose and then he shrugged. "More or less. I've seen them in action, had a few try to use them on me. They didn't take."

"Not surprising. Success of those spells is dependent on a number of factors…but namely your strength against the strength of the witch. A witch of Es's caliber could have a chance."

I saw the flicker of doubt in his eyes, but I didn't say anything. I was good at gauging a person's strength. My life had too often depended on it, and it went deeper than that anyway. It was just part of what I was.

"A lot of independents aren't that strong," I said.

"Is your boy?"

My boy. I huffed out a breath and leaned back against the car. "Damon, I told you months ago that Justin and I used to have something. Then we didn't. That hasn't changed. So just shelve the…whatever."

His stony face didn't change. At all. He jerked a shoulder in a shrug. "It's not like it's any of my business, right?"

"No." Why did it seem like the bite marks on my neck, my wrist, were *burning*? I resisted, just barely, the urge to reach up and rub the one on my neck. Damon's eyes all but burned into mine and I think we both knew we weren't being entirely truthful. I couldn't get involved with another man…not when I was still hung on him. It just wasn't in me. And the bastard knew it.

I'll be waiting…

I glared at him. "Just shelve it, okay?"

"Shelving it."

He didn't even move and the air, the space between us had shrunk down to nothing.

I needed to think about something else, *anything* else but what was in my head just then. I needed something else *in* my head but him. Tearing my gaze away, I focused on the looming monolith of the Lair at his back. "If Justin decided to pull a coercion spell on you, he might be able to do it. You might be able to break it. The two of you would probably end up killing each other. So keep having those happy, bloody thoughts, Damon." I flicked my bangs out of my eyes and tried not to tense when he came around the car, closing the distance between us to just a few inches. It might have been two inches. Three. But it was too close.

I could feel the heat of him, so close, so enticing. Some

part of me wanted to just bury myself against him and stay there. Forever. Instead, I shrugged and tried to feign nonchalance. "Don't go getting a hard-on about the idea or anything. Justin doesn't use coercion spells. It goes against his…sense of fair play. He'd kill a person without blinking but he doesn't use unnatural magics."

"Unnatural…" Damon's voice was a low growl.

I shot him a look.

"What the fuck is an unnatural magic? It's all unnatural."

"No." I shook my head. "It's not. Especially for a witch. *Unnatural* magics require pulling up dark powers and dark shit and darkness you don't want to think about. The darker witches would have Annette look like a sweet little dream and the more you cross those lines, the blurrier they get…and one day, you don't realize it, but you're one of those darker witches…somebody who would suck the soul from your mother, your father, your brother, your sister, your child…all to power up your spell, because it needed a strong life force…and they had the strongest around. There are lines with magic that just can't be crossed. Justin knows those lines…and he stays away. He'll break every line anybody else might draw…but the laws of magic, he'll respect those, and he'll hunt down the people who go over it. He's a good man for me to have at my back."

Read between the lines: I need him right now. Leave it alone.

Damon reached up. I held still as he brushed his hand down my hair. "Why do I get the feeling that you are trying to tell me something?"

"Because I am."

Some of the tension faded away and a ghost of a smile tugged at his lips. "I'm not ever going to like the man, kitten. Deal with it. But he was the one who helped Doyle key in on where you were. That's one thing I won't *ever* forget." His gaze held mine and unspoken words passed between us. My heart slammed hard against my ribs as he cupped my cheek and pressed his thumb against my lip. "He was the one who realized something was wrong. I won't forget *that* either."

Then his hand fell away and he shifted his attention to

stare off past my shoulder. "If he's the man who's going to protect your back in this, I'm not going to fuck with him, either. Now…about the bigger problem…"

I swallowed the knot in my throat and wished I could compartmentalize the way he seemed to do. He didn't brush it off, but he had a way of focusing on the things that needed to be done. The bigger problem. Yeah, let's think about that.

That problem that was likely going to turn me into a messy smear on the pavement once she realized I wasn't going to turn the damn vase over to her. Once she figured out that I planned on giving the damn thing to the witches and seeing if they couldn't do a Hail Mary or whatever that stupid thing was called.

"So, the control thing…" Damon said, a pulse pulsing in his cheek.

I made a mental note. Want to see him tighten up real fast? Mention anything related to an ancient uber-bitch having control over him.

"If I had to hazard a guess, I'd say it would be like one of the coercion spells, but without the spell. If you are her original creation, that means problems for you." I studied his face. "It's one of the basic laws of magic. Do you get that?"

"In theory. Dunno if I agree with the entire thing." He jerked one shoulder in a shrug. "I assume you're leading into the parental law of magic—sadly, that's one of the laws I do think is probably true. We're magical creatures whether we like it or not. Magic follows certain rules and one of them is that fucked-up parental mess. Most of us feel bound—or *are* bound to—those who made us. It's why younger vamps can't leave their masters until they reach a certain level of power—or unless the master dies. Why the lesser were always submits to the stronger." A sneer twisted his lips. "Why in our world, might still makes right and fuck those who get screwed by it."

"Well. Yeah. That's it, in theory…and in a nutshell."

He'd summarized it in a few sentences. Witches studied the laws of magic, including the parental law. And he broke it down to the nuts and bolts. "If she's your creator, the parental law will probably come into play. But success, like most magics, depends on any number of factors—with this, I'd imagine it depends on her will, her target's will and her…state of health."

His brows ratcheted up. "Her state of health."

"Injury always throws a practitioner off. If she's weakened or tired…age could play into it, but she's an ancient. I don't know if age slows her down." If she could be injured, she could be killed. If it bled, it died. I wanted to see if I could make her bleed. If she could…that changed the playing field. A lot.

But the vase first.

"You think the more dominant weres can throw her off?"

Coercion and compulsory spells could be overthrown, if the target had it in him. It was physically and mentally painful, but they could still do it. That wasn't the big problem, though.

I blew out a breath and leaned back against the car, staring at him. I had to make him see. "Whether or not they can isn't the point," I said, watching as his eyes narrowed on my face. "Dominants are outnumbered…what, three to one?"

"Doesn't matter." His gray eyes held mine.

So much confidence. So much strength. Normally, I admired that. I'd love to be able to walk through the world and know so little fear, to know that I had the strength to take down not just *anything*, but a *number* of anythings. I fought and clawed for every damn step I took, it seemed like. Even getting out bed anymore.

But that confidence didn't serve him now.

"Damon, if she can throw them in your way like fodder, it matters."

A muscle jerked in his jaw and understanding dawned in his eyes.

"That's going to be one of your big problems, Damon…her turning your own people against you. And…" I rubbed the spot between my eyes as a headache started to pulse. "Clara."

I could practically feel his confusion.

From under my lashes, I watched him.

"Clara." He shook his head and then, just like that, I saw the knowledge flood his eyes. "She's the one, isn't she?"

"That's what my gut says," I told him. "I didn't want to say anything around MacDonald or any of the others. People are going to panic—"

It's not panic, child. Kill the girl and you take away her options. It's wise thinking…

I squeezed my eyes shut as that voice echoed somewhere deep in the back of my head. Maybe I'd lost my mind for real up on that mountain. Clearing my throat, too aware of him watching me, I forced myself to go on. "They'll panic and think the right choice is to just kill the girl, and her baby."

His eyes were hard as stone. I couldn't figure out a single thing he was thinking.

"She may not be the only one. And you can't let your cats just randomly start slaughtering any pregnant female you come across."

"Anybody who touches her is going to have to go through me," he said, his voice soft.

I swallowed and looked away. "I can't tell you how to protect her. Once she put herself in your hands, she became one of yours and I know that. But the best course of action is to gather up a few of your enforcers, the ones you trust the most, and have them escort her to Green Road. Immediately."

The need to refuse was strong. I could see it burning in his eyes. Instead of saying it outright, though, he turned away, hands braced on his hips, head bowed. "Why? I can protect my people, Kit."

The silence that fell between us was awkward. Awkward and ugly and when he turned back to me, the look on his face was one of…I can't even describe it. He looked like he wanted to just gut himself. "Fuck." It came out of him in an explosive rush. "I guess we know that's a fucking lie, don't we?"

"I'm not one of your people, Damon," I said softly.

"But you were mine…and I failed you."

This time, it was my turn to look away. "It was up to me to protect myself." My throat felt raw and the awful, terrible void in my chest grew larger and larger. "Hell, how many times did I *tell* you to let me have my space?"

Odd…I hadn't thought of that until now. I had been so angry at him—still was. I was just angry in general, but what good did it do? "We couldn't have seen it coming, you know. And if he didn't come after me that night, he would have tried some other night. If we're going to sit around being pissed, being angry, throwing blame, let's throw it where it belongs…at his feet."

I shoved off the car and went to climb in.

"You know I'm already trying to figure out the best way to kill him when he comes out of that box."

Those words, so calmly, flatly spoken made me smile a little. Shooting Damon a look, I shrugged. "I've been trying to figure out the best way to kill him while he's still inside it."

It almost felt good to smile. Too bad I couldn't enjoy it.

"I need to go," I said softly, as the weight on my shoulders pushed down harder, heavier.

"Before you do…" Damon's words came slow, drawing my gaze back to him. "I don't have any right to ask, but I'm doing it anyway."

He wasn't looking at me.

I angled my head and watched as Doyle came striding toward us.

Damon said, "Take the kid."

"What? No. Hell, no. She's going to target on me anyway—"

"Kit. Please."

Well, so much for that nice, warm-and-fuzzy moment I'd thought we'd almost had. Gaping at him, I demanded, "Do you not *hear* me?"

"He asked." Damon took a step toward me, his voice low, all but pulsing with intensity. "He doesn't ask for shit, but he came to me and told me the same damn thing he told me months ago, when you went missing…he said you were going to need him on this. He told me that then and I didn't listen—I was too busy trying to *find* you and he already knew where to start looking. He's the reason we found you and if his gut is telling him that you'll need him, then I'm *not* going to ignore that." He paused and then shook his head. "Not now. Never again, Kit."

CHAPTER TWENTY-THREE

Doyle waited in my living room.

In a very short amount of time, I was going to have to pull out all the stops and do something I hadn't done in ages—breaking and entering, *aneira* style, but instead of focusing on that, I was thinking about Doyle.

The teenaged shapeshifting tiger who was prowling my living room, waiting for me to take him with me while I went all B&E.

I was so pissed I couldn't see straight.

What really bothered me was the fact that my gut said he wasn't going to cause problems.

If I thought he was, I'd find a way to get rid of him. Probably via Justin. Justin knew how to deal with that sort of thing. Temporary fixes, permanent fixes, fixes that wouldn't leave any lasting damage and fixes that weren't really fixes at all.

But I didn't think that was the answer here and the more I steamed, the more my gut told me everything was *fine*.

That just made me madder.

So I made myself stop brooding and locked myself in my room, muscling my bed out of the way.

There were…tools…in here.

Tools. Yeah. Right.

Objects of death and destruction. Cursed weapons,

magicked weapons, some of them were items I *never* should have taken into my possession but once I'd found them…well, leaving any weapon lying in the blood and dirt and gore was a bad idea, but relics? Really stupid.

So, tools.

They were protected by spells and charms and if you didn't know *exactly* where to look for them, you weren't going to find them. Even if you did know where to look, you wouldn't want them. I avoided them at all cost when I was here. As long as I didn't actively seek them out, the spells left me alone, but if I went looking…well. That was when the magic kicked in.

The beauty of the spells. They made the eye not want to see. The spells were made to allow me to touch them, sleep above them, but now as I sought them out, the spells kicked in.

All it took was sinking to my knees and already I wanted to look away…that's how strong they were. It was different on somebody unaware of the spells—they'd just feel inclined to avoid that area of my room, but really, how often did a person go investigating the floorboards under somebody else's bed?

A headache hammered behind my eyes and it only got stronger as I found the tiny little area and pressed. After a few seconds, the specialized lock acknowledged my fingerprint and DNA and then slid out of place with a whisper. The spell screamed louder in my head and I gritted my teeth and I reached down and pressed my hand to its key.

Most of the spells in my home were inactive until I needed them.

The ones protecting these weapons weren't and this son-of-a-bitch here was the spell's focus.

It fed from the magic in the weapons and the weapons were nuclear bomb-type strong so it wasn't going to hurt them.

At my touch, the focus 'unlocked' the spell.

I'd have to have Justin rig it back up for me. This sort of magic was out of Colleen's area of practice and these weapons weren't the kind you could leave unguarded.

The bow lay on top. When I reached out to touch her, the power inside her all but singed my hand. I heard no music, but I'd stopped expecting to hear any, so that was fine.

This music was better off unheard.

She sang of blood spilt, tears wept and death met.

I didn't need that in my head.

Like the other weapons stored in here, she was made for a purpose…filled with magic and raw with it. There were other warrior races out there—like mine—but some of them were gifted with the blade and with the ability to wield magics in a manner similar to witches. Most of them were Druids…and most of the Druids were gone from the world now.

It made me wonder, for a minute, if we'd been created to hunt vamps and shifters, why were the Druids created? Did anybody know? Were they just one of the offshoots? Some sort of mutation? I'd always assumed everybody had always *been* here.

Now I had to wonder.

Now there was no time for it.

The bow had been crafted by a Druid, a man dead for centuries, but his magic lingered on in this. Made from ash and so full of magic she made my teeth hurt, I practiced with her enough to keep my skills up and that was it. She had specially forged arrows, each of them tipped with silver and the arrows themselves were as wide as they could be and still be accurate. Miniature spears, to be accurate. They were also spelled…spelled to fly straight, and true. It was practically cheating, but sometimes, you needed the leg up.

I pulled the bow out, the arrows and laid them to the side.

There were various blades, some spelled, others poisoned. The poisoned ones weren't going to do me much good…there were only a few poisons that were effective against a vamp and all of them had to be ingested to work. The bad part was that in order for them work, one almost had to take enough to make their own blood toxic. I'd take that chance if I ever thought I'd come up against Jude again.

But for this?

I don't know.

Still, I reached for a small pouch tucked off to the side.

I'd do a lot of things, but I wouldn't become a vampire's prisoner. Not again. I'd die first.

I did take a few of the charmed blades. Some of them had spells laid on them that would render just about *anybody* useless for a short period of time. Nasty pieces of work, but sometimes you had to fight dirty to stay alive. I'd learned that lesson the hard way and I had no problem with dirty.

At the bottom of my treasure trove, the mother lode awaited.

Of all the weapons, he was the deadliest.

When I touched him, my arm went numb. That was how much magic he carried.

He had no song, but then again, he never had. His touch was a chilly one and the first time I'd used him to kill a vampire, I'd heard a sibilant whisper in the back of my head. Then…nightmares. They lasted for days. But he was an excellent tool for killing vampires.

I didn't put much stock in named weapons—most of the people who bothered to weren't the actual creators and the only time a weapon's name actually carried much weight was when the creator had bestowed it. But this weapon's name carried weight.

His name was Death.

And I didn't like him.

He was more…*alive* than most of my weapons and that's saying something. All of the weapons I owned had some sort presence, for lack of a better word. They might not be sentient in a way others would recognize, but they spoke to me.

This son-of-a-bitch didn't speak *only* to me.

He spoke to anybody with a lick of magical talent and nobody liked what he had to say.

But…again, he was good at what he did.

It was like he had a built-in homing spell and he could

zero in on a vampire.

And when I carried him, it made it that much easier for me to do the same. I was already fast, but thanks to the spells laid on this blade, I moved faster—like I had the wind at my back…nearly as fast a vampire. Other weird things happened when I carried that blade and not just the odd, distant whispers that I heard every time I killed a vampire with him.

Sometimes I think the maker of the blade lived on inside the length of steel.

I didn't like the feeling.

I didn't like how I felt when I carried that sword, didn't like the way vengeance and chaos and death seemed to drive every single thing I did.

But the weapon served a purpose.

He killed vampires, and he killed them well.

If I was going to creep into a vampire's stronghold with just Justin, a teenaged tiger and a few witches, I wanted every tool I had at my disposal. Including that cursed sword.

When I strode out of my bedroom, Doyle's eyes shot straight over my shoulder to the blades—no…the dark one.

To Death.

"What the hell is that thing?" His eyes were narrow and his voice was full of caution.

I'd felt the same way when I'd first laid eyes on it.

I *still* felt that way.

Doyle flinched and pressed the heel of his hand to his head but I felt the warning prickle against my shields. Justin.

"Justin," I said.

Doyle just continued to stare at me, his pale blue eyes burning. I had the feeling he wanted to put distance between himself and the blade. A lot of it. Didn't blame him. I'd had to force myself to use the motherfucker the first few times I'd thought I'd need him.

I'd needed him.

So I was probably going to need him now.

Didn't mean I had to like it.

And I didn't blame Doyle's obvious dislike.

It was weird how sensitive he was to the magic, though. Most people aside from witches, though, just felt uncomfortable around Death. They didn't look like they wanted to take off and run. If Doyle had been in his tiger form, his fur would have been standing on end and he would have been growling.

I was at the door before Justin knocked and his gaze immediately dropped to the dark sword. A line appeared between his brows. "I hate that blade," he said.

The weight of him seemed to grow heavier. "I don't like him, either."

Then I shrugged and glanced past him to the witches he'd rounded up.

Only three others? That was it?

And one of them, to my surprise…and concern, was Tate.

I managed to conceal my shock, but I don't know if I quite hid the irritation as she gave me a sly smile.

"Hello, dolly."

I thought about pulling out Death and jabbing her with him. She thought she'd been surprised to discover the enchantments on *my* blade? That was nothing compared to the magic inside of Death. He was another one of those ancient relics—the kind that you either just didn't want to mess with, or that you wanted to keep out of the wrong hands. I'd had the choice of leaving him where some fucked up individuals could find him or taking him on myself.

Sometimes the wisest choice was just the only logical one out of bunch of lousy ones.

Just then, though, I thought it might be amusing to draw him and see what Tate said about the little human dolly who carried a sword that had been reputedly forged by godlike beings, a blade that carried the stain of death in his steel.

It was a thought I wouldn't have had a few months ago. Maybe even a few days, a few minutes ago. I wouldn't have wasted much time on it, except my hand all but itched, all but burned to do just that.

Turning away, I crossed the room so none of them could see me.

I'd had no doubt in my mind that Jude had broken me. In that moment, though, I worried if maybe he had done something even worse.

"You okay?"

I'd lost track of how long I stood in front of the sink, hands on the counter while I stared at nothing. It couldn't have been more than a few minutes, but it was a few too long.

Slowly, I lifted my gaze and stared at Justin. "Right as rain." I rolled that phrase over in my mind. "You ever wondered what that means?"

I went to turn and move away but before I could, he caught my arm. "Is it the blade? Or something else?"

This isn't the time, I tried to tell him with just a look.

We hadn't worked together in years, but in a room full of witches and a shapeshifter with very sharp ears, I didn't want to discuss it or try to project it to him, either.

That line remained between his eyebrows but he just watched me for a minute and then moved away.

He looked over at Doyle, his mouth compressed. "What's with the cat? Thought we'd decided it was us handling this end."

"I need to be there," Doyle said from the other room before I had a chance to respond.

Justin's brows arched as Doyle came prowling into the kitchen. "Oh?" He drew it out, long and slow. Then he leaned back against the counter and crossed his arms over his chest. "Tell me. Please. I'm all ears."

Doyle flashed him a toothy smile. "I don't need to tell you shit, witch. I'm going. Try to stop me and I'll just track you."

Justin lifted an arm and silver released from his sleeves,

spinning in dizzying threads around it. "What if I decide that's not in our best interests, cat?"

"Enough." I caught the silver in my hand, ignoring the jolt of magic that shot up my arm. Damn. If that silver ever touched shifter flesh, they'd be in a world of hurt, and not just from the silver. He'd laid some ugly spells in the metal. Catching Justin's eyes, I stared at him. "The kid wants to go. If my gut said it was a stupid idea, I would have argued and Damon would have listened to me. Since he's here, you know that's not the issue. Are you going to push this?"

Justin's gaze dropped to my face, studying me closely.

I heard somebody grumbling in the other room—quietly, but the sentiment was clear enough.

Tate didn't bother being subtle. She came storming into the small kitchen, full of attitude and temper, her eyes glinting. "What is this? We're fucking around with the *ultimate* queen of the jungle, so to speak and you want to let Beast Boy come along? That's insane."

I shot Tate a dark look. "Not your call. You don't want to come along, you can go play elsewhere. Otherwise? Shove it."

"Look, maybe you like playing with furries, and maybe you don't worry about them turning on you, but—"

I had him in my hand.

He didn't come to my call, but I never would have called Death.

But I drew him, just that fast and now he was pressed to her neck and I stared at the dull gray tip of the sword touching her flesh.

The reaction was instantaneous. Her skin went white and I felt the shock reverberate through her even as her magic reacted, the heat in the room jacking up. The room didn't go up in flames—that was probably thanks to the wards laid on my home by Colleen and Justin—but I could *feel* the heat and the pressure on the wards grew, slamming into me. They were connected to me and the more *they* felt, the more I was going to feel.

"Enough," I told her.

She stared at the blade, shocked into momentary silence. Then: "Anybody carrying a blade like that must have a death wish…what is that thing?"

I smiled a little, a joke between me and the blade.

"Death," I said, amused. Then I looked into her golden eyes, saw the flames dancing there. "I'm tired, Tate. I'm tired of you. I'm tired of everything. I want this job done. If you don't want to go along and see about getting your pound of flesh for what was done to Es, then the door is there. But you can't *do* this without me…and I don't care if you go along or not. So either shut up. Or get out of my way."

Doyle rode with Justin and me.

He was a quiet, hot presence in the back seat. Once we were on the road, he stripped out of his jacket and unrolled a supple length of cloth.

I heard the familiar hiss and scrape as he started to sharpen blades.

Justin's eyes widened, betraying his surprise.

If I hadn't already noticed Doyle's fascination with weapons, I might have asked him about it.

A tiger that carried around throwing daggers.

Weird, that.

But some people just liked shiny objects. I was one of them. Who was I to question what gave Doyle's mind that much needed focus and calm?

The drive to Allerton's house would have taken close to an hour, but we couldn't drive straight there.

We would have to leave our cars some distance off and move the rest of the way on foot.

Under normal circumstances, I'd rather take a few days and plan this out, map out a nice, neat little plan of attack.

We didn't have time.

I could all but hear the countdown in the back of my head, see the flashing of the clock as the hours and minutes ticked away. We had hours. Maybe even a day.

But *days*…no. My gut said the time was now. The *only* time. Pandora was ready to make her move. Maybe she even had a way to key in on me and Justin and once *we* had figured out who had the vase, she would zero in on the target, too.

We had to move now and I had to figure out my next step.

I couldn't do that until I had the vase in my hands.

Destroy the vase. Cut off her path of retreat, a calm voice murmured in the back of my head. *Cut off her source of power. While she is a state of panic, make your move.*

Eminently practical.

Except for the whole *cut off her source of power.*

Because her source of power came from the weres. If she got her hands on Clara, she'd get a new body, and a whole new power source in the form of a baby.

Already handled that. Damon had sent me a message earlier—Green Road had taken in both Clara and Marcus, and they were under wraps. Damon wouldn't give me any more than that, although he did tell me he was now short four of his enforcers.

So…source of power, check.

Well done, Kitasa…now focus on her path of retreat.

I tensed. What the ever-loving hell…?

CHAPTER TWENTY-FOUR

Night wrapped around us, a cool, welcome kiss against my flesh. I wanted to take a blade and use it to carve that voice out of my head, except I sort of needed my brain.

That…echo…or whatever I thought I'd heard hadn't come back. I was alone in my head, left alone to think, brood…panic. There had been moments up in the mountains, when I'd been trapped…I'd heard voices. Insanity had been a sweet dream for a while, then just another torment as delirium seemed to hover out of reach, but never consume me.

I didn't want those voices coming back.

I didn't want to lose myself again.

Not now. Just one of many things that would have to wait.

I'd dressed in close-fitting garb designed to hide my pale skin from the light, mask my scent. I couldn't completely cover all sight, all traces of myself, but I had tricks up my sleeves. There was a thick, magic-based ointment that I'd slathered over my skin on the walk in and it had faded enough to not stand out.

Three miles earlier, I'd told Doyle to let me get in front: *Five minutes,* I'd told him. *Then try to scent track me.*

It had taken him another full five minutes to find me once I'd left the path.

His sense of smell was keener than a vampire's, as long

as I didn't bleed. I didn't plan on bleeding today.

The salve once it was absorbed by my skin was just a sort of olfactory chameleon. It worked with my body chemistry and the environment…and magic, of course, and let me blend my smell with everything around me. The spell wouldn't last more than eight hours, but if I was in the Allerton compound longer than that, I wouldn't need the spell. I'd need the little bag I'd grabbed from the floorboards under my bed. The little poison pill.

None of the witches would use the salve, but I figured they had their own ways of blending in.

The stuff made the skin burn and itch, a side effect of the magic—*all magic comes with a price*!—but it wasn't anything I couldn't handle.

Doyle moved along at my side, cover from neck to foot in black. His hair, pale as mine, was covered under a skull cap. I approved. I offered him the salve, but he wasn't interested.

I didn't blame him—it made my nose and senses burn like hell and would be doubly hard on him. Hopefully, the kid could handle it if a bunch of vamps came after his ass.

He was a dominant shifter and fast as hell, but even Damon could go down if you threw enough vamps at him. Doyle wasn't Damon.

He was just a kid.

"My intel says that Amadeus is out attending the opera tonight," Justin said, his voice low as we skirted around the house. "Skeletal staff on hand. His stable of humans—thirty of them. He has a bigger group than that, but he takes half of his women with him whenever he travels. I can knock the remaining humans out without hurting them. Vamps on patrol, ten. More inside—feels like about another twenty. Varying ranges of power."

I drew Death.

Justin gave it a narrow look.

"Who does he have on the outside?"

Justin squinted, assessing. He wasn't looking with his eyes. Justin had an affinity for sensing an enemy, rather like I did, but his was more acute and he ramped it up with magic. "Fodder mostly."

Stupid. Always good to have at least a few good men on the outside. The weak ones might do a good job at slowing us down, but it didn't last long and with the right group, they could go down in no time.

Justin knew how to put the right group together.

"I take it he's not expecting company."

Justin flashed a grin. "Now, Kit…I'm not *that* out of practice."

He glanced at Tate.

She moved to the front.

Hell opened up.

CHAPTER TWENTY-FIVE

Getting inside the compound wasn't hard. I don't know if Amadeus was stupid or just arrogant, but when Justin said *fodder*, he was almost being kind. Damn near everybody on the outside had less than a few decades on them, and very few functioning brain cells, apparently.

Tate had most of them down, caught in the web of her fire and they died in moments.

Vampires didn't really grow into their full strength until they saw at least a couple of centuries. Even the babies—those dead a few days—could make mincemeat out of humans, but if they wanted to do any real damage to other vampires or shapeshifters, or have any chance against a warrior witch, they needed to see a century or so pass. None of these would ever have the chance. I couldn't even feel bad about it.

Closer to the house, I could sense the stronger ones and my skin crawled, my instincts screaming with the urge to run.

They'd retreated into the house and I could feel the chill of their anger dancing in the air. We'd have to go in there. I didn't want to.

Justin had done his homework and he'd planned *damn* well for this. The second witch, Paddy—a man I vaguely knew from some other jobs—moved to stand next to me and I felt the cool kiss of his power against my flesh as he readied himself. "You and your furry friend need to get ready, Kit." Paddy flashed me a smile.

I sank to the ground. "Doyle. Get down."

A windstorm kicked up as Doyle hunkered down next to me. Paddy's magic always made me think of rolling, green hills and stormy oceans. Right now, those rolling, green hills were being battered by an unseen wind and it slammed between Justin and Paddy, the two men protected by their magic. Tate stood a little farther away and I saw her clothes flapping around her, but she must have shielded herself against it as well, because that wind had the strength of an F-5 tornado behind it.

A focused F-5 tornado—and it slammed into the front wall of the Allerton compound, turning into nothing but rubble.

I slid Justin a look. *I hope you know where in the hell that vase is.*

He wasn't looking at me, but he had a knowing grin on his face.

Although, really, would it be so bad if the damn thing was smashed into smithereens?

I just didn't know.

But that was just one of those bridges I'd cross when I came to it. First, we had to find it.

I went to rise but before I straightened up, Doyle yanked me down. A bent, twisted piece of metal came flying my way, moving faster than my eyes could track. A vampire lunged at me, his jaw elongated, mouth open and fangs extended. As I twisted out of the way, panic and adrenaline clashed through my veins.

A monster exploded from Doyle's skin in the span of seconds—a bizarre looking creature, caught between a man and giant cat, his pelt orange and sliced with black stripes.

The cold, cloying stink of vampire blood filled the air as Doyle decided to remove the vampire's head.

Expedient.

More of them flowed out of the house—I counted five as I pulled my swords, Death in one hand, the leaf blade from

Damon in the other. I scented metal and magic on the air, over the stink of vamp blood. Panic continued to sing inside me. Next to me, silver flashed through the night.

"Kit."

That was all Justin said, but I heard the warning.

If I panicked here, we were screwed.

I was screwed.

Yeah. I know that. I got that. Still, the metallic taste of fear threatened to choke me.

Couldn't fail…

I will not falter.

I will not fail.

I wanted my other blade. I settled for gripping the other two tighter as I squared my shoulders. Fuck this. Fuck it all to hell and back. I could do this. I'd faced this and worse, and lived to tell about it.

From the corner of my eye, I saw one coming at me and I pivoted to face him. Instinct took over and Death drove into his heart.

The dark, awful magic of the blade took over and I heard his voice, that ugly, malevolent whisper in the back of my mind where all I wanted to hear was music. The song of my weapons. I'd rather have heard nothing.

Yes…give me more…

And he laughed as I yanked my blade back and swung, taking the stunned, weakened vampire's head.

Of course I'd give him more.

He stole the fight out of any foe I faced.

How could I not *use* him?

The pulverized thing under my feet had once been a vampire. As I crossed over, dully aware of the silver unwrapping from its body, I extended my senses.

"They aren't all dead."

"Be quiet," Tate hissed.

I stared at her, the alien presence in my head strong,

stronger than I liked. He didn't like Tate much, either…but he made me think about reaching out and bringing the flat of my blade down across her head. Just to see the shock in her eyes before she went down.

A hand closed around my wrist.

Magic sparked up my arm.

I jerked away but before I could do anything more, Justin caught my face in his hands.

Dimly, I heard a tiger growl. The sword thought maybe it would be fun to…

No.

"Damn right, no," Justin said, his green eyes glowing as he stared at me. "Kit, look at me. Focus."

"We need to find the vase," I said.

Find me more…

Why was this happening?

In the silence of my mind, his alien voice seemed so very, very loud.

"We'll find the fucking vase." Justin squeezed, his hands tangling in my hair. "But you have to push him *back*."

Push him…

Find me more—

With a scream, I tore away from Justin and flung the blade down. I stared at the dark, ugly metal of the blade for a long moment and then shot Justin a glance.

"His call is stronger. What the hell?"

A look of distaste rolled across Justin features and I felt the ripple of his magic as he extended out. "He senses something is off. He's pushing, trying your limits. You can't let him in."

I *knew* that. Eying the sword, I rubbed my hand against the leg of my pants and braced myself. I didn't want to pick him up.

If I could, I would have left him lying there, but that wasn't an option. Like the vase, he was a relic and you didn't leave relics of power lying around. Breathing out through my teeth, I grabbed him and sheathed him, ignoring the ugly, insidious whispers in the back of my head. The prickling heat of shifter energy rolled across my skin and I looked up, saw Doyle staring at me. I reached down and grabbed the knife belt he'd lost when he shifted.

"If you're going to carry blades, you need to find a way to do it so you can carry them while you shift," I said, hurling the belt at him.

He caught it, still staring at me with worried eyes.

And to think, they'd all been worried about *Doyle*.

I kept the leaf blade in my hand.

Encased in the muffling, enchanted leather of his sheath, Death couldn't talk to me now. Or bewitch me or whatever in the hell he was trying to do. Possess me, maybe.

Utter devastation surrounded us, but the farther we got from the wall Paddy had taken out, the clearer our path became.

It was still quiet, though.

Too quiet.

I could feel the crawl of their presence.

All over me.

I knew they were there.

We'd killed a lot of them, but not all. And the ones that remained were the strongest.

I could all but feel them…

And something else.

Something alien and cold. I heard it in the back of my head, in my ears…in my *gut*.

As we moved deeper into the house, whatever it was, the call of it grew louder.

The good news, the louder *that* call became, the weaker Death's got.

The bad news…this alien presence wasn't any better.

"Justin?"

"Yeah. Me, too."

Tate had a strained look on her face.

Happy-go-lucky Paddy didn't look so happy or lucky just

then. He looked like he wanted to call up the wind and wipe this entire house from the face of the earth.

And the other witch, a man by the name Torrance, was muttering under his breath. None of his words made sense until suddenly he shouted, "*Wood*!"

That made sense—sort of.

Paddy went to his knees and Justin grabbed me. I couldn't even comprehend how fast he had me on the other side of the hall. Screams rose in the air as the earth ripped open right where we had been standing. My eyes tracked it, *barely*, as forms were swallowed up by that hole. Some were almost fast enough to get away, but Paddy's magic slammed into them and drove them down. Into that hole.

Fire swarmed over it.

Tate was laughing.

Torrance snarled when I tried to pull away from Justin.

"Doyle, stay down!" Justin shouted.

Something whistled…

The fire winked out.

I blinked, stunned, as huge pieces of wood—chunks of timber, thick pieces of board came flying through the air—and arrowed down into that hole.

The stink of vampire blood rose thick in the air.

"Earth. Air. Fire. Magic," I murmured, looking at each of the witches.

"You got it, kitty-kitty." Justin smiled, the magic around him sparking hard and cold.

He'd brought a veritable army…masters of the elements and they were turning the vampires into nothing.

His arms fell away and I put distance between us, following that alien music.

The vase.

"Know where it is?" Justin asked.

"Down." I swallowed and searched the area. The feel of vampire was still strong enough to make my skin crawl. And somehow, I knew where they were. We had to go down. Into the basement. Surrounded…trapped…

My gut crawled.

I squeezed the blade and forced myself to ignore the sound of the silence in the back of my mind.

The music grew louder.

"What am I hearing?" Doyle asked.

If I'd had the brain cells to spare, I might have been surprised that he felt it. The magic was strong, almost overpowering, but I wouldn't have expected a shifter to *hear* the power of it.

I didn't have the brain cells, though, and I was trying hard not to focus on anything but the steps that unwound in front of me.

And…her.

I looked at Justin.

Sometime in between one heartbeat and the next, she'd arrived.

Maybe the magic of the vase had blunted her presence.

Maybe the magic of the witches had made it harder to feel her.

Maybe the battle had blinded us to her.

I just didn't know.

But she was here.

And if luck would play out the way it always did…she would be down *there*…

"You truly are a clever, silly girl."

I rounded the final curve and stopped, my back pressed to the wall.

We hadn't yet seen the humans and now I knew why.

They lay in a neat little pile, like puppies.

Around them was a wall of vampires, all of the ones that remained, I suspected.

Every single one of them had more than a century behind them. The look in their eyes was something bright and blank and…avid.

"The lights are on but nobody's home," I said, wondering if anybody would realize what I was talking about.

Justin grunted.

"I can just turn the room into an oven," Tate said.

"No. Humans." I stared at the people for a long moment

and then shifted my attention to Pandora. "If you already found the vase, why did you need me?"

"Because I *hadn't* found it." She smiled, her voice bright and cheerful, like a teacher encouraging a young child as she fought her way through a problem. And her eyes glinted with promises of pain. "That was why I needed *you*. I'm tired…this body is tired. I could only reach so far and why should I extend myself if I could let somebody else do the work?"

She smiled at me and then moved away from the gathered knot of vampires, lifting her arms and turning in a circle. "I can feel it now…it calls me. Don't you hear it?"

Bat-shit crazy bitch.

Her head whipped around and she stared at me. "You annoy me, Kit. Don't push your luck or I'll just kill you now and be done with it."

She turned her back on me and strode across the room. "Kill her keepers but leave the girl alive. She might be of use yet."

Well.

That was stupid.

I didn't have time to panic as vampires lunged for me.

I didn't have time to scream.

I didn't have time to *think*.

Just move.

Their blood was a stain on my skin and still there were more.

In the air, Pandora's voice was a mocking laugh. I fought with my back pressed to Justin's, his magic an extra shield around us.

More specifically…around Tate.

Her cockiness had gotten her in trouble and the only reason she was alive was because Doyle had ripped the vampire who'd been feeding on her in two. Literally. Justin had slapped a magic-charged fielding dressing on her jugular but she was unconscious.

At least she was alive.

Paddy was alive.

Torrance wasn't.

He'd used that freaky ass power of wood to impale several vampires, but one of them, even as he was driving the wood into the vampire's heart, the vampire had impaled *himself*...on Torrance.

The two lay locked together in a grim, obscene embrace, the image forever smeared across my memory.

Silver slashed out. Blood sprayed across my lips and I wanted to wipe it off but I didn't dare. Two of the vampires had been strong enough to power through Justin's shields. They'd almost gotten Tate.

The strongest one tried to shove through again and I swung. At the same time, something attacked Justin's wards and he bellowed—the sound cut off abruptly. His wards flickered—died.

Justin—

Hands grabbed me.

Panic screamed inside me and without realizing it, I drew Death and swung.

He met undead flesh and cleaved through it, and in the back of my mind, over my panic, I felt his near-orgasmic pleasure.

Get out—get out—get out! I screamed at him.

He only laughed.

Fangs flashed at me and I raised the blade, drove him into that snarling mouth before the vampire realized the game had changed. He was dead a second later and I moved on. Another fell.

Their blood painted me now and dully, over the roar of my blood, I could hear Pandora. I heard her laughter...those bell-like tones. *Ask not for whom the bell tolls...*

Silver flashed out and closed around my wrist. Another strand caught the sword.

I jerked back and looked up as Justin rose from the floor, his clothes dripping with vampire blood. He barely managed to stay on his feet.

Doyle pounced, landing on four paws between us, opening his mouth to scream in fury at Justin.

Justin glared at him. "Not impressed. The sword is trying to take her over and she's got a void in her mind right now—she's vulnerable. You want to lose her to a devil blade like that, cat?"

The words were enough to make the giant tiger look unsure.

I swallowed and looked at the blade, threw it down. "Justin, I'm fine."

He stared at me, his eyes hard. Then he nodded and turned to face Pandora. I followed the line of his sight and found myself staring. Pandora sat on the pile of humans, all of them unconscious. Unconscious, thank God, not dead. She sat on them like they were some sort of living, breathing throne. Next to her, lying almost negligently, was a vase…and it was a massive son of a bitch, too. Nearly two feet tall. She held it in place, one hand curled around what looked to be a curved, sweeping handle.

It was deceptively simple, black with images painted on the side. Images of monsters. Creatures of nightmares. The monsters that had broken me…and they surrounded a woman.

Pandora's Box.

Doyle made a deep grumbling sound in his chest.

Justin tensed next to me.

Decision time.

"Where is the girl?" she asked.

I blinked.

Instinctively, I flexed my hand and she started to laugh. "Oh, that's so precious. Even with the bond broken, you still long to call it. And you have the stupid, silly blade *with* you…"

No. No, I didn't.

I carried the leaf blade.

I breathed shallowly.

She knew so much. But maybe not as much as she thought.

A coy smile curved her lips as she watched me. "Where is the girl, Kitasa?"

"What girl?"

She reached down and stroked her hand down the flank of the one of the humans she used for her perch. "Don't be a fool, *aneira.* You know which one." She rose and it was all fluid grace and boneless movement. Nobody should be able to get off a pile of humans and look graceful, but she did it. "I sought you out because I *knew* it would all come together for you. My wolf told me the girl was seeking you." She looked off to the side and fury exploded through me as Gio came slinking out of the shadows. He went to his knees and pressed his face to her leg.

That son of a bitch. Part of me realized she had compelled him, controlled him. And it didn't matter. She stroked a hand down his hair and he watched her adoringly. The bastard had spied on me. Betrayed TJ. Betrayed all of us…and he was staring up at her like he wanted nothing more than to hump her leg. Pandora gave me an amused look. "He told me that you had this…softness for children. Then she came to you. I know my offspring, silly girl. I felt her there, and I knew. I knew it would all come together…for me. Because it's your nature. That nasty, amazing luck."

I felt like I'd been punched.

It must have shown on my face because she started to laugh again. "Don't look so upset, Kit." A smile curved her face. *Come on…it's no big deal!* "I needed your help. And it's only fair…all of the things I could give to *my* creatures and I could never quite duplicate something like that. How everything neatly falls into place for you?"

"*Neatly*?" I snarled, damn near choking on the world. "You think my *life* has neatly come together, you crazy bitch?" Fear took a back seat as she stood there, practically patting me on the head like a pup that had done a good job chasing down a bone.

"So touchy. You didn't spend centuries *trapped*," she said, ice dripping from her words. "*I* did. Centuries, Kitasa. I spent years trapped, my power fading away bit by bit, my body wasting away…then those fools take me from the witches…"

She shrugged and looked at her vase. "They didn't even realize what they'd done. Once I was out of their spells, I was free to come and go, but they didn't *get* that. They had their *own* witches…imbeciles, all of them, chanting over the vase, like they were trying to conjure up the devil. I waited until I was alone because it was time. I had to find my new vessel so I left." She frowned, a line between her eyes. "The world…it's become so big."

"I thought the vase was *stolen* from you."

She blinked. "It was. When I emerged, it was in this dull little gray room." She flicked a hand as though she was brushing away the memory. "A dull grey room with a huge lock for a door, as though that would keep me in."

Likely to keep others out, I thought. A vault, probably. A walk-in sort in one of the Allerton homes in the city.

"But when I went back…the vase was gone. I hadn't found the girl. I couldn't find my vessel…"

She looked confused. Lost.

Poor thing.

"Let me get this straight," I said slowly, tightening my grip on the sword and trying to decide if she'd die if I took her head. Probably. Most things needed a head to survive, right? Maybe even *all* things. "You hired *me* because you couldn't figure out where they'd taken the damn thing after you climbed out of it."

Pandora gave me another one of those inhuman stares. In the back of our souls, we all remember what it's like to cringe and hide in the dark. We know what it's like to be weak, to fear that dark.

Pandora *was* the dark.

"I think I tire of you," she murmured. "I'll find the girl myself. She's of my blood, and carries the child of a cat, I already know that. If I must cut them all down to find her, I will. I have my vessel. I no longer need you."

Justin's magic flashed, hard and bright.

I bolstered my own shields although I didn't know what good it would do.

Pandora turned her back on us, chuckling. "As if I'd waste my energy. Cat…kill them."

Doyle growled.

Chapter Twenty-Six

His growl rolled around the room and sweat dripped down my back, icy and cold as I shifted my gaze to look at the tiger. He lay low to the ground, body tensed and ready, eyes glowing as he stared at Pandora.

She drew the vase down as though it weighed nothing.

"I said kill them!" she snapped.

"Kit," Justin said, his voice ragged. "I have to—"

"No."

I drew my gun.

Doyle lunged.

Justin's wards screamed as the tiger fought his way through them and then Pandora's scream joined them. "You stupid—"

Blood, the hot, iron scent of it, flooded the air. Shifter blood. *Wolf* blood.

Doyle took Gio down, his face buried in the werewolf's neck and the smaller man struggled under Doyle's weight, but he was outmatched in so many ways. Blood sprayed in an arc and I heard a heartbeat stutter, then falter, then end.

Pandora bellowed and lunged.

Doyle met her halfway.

Please don't die—

Leveling the Desert Eagle, I aimed at the vase. How nice of her. She'd set it up and all nice and steady—

I unloaded and watched as the bullets pounded into it.

One.

Two.

Three.

Charged ammo—but the vase was magic. Old magic and the first one didn't penetrate.

Pandora shrieked and she threw Doyle off. More blood; this time it was Doyle's. But she had blood dripping down the front of her body and my nose had caught the scent. It wasn't cat's blood. Talon claws raked her face and there was a gaping bite mark in her neck, already knitting itself together.

She bled.

That meant she could die.

She came for me and I shifted my focus.

Time slowed to a crawl as I took aim.

Es's voice seemed to wrap around me.

She hasn't been of our world all that long…she's won't expect some of the tricks you might have up your sleeve.

I pulled the trigger.

Pandora stumbled to a halt as the bullet ripped into and took away the top half of her skull.

I shoved my gun into the sheath and, without blinking, grabbed Death.

His scream of joy rang in my head as I spun and whirled, taking off what remained of her head.

The vase exploded.

I wasn't going to get sick.

As long as I didn't think about the fact that I was covered with vampire blood and as long as I didn't think about the fact that Death was still trying to whisper to me, his voice louder than ever.

"We need to move," Justin said, his voice urgent. "Come

on, Paddy. I know you're tired, but we need—"

A pale figure stepped out from behind a tree.

For one second, my heart knew nothing but icy terror. Pale hair. Pale face. Terrible power. Vampire—

Another ghost from my past came back to whisper to me…Goliath, his voice deep and gruff, his hands big and gentle as he patted my back and tried to comfort up on that horrid, hellish mountain.

She's going to remember this, every second of it for months, probably years. And if she can't think back and remember seeing the box that hauled him away, part of her is going to wonder if he's after her.

Goliath had all but forced me to watch as they'd put Jude away.

Jude was gone. Locked up for the next fifty years. Staring across the ruin and rubble at the pale vampire, I reminded myself of that. That vampire wasn't Jude. And the similarity was only superficial. They were both blond. All vampires were pale, because they never saw the sun.

And this man was handsome but he lacked the completely angelic beauty that Jude possessed. Angelic beauty, unholy evil.

"I take it that's Amadeus," I said softly as he started to come toward us, his cloak flaring open to reveal a blood red lining.

"You take it right. Has a flare for the stupid."

My blood roared, pounded.

"I'll have you both jailed for this," the vampire said, his voice cool. "You had no business—"

Shapeshifter magic prickled, rolled, the energy of an angry cat shifter beating against my skin. Doyle stepped between us. Gently, he put Tate at our feet and then he rose and faced the vampire.

"I do," he said.

Amadeus gave him a bored look. "Go away, cub, before I decide I'm hungry. My quarrel isn't with you. You're just…in the way."

Doyle's hands hung loose at his sides. A strange smile

curled his lips.

"Oh, I don't know about that," he said. "We've got blood to settle. You owned shares in a company that Jude sold a few months ago—Blood Games. Remember it?"

Something glittered in the vampire's eyes and a grin stretched across his face. "Oh. Oh, yes…interesting pursuits we had there. Some problems. We had to distance ourselves from it."

Something uneasy danced down my spine. "Doyle."

He didn't look at me.

"You didn't distance yourself enough."

He lunged, going from human form to that awful half-monster, half-animal in just seconds. The laughing, taunting boy I was so familiar was gone, and in his place was a killer.

But the vampire was older. Stronger.

Amadeus crashed into him and took him down. "Stupid *boy*," he snarled, slamming him down so hard I heard bone crunch.

I tensed.

Justin grabbed my arm before I could move.

"Let me go!" I whispered, my voice low and furious.

"Not happening," he said, shaking his head, his eyes on the two in front of us.

I jerked on my arm again. "Justin, you son of a bitch—"

"Kit…" He looked away for one brief moment, his eyes grim and dark. "This isn't about the vase."

I had figured that much out.

"Look." Justin jerked his head.

I saw the vampires spreading out behind us.

Eight of them.

We were outnumbered. Cold spread through me.

And I didn't have to ask Justin how he felt. He was about tapped out. And this…*Blood games*—blood *games. Jude*—

Understanding slammed into me. The Everglades. Doyle's kidnapping…the days he'd spent as a prisoner. Trapped. Helpless.

"He said there was blood between them," I whispered.

"Yes." Justin's eyes stayed locked on the two grappling

forms. His hand closed around my arm and his answer came in images and barely formed words. Empathy wasn't his strong suit, or mine, but it worked.

Amadeus had made it personal. As long as we didn't get involved from this point on, it would end here.

Otherwise Justin and I were going to have to fight our way through the vampires. And the ones across from us were older. Strong ones. I could feel the weight of their years slamming into me and dread spiraled, climbed inside me as panic threatened.

Justin's fingers dug in. His magic arced through me, shocked me.

Hold it together, damn it!

I don't know if he shouted that at me or if I did, but I shoved the panic back, locked it down, locked it away and forced myself to stare at the bloodied tiger as the vampire tore awful, terrible strips from him.

And he laughed. The bastard laughed as he did it.

What was Doyle thinking—

But I knew.

He was just a stupid, idiotic *brave* kid…who saw a way for us to get out.

I couldn't let him do this. He'd saved me once already. It didn't matter what happened to me—

Vaguely, I felt the weird, familiar prickle of magic. Although my mind was so painfully, painfully quiet.

Justin shot me a look. "Kit—"

My breath hitched.

Light exploded—*from Doyle.*

And Amadeus screamed, his body jolted upright as Doyle drove the wooden handle of an axe through his chest.

Doyle…

I stumbled against Justin as the shock slammed through me.

Doyle's upturned face…when I first saw him in that hole. So much like a face from my past. My cousin, Rathi.

His fascination with weapons. That unnatural affinity for them…

From the back of my memory, a moment out of time rose. Goliath's voice, as we crouched in the forest, waiting for Justin and Banner.

Doyle's a tracker, Kitty. Almost as good as you. Never seen the like of it. He didn't track you by scent. It was...It was amazing. I ain't never seen anything like it.

"Like me," I said numbly.

Doyle shoved Amadeus's lifeless body to the side and with a savage snarl, he jerked the axe out. "Blood debt," he growled at the vampires as they swarmed closer. "Fuck with me and the cats will eat you alive. Your house will die."

Blood debts, another old, archaic law of the council, but one they hadn't done away with. Some part of my mind tucked it away—I'd process it all later. Much, much later. Doyle came toward us, still in his half-form, clutching an axe that looked like a toy in his giant paw-like hand. There were runes, I realized. Runes on the bloodied blade.

And in his blue eyes, I saw confusion when he looked at me.

"Kit—"

I gave him a minute shake of my head.

"Get Tate. You got your blood. And then some. Let's go."

"What do you make of it?"

It was the first time Justin had managed to corner me alone since…*it.*

I held Doyle's axe in my hands while the clan's healer, Ella, finished patching him together. Amadeus had done him some damage and he'd lost enough blood that he actually *needed* the healing.

"Damn it, Kit."

Slowly, I forced myself to drag my eyes away from the axe and meet Justin's.

"It's…" I stopped and rubbed a hand over my face. "There's power in it. The runes are familiar, although they aren't *exactly* like mine. The weapons come down a family line and these are..." I touched one of them, felt the answering burn of magic. It was alien and didn't like me touching it. No. Not *it.* He. *He* didn't like me touching him. "Think of them as family crests. Somebody meant for Doyle to have this. But I don't know who. One of my aunts, my grandmother, even my cousins could have read this, told you who his family is. I can't. None of that even matters, though. Because the axe is his. He calls Doyle…and Doyle calls him."

"Calls him." Justin turned his head and stared at the young man on the bed. He was pale, almost as pale as the sheets. On the far side of the bed, Damon sat down, his mouth a thin, flat line as he listened to Ella.

We hadn't told him yet, how this had happened.

Did Doyle even know?

But then I remembered the shock in his eyes as he came to me. He hadn't known. At least not about the weapon bond.

I hadn't known. Because nobody had told me. Nobody had told Doyle, either.

Like me…

◊◊◊◊◊

Once more, we were back in Damon's quarters. Ground zero.

"How is Doyle?" I asked, even though we'd just left him to the tender mercies of Ella and several of Damon's bodyguards.

Gray eyes burned into me. "He'll be fine. He's a cat, baby girl. Blood loss and an ass-kicking from a vamp isn't going to slow him down for long."

Before I could think of anything else to say, the door opened and Chang slipped in.

I blinked, caught off guard at the sight of him. He was dressed in battle gear, I suppose. Black shirt that hugged close, black utility pants that would have looked right at home in my closet…if they were an inch or two shorter and broader through the hips. "I didn't know you owned anything other than suits, Chang."

A ghost of a smile danced around his lips as he settled himself at Damon's shoulder. Ever the shadow.

"So, Doyle's resting," I said, parsing out the words while I tried to figure this out.

Next to me, Justin sighed.

I shot him a murderous glare.

He lifted his hands. The silver in his sleeves looked tarnished, dull.

Be quiet, I said, focusing my thoughts, my emotions as hard and loud as I could. I didn't know if he'd pick them up without me touching him, but he ought to pick up on *some* of that.

"Something…weird…happened," I finally said, slumping in my seat as exhaustion crept in.

"Weirder than…what? You using a gun to take out a vase? Or the evil bitch?" A sly smile lit Damon's face. "Although, kitten, I didn't realize you had such a thing against interior decorating."

I narrowed my eyes at him.

He leaned forward, elbows on the table. "Why don't you just ask what you need to ask?"

"Who was Doyle's mother?"

"We don't know." Damon shrugged, his eyes darkened to almost black. "She left Doyle's dad. Nobody ever saw her after she took off."

"Actually…" Chang spoke up, drawing my eyes to him. "Few people saw her *before* she took off. Doyle's father, Malcolm, was rarely seen anywhere with her. She was…shy, I've heard. Once the baby was born, she stayed long enough to wean him, then she left."

"She just abandoned him?"

Damon shrugged. "Not unheard of with half-breed kids, baby girl," he said, his voice low and edgy. "After about a month or so, the shifter parent can tell if the gene is going to be recessive or not. The kid may never *shift* but it becomes pretty damn obvious if the child will be more...or less…human. She probably looked at Doyle one day and decided she didn't want see him coughing up hairballs."

I had a dagger buried in the surface of the table before I realized I'd drawn it.

Next to me, Justin went still.

Chang's eyes were cautious.

But Damon just smiled. "Why so angry, kitten?"

"How long have you known?" I demanded, forcing the question out.

His lashes swept down low, shielding his eyes.

He sighed and rubbed his hands over his face and then looked up at Chang. "Chang and I…we always knew something was different on him. We didn't know *what* it was, though."

"When did you know?" I shouted.

"The day Harry Potter brought you back from Wolf Haven," Damon said, his voice flat, level. "It was after you'd been attacked—you had that big bite taken out of you."

The day he'd marked me…

I tensed. Against my will, I reached up and brushed my hand down my neck, feeling the ridge of the scar.

I saw Damon move but I couldn't get away fast enough as he came across the table, landing on the balls of his feet in a crouch just in front of me. Body bent in a position no human could hold, he put his face in mine. "No," he murmured. He reached up and covered the bite with his palm. "It had nothing to do with Doyle. Everything that ever happened with us is just because of us. Nothing else."

"You sure about that?"

He brushed his thumb against my lower lip. "Never been more certain of anything. And I'll keep waiting until you're ready."

With a whisper of sound and a sigh, he was gone, moving back into his seat and it was like that moment had never happened.

Chang cleared his throat. In his smooth, perfect voice, he said, "There was an…incident. Sam took it upon herself to try and discipline Doyle and he was bloodied. Nothing major, but the scent of his blood…and yours. Too much alike."

"He's got *aneira* blood," Justin muttered.

"You just now figuring that out, Harry Potter?" Damon curled his lip.

Justin flipped him off.

CHAPTER TWENTY-SEVEN

Two days later, I stood in my apartment and realized I'd come to a decision.

Or maybe the decision had been made a while ago. I couldn't go back to Wolf Haven. TJ and Justin were right—I wasn't made for standing behind a bar. There was only one thing I was really good at.

So I guess that meant I was back in business.

But first, I had to attend to a personal matter.

If life hadn't kicked me in the face, I would have done it months ago. Now, though, thanks to TJ, I finally felt strong enough. All because she'd kicked me in the butt. Again.

Her voice, so sad and gentle, echoed in memory.

Kit, you're stronger than I am. Please don't turn into me. Don't let him win like this.

There were much, much worse things, in my mind, than being like her. She'd been the first person to show me any real kindness. The first to care about me. She had given me my first real home and whenever things were really bad and I needed to hide, needed to get away from anything and everything, she would *always* have a place for me.

She had been there for me after a monster had broken me, and then, when the time was right, she'd forced me to face myself.

It was time to pay that kindness back…and take down

the monster who had broken her.

It was something she wouldn't be able to do. I knew that. TJ was a mean, smart bitch, but the wolf in her was weak and if she wanted to face down the monster who had hurt her, she'd have to be a dominant. A leopard couldn't change its spots and a wolf couldn't go from beta to alpha. It just didn't happen.

But I could kill that son of a bitch for her.

Well, as long as I had some back-up with me…and I knew just the right people for the job.

I gathered up the weapons I needed. Justin had already re-keyed the spells that protected the darker weapons I owned. Death was back in his place. He had other names, but Death was the one he answered to. He didn't care what the legends called him; he didn't care what history called him. He cared about death, blood and chaos…and even now, I could hear him whispering to me. The power of his magic was too strong and until I had a better grip on myself, he was off limits.

He'd almost gotten too deeply inside me. It was fear, I suspected, that let him root so deeply within me.

He hadn't even been the equalizing force, really. Not with Pandora. It had been a gun. A modern weapon to kill an ancient. Maybe I needed to start showing those modern weapons a bit more respect. And it was time to start trusting myself more, as well.

On my way out the door, I grabbed my phone and dialed a number.

Goliath's voice was a deep, bass rumble and just hearing him made me smile.

I'd been wanting to do this for a long, long time.

The next call I made was to Justin. I needed to restock on my ammo and he had the best suppliers around. Plus, I wanted to see if he was interested in joining Goliath and me on our little road trip.

He absolutely did. We made our plans. We were heading out in the morning. Goliath would get a few more wolves lined up to take with us and I'd make another call or two.

Goliath was also going to need to figure out what to tell TJ. He had to disappear for a day or two. She couldn't know. Not yet.

We'd tell her…after.

I had one stop to make before heading to Wolf Haven.

This time, I didn't even need to distract myself as I drove to the Lair.

Parking my battered car into my spot in front of the Lair, I climbed out. Silence fell as I drew near, but it didn't last long.

No massive tiger came running out to greet me.

He'd have to stay in one form or the other for a few days, Ella had said. And rest. He needed a lot of rest.

But I wasn't here to see Doyle.

I wasn't even here to see Damon.

Which was good…he wasn't on the grounds. He would have met me and I wasn't ready to see him. Not yet.

A few people glanced at me. One or two even half-smiled as I made my way to Damon's quarters.

That familiar scent wrapped around me as I slid inside.

I lingered by the bed after I'd left my message. Because I missed it so much, I caught one of his pillows, lifted it to my face, breathed it in. I was tempted to steal away with it, but I had at least some pride.

Forcing myself to put the pillow down, I moved away from the bed and headed to the door. Once there, I paused and looked back, my vision narrowing in on the note I'd pinned to his headboard with one of my daggers.

Subtle. That was me.

The message itself was simple, but he'd get the point.

Keep waiting. I'm getting closer.

For the first time in what seemed like a long, long time, the scars and shadows weren't choking me…and I had a job to do. I turned around and walked away.

About J.C. Daniels

J.C. Daniels is the pen name of author Shiloh Walker. Shiloh/J.C has been writing since she was a kid. She fell in love with vampires with the book Bunnicula and has worked her way up to the more…ah…serious works of fiction. She loves reading and writing just about every kind of romance. Once upon a time she worked as a nurse, but now she writes full time and lives with her family in the Midwest. She writes urban fantasy and erotic under the pen name J.C. Daniels and romantic suspense and contemporary romance as Shiloh Walker.

Read more about Shiloh & J.C. at www.shilohwalker.com